Seán Moncrieff has hosted various television and radio programmes over the last decade. A journalist by training, he lives in Dublin. This is his first novel.

www.booksattransworld.co.uk

Dublin

SEÁN MONCRIEFF

Doubleday

LONDON · NEW YORK · TORONTO · SYDNEY · AUCKLAND

TRANSWORLD PUBLISHERS
61–63 Uxbridge Road, London W5 5SA
A division of The Random House Group Ltd

RANDOM HOUSE AUSTRALIA (PTY) LTD
20 Alfred Street, Milsons Point, Sydney
New South Wales 2061, Australia

RANDOM HOUSE NEW ZEALAND
18 Poland Road, Glenfield, Auckland 10, New Zealand

RANDOM HOUSE SOUTH AFRICA (PTY) LTD
Endulini, 5a Jubilee Road, Parktown 2193, South Africa

Published 2001 by Doubleday
a division of Transworld Publishers

Typeset by
Phoenix Typesetting, Ilkley, West Yorkshire

Printed in Great Britain
by Clays Ltd, St Ives plc

1 3 5 7 9 10 8 6 4 2

I could have been important, if I'd been somebody else.

— The Fatima Mansions, 'A Pack Of Lies',
from the album *Viva Dead Ponies*

Nightbird nightsun nighttown. Chase me, Charley!
(he blows into Bloom's ear) Buzz!

— James Joyce, *Ulysses*

The Millennium Spire

In November 1998, the Irish Government announced that it was to build a monument on Dublin's main thoroughfare, O'Connell Street. When constructed, it would be the centrepiece of Ireland's millennium celebrations. Officially titled the Monument of Light (and more familiarly known as the Millennium Spire), it was a 120-metre stainless steel needle. When completed, it would be the tallest structure in Dublin and visible from virtually all parts of the city. It was to be sited on the part of O'Connell Street previously occupied by Nelson's Pillar, which was blown up by the IRA during the 1960s (that organization having regarded Nelson's Pillar as a monument to British imperialism). The government planned officially to 'unveil' the spire on 31 December 1999.

However, during 1999, Mr Micheál Ó Nualláin, the brother of writer Flann O'Brien, challenged the project in the Irish High Court. Mr Ó Nualláin – who had submitted his own designs for the O'Connell Street project – successfully argued that Dublin Corporation was required to produce an environmental impact statement before the spire could be built.

As a result, work on the spire could not commence until the environmental impact statement was completed. This statement, however, which took some months to produce, was generally favourable to the spire's being built. Finally, in late December 2000, Ireland's Minister for the Environment, Noel Dempsey, announced that the Monument of Light would be constructed. The work is expected to be completed by the end of 2001. The action of this novel takes place some time after that.

In February 2001, Dublin Corporation also announced that the Anna Livia monument, which currently resides in O'Connell Street, is to be moved to another location, thus cleverly evading its destruction as outlined in this novel. But I'll get it the next time.

one

My name is Simon Dillon, and I know I'm going to die soon.

I am thirty-five years of age, tall, pot-bellied and greying. I have a dead mother, a mad father, no friends left and a wife who will never void the bitterness I have injected into her.

All I do is lie in bed and scratch, chasing the hot itchiness which moves beneath my skin. I claw at it, until my fingernails are crusted with blood, my legs and arms latticed with tiny scrapes.

But this does no good; the itch creeps to a new location, until I am smacking and pounding myself, tearfully at war with my own limbs.

Fucked in the body, fucked in the head.

The itch taunts me, denies me sleep; a vicious revenge for my excess.

Yet I still try to lull us. I close my eyes and go to the base of Mount Monadnock, my booted feet crunching into pristine snow. The sky is a tense, liquid blue. The day is cold, but enjoyably so. I'm wrapped up well, the Sabres of Paradise thumping

'Inter-Lergen-Ten-Ko II' into my slightly numbed ears. But it's inappropriate to my surroundings: the extravagant space here easily dissolves the force of the music, so I click off the Walkman and head for home, stumbling down the mountain and onto Main Street, where wood-panelled station wagons glide by, windscreen wipers swishing hello. I know that when I get there a fireplace will be crinkling warmth, that I'll be handed a hot whiskey, kissed wetly on the cheek, that children will scramble up to hug my legs.

But when I reach the front door, my body has already guessed what I'm at: it jerks me back to a dry-throated consciousness, the stiff sheets and hot air of my grey room. I have a slug of water, reach for my cigarettes, and remember again that I've foolishly given them up.

I get to sleep eventually, but in my dream it's never where I want to go: like that guy in *The Prisoner*, I always end up back here. Panting up Carrickbrack Road towards Howth Head, up to the lay-by that overlooks the extravagant sweep of Dublin bay; where busloads of mildly interested tourists come to watch the ferries chug into the outstretched arms of the city.

I jump the barrier, struggle closer to the cliff and sit down on the grass. I fumble in the pockets of my black suit. They are full of something, warm objects, I don't want to think what. I finally extract twenty Major and a brass Zippo I lost years ago. I light a cigarette, then fling the rest of them towards the sea where they scatter like snow from the packet. Seagulls jet in to investigate. The still-lit Zippo I throw at the brittle gorse to my right. Desiccated by the sun, it catches light immediately. I watch as the flames expand like poisonous orange clouds and start to eat their way down the hill, through Sutton Cross and back towards Dublin, gobbling everything until the coast before me is mutated into a curved sheet of flame, doubled in size by the glassy sea.

And I remember that the word Dublin comes from the Irish

dubh linn, meaning black pool. Filthy. Black. Pool.

I do this because there is nothing else left for me to do. In my position, you become unapologetically self-absorbed. I attempt to decode my dreams, mock myself with questions about the worth of my life. I write a moral report-card, and find nothing but degrees of irony.

But enough of that: I want to be clear about why I'm going to present my account of what happened.

I have no interest in explaining my side of this story; I'm not looking for your sympathy or understanding. I'm doing this for the money. They think it's a good yarn, and I suppose it is.

So let's get on with it.

As you may know, my involvement lasted just one day, but first you should know about the events of the night before, on 15 June. You've probably read about this: at the time it made all the head-lines.

It started in the centre of Dublin, at about 7:45 in the evening; a noisy, agitated time of day: foreign students wearing cheap plastic shades sat in clumps under the Daniel O'Connell monument, believing this to be a cool thing to do. There were late shoppers and early drinkers, beggars on their cardboard thrones, workers going home, and others just starting: handing out leaflets proclaiming cheap pizza and socialist liberation. Jerky traffic filled the six-lane width of O'Connell Street, forcing pedestrians to cross the road in short stampedes, controlled by the computer bleep of traffic lights. The tang of carbon monoxide thickened in the air and the summer evening light was starting to turn dirty.

Two men moved through the crowds along the western side of the street, northwards towards the Millennium Spire. These were the men who later became known in the papers as the Beer Boys.

They crossed Middle Abbey Street and came to an uncommitted halt outside Eason's. Nearby a pack of neurotic wasps circled an erupting rubbish bin. Everyone else on the pavement made a wide detour around this bin, but not the Beer Boys, who seemed not to notice. They let the wasps flurry around them, as indifferent as grazing cows. They squinted, studying the bus signs.

Private buses also flock in O'Connell Street. On Thursdays and Fridays, convoys of them arrive in the centre of town and park wherever they can, defiantly clogging up the edgy city traffic while they wait to ferry loud students and timid nurses back to Glenamaddy or Gortnamuck or wherever. It's like a UN evacuation from a warring city, the buses displaying their friendly rural intentions with squat logos: Burke, Murphy, Kelly. Comforting, country names. They fill up quickly and move out; another group of desperate souls rescued.

Our boys weren't here to catch a bus. They were obviously not students or nurses. Big, squat, deep-set bastards, they were; tall, with tree-trunk necks. At a glance, they looked like idiot twins: both wearing shabby raincoats (it was summer, but this was Ireland), and scuffed purple patent-leather shoes that looked strangely effeminate on men this bulky. Their black curly hair was untidily dolloped on their heads, like it had dropped from the sky and landed there by accident. They were swarthy and dark-eyed, unhealthy. Obviously not Irish, probably from Eastern Europe: the kind of ungrateful-looking men who sell the *Big Issues* in dirty train stations and live in social welfare hostels while fighting deportation.

One of the Beer Boys wore a ridiculous moustache, a furry creature nestling beneath his nose. He shoved his friend and pointed at one of the buses.

'*Sligo aftobu. Sli-go.*'

The other shrugged and nodded, as if not entirely convinced but ready to give it a try.

'OK,' shouted the moustached one. They marched towards the bus, hands plunged into their coat pockets. The wasps followed them, like an insect halo.

Inside, it was dark and dramatically quiet. There were six passengers on board. The driver had gone for a drink in the Oval Bar around the corner. From the back of the bus came the tinny sound of music leaking from a cheap Walkman. The men looked towards this. They grinned.

'Meat Loaf!'

The Beer Boys fell silent, craning their heads forward like hungry chicks to catch the distant aural scraps from the chubby singer. They swapped a fond look and joined hands, like ecstatic middle-aged women at a religious event. Then, in a crude baritone voice, one of them sang:

> '*Bab-bee*
> *I love you—*'

'*Nyet, nyet!*' fiercely interrupted his moustached friend. The other shook his head in agreement: these were not the right words to the song. In an attempt to remember, they softly hummed the tune together, but seemed to make no progress in recalling the lyrics. As if by way of compensation to their startled audience, the Beer Boys gradually began to sing louder, now employing the word *La* to fill in for the forgotten verse.

> '*La La La*
> *La La La,*
> *La La La la-la-la-la-la.*
> *La La La Laaaaa*
> *La la-la-la-la La Laaaaaah!*'

Like thirsty men who have finally found water, the Beer Boys stretched out their arms and threw them around each other. All pretence of singing now abandoned, they yelled out the one bit of the song they could be sure of, its title:

'Two Out of Three Ain't *Baaaad*!'

'JesusfuckingChrist.'

The Russians released each other. The bemused travellers now switched their attention from the singers to one of the other passengers: a woman in her early thirties with shoulder-length dyed-blond hair. She was wearing a bit too much gold jewellery and a peach-coloured Dior trouser suit. She was standing, staring goggle-eyed at the Beer Boys. In her arms she held a toddler, a girl, maybe three or four years old. The girl was dressed in Baby Gap denim overalls. The two outfits clashed.

The Meat Loaf fans studied the woman for a moment, and again they grinned. The man with the moustache had brown teeth.

'*Privet!*'

Uncomprehending, the woman shrugged faintly. The non-moustached Beer Boy clasped his hairy hands to his chest and shook his head, camp in his self-criticism.

'*Prasteetye! Ya ne gavoriu po Angliski,*' he sang, as if the words were an advertising jingle.

'Mary Barton!' exclaimed the other.

He pronounced it *Maribarton*, like it was the name of a flower.

'Look, lads, Jesus, I'm leaving. I'm going.'

'Mary Barton!'

The woman didn't answer. Now having apparently established that this was indeed Mary Barton, the Beer Boys reached under their coats and took out what one witness thought were Uzis, but were in fact BXPs, South African 9mm semi-automatic pistols. With something of a theatrical flourish, they folded out the butts of their guns (unnecessary, given their proximity to the woman) and clicked off the safety catches.

According to the witnesses, Mary Barton at this point remained still, petrified; a frozen, terrified animal.

The Beer Boys pointed their guns at her.

The other passengers were not bemused any more.

'Jesus, lads. Jesus,' the woman finally managed to say. It came out as a distended, comical squeak.

With stiff arms she held out the toddler, as if by some chance they hadn't noticed it. The child gabbled delightedly, stretching out podgy hands towards the weapons.

'Hiya,' said the toddler.

The men were amused by this.

'Hiya,' one of them replied. Without a word they moved their guns slightly to the left so that now the barrels were within inches of the child's soft and pink-smelling head.

They fired.

I have given a lot of thought to what happened to Mary Barton, and I think there are worse ways than this to die. The magazine of a BXP holds thirty-two bullets. The gun has a firing rate of eight hundred rounds per minute. So it was perhaps five seconds before they had to reload. According to the witnesses, the child disintegrated in a red blur within Mary Barton's hands. By some vicious fluke, not a single bullet hit her.

Yet while the Beer Boys carefully reloaded – an action that took, perhaps, ten seconds – Mary Barton continued to stand as she was, mouth open, arms outstretched, a waxen copy of the person who had stood there seconds before, holding the fleshy strips of a child who no longer existed.

The little girl died instantly, without pain, while Mary Barton's mind slammed down a shutter between her and the hopeless truth of what had just occurred. Refusing to admit such information, her brain and body froze, leaving Mary Barton outside the universe of cause and effect, safe from the ineluctable horror of that death, without fear as the Beer Boys snapped the fresh magazines into their guns and unloaded sixty-four bullets into her head at point-blank range.

No-one saw them get off the bus. There was too much smoke and blood. But they were heard. Above the screams and coughing, one of them sang out:

'*Bolshoye spasiva! Priyat na svampi poznakomitsa!*'

His friend laughed: a throaty honk that descended into snorts.

'*Peevo!*' said the first man.

'*Peevo!*' cried the second.

No-one on the bus had any idea what the men were talking about, except for their final word. The woman at the back with the Meat Loaf Walkman had once been on a stopover in Moscow and recognized the word *peevo*. It means beer.

two

The following morning I couldn't open my eyes.

They felt tender and gritty, as if during the night someone had spitefully sprayed sand onto my eyeballs and then sewn the lids together. But this didn't bother me unduly; I didn't want to open them. I knew that when I did, I would be admitting a new universe of dislocating physical pain, along with the Euclidean problems of getting up from where I was, washing, dressing and debating the relative merits and demerits of going into work.

What's that phrase? Drunk as a boiled owl. We'd started early the afternoon before, G&Ts at first, after a few spliffs on the way there. Then there was pizza and wine in some place in Dawson Street. I had dough balls. I like them. We ran into a journalist. Writes about theatre. Self-important arsehole. Has a Dutch or German name. Hans somethingorother. I kept singing it out at the top of my voice.

'*Hans! Hans! Hans dat do dishes!*'

Hilarious at the time.

We switched to pints afterwards. In Kehoe's, I think. Then the cocaine was produced and suddenly we were Gods Among Men. Went to some other bar after that, can't remember where. Place full of chrome. Good music though. Didn't talk a lot, just bobbed our heads around.

For the rest of the night . . . it's blurry. I know we ended up in the Sidebar, because that's where we always end up. It's a club which intends to project a stately ambience by being brown and musty. Musicians, comedians and TV presenters collect there every weekend and pretend to be pleased to see one another, along with dozens of people who want to be musicians, comedians or TV presenters. Of course we hate it: full of wankers. But there's a VIP section where we can usually get in, except if there's actual VIPs in town. We've been going there for years, yet whoever I'm with, there's always the same discussion at closing time: *where will we go? Where will we go?* Everyone looks puzzled and hums and haws, waiting for some arse to say: *what about the Sidebar?* Just so the rest of us can cry: *oh no, I hate that place. There must be some place else*, knowing full well there isn't.

Not that it matters where we go at that hour. All we really want is what the Sidebar provides: seats at one in the morning (we're old fellas now), drink and a nice comfortable toilet in which to take cocaine. On the nursery slopes of early middle age, one's needs become simple.

This was the kind of thing that was going through my mind prior to opening my eyes that morning. It was quite enjoyable, but not destined to last: my oldest friend in the world had decided that the time was right to give me a good root in the hole.

'Dillo! Story?'

Bongo Mannion had the occasionally annoying habit of speaking in working-class Dublin vernacular, despite the fact that, like me, he was a middle-class kid from Dalkey and, like all such kids, could probably speak better French than Dublin.

Most people found his jollity annoying, but I liked him. We'd been at school together, and after that in a band. At one time, Bongo and I were considered one of the best rhythm sections in the city; me on bass, him on drums. This, however, was not how Dermot Mannion got the name Bongo. Most people thought it was because he was a drummer, while in fact he'd never played the bongos in his life. His original nickname was Bong, due to the startling amounts of grass he liked to consume.

Bongo's friendly kick jolted my eyelids open, giving the morning sunlight the chance it needed to microwave the meagre contents of my head. It hurt.

'Fuckya, Bongo.'

'Come on, Simo, up you get,' he said, unreasonably jaunty considering the hangover he should have had. 'I've got to get in for a meeting, and you should go into your place as well before they forget what you look like. And what do ya look like?'

I probably didn't appear my best. I was lying where I had fallen asleep: on the parquet floor of the living room in Bongo's apartment. I was wearing a black John Rocha suit which had looked good when I put it on two days before.

Bongo poked my clothes with a chubby toe.

'Yuk.'

It was an apt adjective, but one which could equally have been applied to him. There was a time when Bongo was eleven stone and couldn't put on an ounce. But somehow, when he hit his thirties, he contrived a way around that problem. Now he was fat. He was just out of the shower, his black hair gelled back like Lord Snooty in the *Dandy*, his jowls covered in shaving cream. He wore only a huge yellow tee-shirt which strained across his belly. On the chest were the letters BUM, which, Bongo was fond of telling people, stood for Big Ugly Motherfucker. You could never accuse him of not having a sense of irony.

But for all that, Bongo was the most successful person of my age that I knew. He'd done some sort of master's degree in business and got a job in the Financial Services Centre selling bonds and Deutschmarks and all that kind of crap. He didn't talk much about it. Still, when we were out in the Sidebar and the assholes there talked to him in their rehearsed tones of weary exasperation, I enjoyed the knowledge that in reality Bongo Mannion could buy and sell the whole lot of them.

Naturally, I never told him any of this.

I squinted up at his snub-nosed face.

'Put some trousers on, will ya,' I said. 'I can see your bollix from here.'

'I can see a bollix from here too.'

He spun on his heel and pranced back to his bathroom.

'And that goes for the rest of yeese,' he hollered. 'Everybody up!'

Two other people were also in the apartment that morning, though at that point I paid little attention to this. My priorities were:

a) Get off the floor, an objective I achieved with little dignity and much pain.

b) Have a piss, during which I had to endure the sight of Bongo shaving while he emitted a series of well-worn barbs about the size of my penis.

c) Quench my thirst.

d) Escape the murderous throbbing in my head.

Bongo's kitchen was always equipped with reservoirs of Libby's orange juice (with added vitamin C: good health was paramount with us), and a monster box of soluble Solpadeine, our headache-killer of choice. There was little else there, apart from tea and coffee, a suspect litre of milk and several large bags of KP salted peanuts. Bongo was addicted to peanuts.

It was a beautiful kitchen, though: sleek marble, redwood and subdued lighting. It was a beautiful apartment, if a little cold: impressive to see, but somehow intimidating to live in; as if the very furniture was slightly disgusted by the unfashionable humans it had to share space with. It was located halfway up the modestly titled Proteus Tower, a pricey glass-covered box on the South Quays. Indifferent to the joys of home decoration, Bongo had bought it as an all-in job: the walls, the chairs, the integrated stereo system, the bed sheets, the cups and cutlery; all of it designed to death. He didn't cook, so in the two years he had lived there he never left so much as a thumbprint on any of his stylish pots and utensils. Bongo had a very clean kitchen.

I filled two thin, blue-tinted glasses: one with orange juice, the other with Solpadeine and water. I drank the juice while the tablets fizzed, then threw back the bitter headache mixture. I poured out some more juice, went back into the long living room, walked down to the picture window, sipped my orange and waited for the pain to subside. I liked standing there in the mornings. When it was bright, as it was that day, you could see across most of the city: a wide, shiny convulsion of shapes and colours scattered along the eastern seaboard, given life by the windy strings of traffic. All the people in their little tin boxes, listening to the scandals on *Morning Ireland*, anxious to be on time so they can get off a bit early and avoid all the other people in their cars trying to avoid them. Like ants, carefully controlled by an invisible intelligence. The Celtic Tiger, run by kittens.

The skyline was a jumble of cranes. It seems to have been that way for years in Dublin, though when I was a kid I can remember that even one new building was regarded as a major event. Now you can turn into a street and find that it has suddenly disappeared, or been transformed into some huge concrete seashell called the Centre for European Twig Lacing. All this change scares and befuddles my father, who never leaves the house in Dalkey. *Not the Dublin I know, the Dublin you were born in. Looks like toy town. Greedy drones with those dreadful flat accents. Where did they get those accents? Spoiled brats. Like you, full of education and good for nothing. The decency is gone, the purpose. That's why you are the way you are.*

The way I am.

My only living parent regards me as a complete waster. In fairness, there is some element of truth to this. Then again, my father is a complete prick.

'Good morning, everyone. And what a beautiful morning it is too. Bongo, I must declare yet again that your apartment is exquisite. Particularly salubrious on a morning like this.'

Speaking of complete pricks, here was another. The words, along with the south-Dublin *yah* accent they were spoken with, came from Brian Blennerhassett, who, I now realized, had self-lessly slept in the guest bedroom, leaving me to luxuriate on Bongo's parquet. Brian Blennerhassett was one of those people who everyone knows because he seems to be everywhere, doing everything and paying for nothing. He made his living, as far as I knew, from writing crap advertising copy, though his real career was self-promotion. Brian Blennerhassett liked to be regarded as a Literary Man About Town – he had, of course, been working on a screenplay for years – and spent most of his time attending openings and parties and press receptions: anything where he might get his picture on the back pages of the Sunday newspapers. He also adored going on radio and television shows to share his apparently limitless range of 'controversial' views.

Brian had manufactured himself into pure image. This is not an exaggeration: Brian Blennerhassett always wore a pair of jet-black, round John Lennon-style shades. Always. I had never seen him take them off, even for a second, even in the middle of the night. He also always wore a black suit with a white shirt and black tie. Sometimes he would take off the jacket.

And then there was the way he talked: like a character out of *Pride and Prejudice*. Brian Blennerhassett loved nothing more than quoting authors, especially if no-one else had read them, or even heard of them. *You've never read Denton Welch? Reeeeally? Never?* He would always pause for just a second too long, and grin, showing his uneven, gapped teeth. Brian, or BB as he liked others to refer to him, or the Dick as others liked to refer to BB, was an ugly pug: he had a great hooked nose and a constant spate of spots around his mouth and neck. Yet he did seem to get a lot of sex, mostly because his chat-up technique consisted of grabbing women and fondling them until they either gave in or thumped him. I suppose some of them bought the literary bullshit or just wanted to get off with someone famous: as a reward for his tireless efforts, Brian Blennerhassett was now a minor national hate figure.

Unfortunately, for me at least, he enjoyed being a national hate figure, a position which somehow immunized him against all criticism. If you said to him, as I often had: 'But BB, everyone loathes you. Not one person on this planet thinks you are likeable. The whole country detests your existence,' he would smile, satisfied, stick that huge hooter of his imperiously in the air and declare:

'Of course they do.'

Brian Blennerhassett had convinced himself that the hatred was genetically predetermined, a natural reaction to his sparkling brilliance. He was born to suffer for his art: an art that consisted of going to parties, talking shite on the television and writing ad copy for Bernie's Cut-price Carpet Barn.

However, the main reason I disliked him was because he was

mean, and not just in the financial sense. Brian Blennerhassett never bought a drink and shamelessly scabbed fags and drugs as if this was his inherited right, making Bongo – a wantonly soft touch – one of the Dick's best mates, at least some of the time. The Dick assumed that I hung around with Bongo for the same reason, and would smirk at me conspiratorially. I often gave out to Bongo about him, but the Bong would shrug shyly and say: 'Ah no. He's all right. You have to get to know him.'

He wasn't all right. He was a prick. Take my word for it.

And there he was, shades on, jacket off, leaning against the doorway while spraying out the verbal fertilizer that he was convinced just charmed the pants off everyone within earshot.

'Simon, how are we today? A little shrivelled in the soul perhaps?'

'Shove it up your hole, BB.'

Is what I should have said. Instead I shrugged and grunted.

Bongo wandered back in, plump, besuited and chewing peanuts. He offered some to us, we both refused, and then Bongo did something which for him was quite unusual: he stopped eating. Instead he slowly stretched out an arm and pointed at the far wall of his living room, as if the wall itself had suddenly morphed into some shimmering exotic wonder.

It wasn't, however, the wall he was looking at. Against it was his sofa, and on the sofa was the source of his wonderment. Her back was turned to us, so all we could see was her straight, ink-black hair which fell to the side, revealing a flash of velvety chestnut skin, almost down to the small of her back where a blanket covered the rest. She had beautiful shoulders: square and quite muscular. The right one carried a small tattoo: a skull. Her muscles glided against each other as she gradually awoke, the rest of her gently squirming underneath the blanket. Slowly, she moved her brown left arm into the air until it was fully extended, stretching it like a lazy cat in a hot Greek courtyard.

We gawked.

There then followed a brief and silent exchange of information between the three males in the room. Assuming Brian had once more triumphed in love, Bongo prodded him in the back, gestured towards the woman and widened his eyes interrogatively. But Brian shrugged and shook his head in the negative. He pointed at the woman, then pointed at me. Bongo widened his eyes even further and silently applauded.

I didn't feel I deserved his plaudits. There were a number of reasons why bringing a woman back to Bongo's apartment was a mistake, and at that moment chief among them was the fact that I had no idea who she was and no memory of ever meeting her. Worse still, I was well aware that I could have talked to her for hours the previous night. We might have even done the Wild Thing. I simply couldn't remember. I am prone to drunken black-outs; some of them so blanketing that I have, on occasion, invited people to my house for dinner, only to fail to recognize them when they turned up on my doorstep the following night.

I upturned my hands helplessly. Bongo smiled and chomped more peanuts.

Our mimed conversation was suddenly cut short: the woman started to move again, slowly pushing herself up from the couch with her right hand and brushing the hair from her eyes with her left. I could feel my heart start to gallop in my chest. The expectation in the room was now suffocating, and not just for me: we all wanted to see her face. She also appeared to be topless. We all wanted to see her breasts.

We were doubly disappointed.

She was actually wearing some sort of singlet that fastened at the neck and was low in the back, and her face didn't match – it couldn't have matched – the loveliness we had all imagined. It was pointy and a little pinched, as if she was constantly irritated by something. Still, she did have striking green eyes, almost perfectly round, and when she finally smiled her apparent irritation dissolved so completely I wondered had it ever been there at all. The smile made her seem painfully vulnerable, like children behind barbed wire.

'Good morning. Oh, I am a little bit wrecked. Bongo, can I use your shower?'

She wasn't Irish. French, perhaps. She pronounced Bongo *Bongooh*.

Bongooh spread his arms wide in a gesture of welcome.

'Sure, sure. Let me show you.'

He led her from the room. She had sleek, dark legs. From down the hall, I could hear Bongo offering her peanuts.

I didn't want to stand up any more: the potential sight of Gallic breasts had drained me. The pain in my head had gone, to be replaced by a vague, dizzy sensation, like my brain had lost the ability to hang onto thoughts for any longer than a few seconds. My skin felt oily from too many cigarettes. I stank. There was no way I was going to get to work. I didn't even know if I could manage to leave the apartment. I flopped down on the sofa, still warm from the woman's body and smelling faintly of White Musk. I cupped my face in my hands.

Smoothing down his greasy hair, Brian Blennerhassett went about locating his neatly folded jacket.

'From your perplexed expression I take it you do not have full recall of the night's festivities, Simon. I'm afraid I cannot help you that much, I never caught the lady's name. I can tell you we met her in the Sidebar and you and she chatted for some time.'

I really hated this: being helped in any way by the Dick. But I had to know.

'Brian, can you remember whether me and her . . . ?'

'I cannot help you there, Simon, alas. Certainly I, alas again, witnessed no such activity, but I was away to the Land of Nod as soon as we arrived here.'

He went to the mirror over the fireplace and checked his tie was straight.

'I'm afraid, Simon, that is all I can tell you. I must depart. I leave you with my good wishes and trust you will enjoy what no doubt promises to be yet another interesting chapter in your life.'

He stressed the words *your life*. We both knew what he meant. Prick.

As Brian Blennerhassett was well aware, I was married, though not happily.

Angela and I had been together for a few years, the first six months of which we'd spent in a stoned miasma in Amsterdam, me busking, her working as a tour guide in the Rijksmuseum. We'd returned to Dublin with a Dutch marriage certificate and two heads full of big plans, some of which Angela even followed up on by getting herself a scandalously well-paid job in software development. I sold all the dope I brought back from Amsterdam, then spent the money on drink. And dope.

She finally threw me out, took me back, threw me out again. She kept cutting her hair shorter, as if to better show the hardening of her eyes, the bitter twist of her mouth; suddenly she seemed worn, and I didn't want to look at her any more.

We did manage, however, to produce Emily, a chubby wild-haired two-year-old who squealed with delight whenever she saw me, and out of a dull sense of responsibility I felt I should try to reunite the family unit; I just hadn't done anything about it. We'd been separated for three months. I missed Emily.

Brian left, mobile already stuck to his ear. Bongo returned, still chewing.

He stood in front of me and rotated his groin.

'Meester Lurve-stud.'

'Bongo.'

He stopped gyrating and sat down beside me.

'Don't worry. You didn't violate the sacred vows of fidelity you hold so dear.'

Bongo was of the opinion that I should never have married. Too immature.

'Were you talking to her last night?'

'Barely. But I don't remember bringing her back here. Lucky for you I'm such a charming bastard. I was able to admit all that to her just now. She's French. From just outside Lyons but now lives in Paris. Only got off the plane yesterday and this is her first time in Ireland. Her name is Odette Doherty.'

'Doherty? Doherty? Fuck off.'

'No, really. I swear to God. She's actually here to do some sort of roots thing. Her father – who's dead, I think – was from Westmeath or some place. Un *boggeur*.'

'Odette Doherty? Fuck off, Bongo.'

'I'm serious.'

I didn't know whether to believe him or not. Her name, I decided, was irrelevant anyway.

'I should get out of here before she leaves the shower.' I stood up and sat down again. 'I'm fucked. I can't even stand.'

Bongo patted me on the back.

'Relax, Simon. Have a shower, borrow a shirt. Take your time. This woman is cool. She's not going to be following you home or anything. She just had a laugh with you and that's it. Apparently you spent the whole night talking to her about immigration.'

Despite my grumpiness, I smirked back at him.

'Really?'

At the time I was just into my latest career change, and it was going pretty much the way they all had.

By any reasonable criteria, I am a failure. I'm intelligent, I have some talents, and I had assumed that at some point in my life a desire to succeed would grip me the way it had most of my peers. But this ambition never arrived. Any career I could have had I didn't want, and anything I found even mildly attractive it seemed far too troublesome to pursue.

On that day I was a researcher for a television production company making a series of documentaries about immigrants from Eastern Europe. I'd been with them a couple of months, and started out with all the enthusiasm of a woman faking an orgasm, hoping it will turn into the real thing. I'd worked in an enormous flurry: building up lists of contacts, interviewing immigrants, typing up research notes. The company were delighted with me, until I came to a dramatic halt. Getting up, going into the office, making appointments, suddenly all of it seemed to require huge amounts of effort, far more than I was capable of. There was even a dull horror about going to work: sitting in a tatty office like all the others I've worked in, breathing in the hot air, planning lunch and the next fag break.

So I did what I always do: started showing up late, phoning in sick, inventing dead relations whose funerals I had to go to. For the two days prior to this, I'd simply been on the piss: anything to avoid thinking about the work I should be doing.

That I should now tell Odette Doherty all about this work was obviously ironic, though on that morning it also struck me as somehow hopeful: if I was prepared to talk to her about it, perhaps, behind all my own bullshit, I might be interested enough to keep going, to finish something. For a change.

I rubbed my face as hard as I was able.

'I should go to work.'

'You should.'

'But I am absolutely destroyed.'

'So?'

Bongo already knew where I was going with this. He made me say it anyway.

'You know I don't normally do this. Bongo, I wouldn't ask unless I was desperate. Just a couple of lines so I can get my shit together.'

Bongo made a face.

'I'll fucking kill you if you don't go into work.'

'I will. I swear it.'

I was lying of course. Not about the cocaine: I have a vulpine streak that has kept me, for the most part, out of trouble with drugs. Today I simply needed them to get back to my tiny grey flat in Monkstown. Sleep, I needed. Then I'd embrace my new-found professional enthusiasm.

Bongo adopted his most penetrating glare. He didn't believe me, but he hated to say no.

'Just this once. I'll get me Bible.'

Bongo kept his drugs inside a hollowed-out copy of the Bible. There were three reasons for this:

a) Security. Bongo reckoned that no-one ever flicks through the Bible. His reasoning, as I'd often told him, was flawed on this point. Apart from a few hundred CDs and at least two dozen pictures of various family members, Bongo had no personal effects in the apartment: the Bible was the only book in the place, and thus far more likely to be leafed through by nosy visitors.

b) He needed something big enough to keep all his drugs in. Bongo always had a supply of grass and coke, and not your few lines folded inside a torn-out page from *Hello!* magazine. Bongo would keep a *bag* of cocaine: he would buy thirty grams at a time; enough to send him to prison for a long stretch if he was ever caught.

c) He thought it was funny.

He came back into the room and threw the bag over to me.

'You better do it quick before your girlfriend comes out of the shower.'

I set about chopping up the lines on the glass coffee table while Bongo loitered by the door, watching out for the reappearance of Odette Doherty.

'Your woman is cute though,' he said in a stage whisper. 'If you change your mind about her, you know that I can give you a few tips about French chicks.'

He clicked and winked at me, every inch the chubby playboy. Years ago, we did a gig at the Bataclan in Paris and then afterwards, I can't remember how, we were brought to Les Bains Douche, a club stuffed with trendy Parisians trying to look tragic. Bongo, much to his own amazement, got off with a model with a thing for musicians. She brought him back to her apartment where, in the course of copulation, she cried out: 'Bongooh, sing to me.'

Not wishing to disappoint, Bongo gave her a few bars of the only song he could think of.

'Doe, a deer, a female deer . . .'

I was trying to roll a crinkled fiver into a tube when the doorbell rang. Bongo, always a rock in crisis situations, started flapping his arms at me. The gesture brought back one of the few memories I think I have of my mother: shooing cows out of our front garden. I must have been four or five. What cows were doing in Dalkey, I've no idea. I put a yellowed copy of the *Irish Times* over the lines and slipped the bag in my pocket. Bongo, hand on his heart, went to answer the buzzer. I slumped back on the sofa, annoyed by this interruption.

From where I was I couldn't hear the conversation over the intercom, but from Bongo's tone I knew something strange had just happened. He came back into the living room, his face scrunched up with puzzlement. He pointed back towards the door, but didn't say anything.

'What?'

Again, Bongo just pointed at the door.

'Bongo. Who is it?'

'It's the Guards. They're coming up.'

The thump at the front door shuddered through the apartment.

My first thought was the same as Bongo's: it must have some-thing to do with drugs. Yet it couldn't be. Bongo had never been in trouble with the police before: my brilliant logic at that moment being that if you have never been in trouble before, then you get some sort of exemption, even if you do keep large quantities of class-A drugs in your home.

Whatever it was, it was too late to prepare for this visit. Bongo went to open the door and I stayed where I was, a new wave of nausea and exhaustion breaking over me. I briefly considered going into Bongo's bedroom and lying down, but then rejected this idea: he probably needed some moral support, and anyway I wasn't able to stand up.

Bongo came back in, strode halfway down the living room and turned around. This, I realized, was strategic: it obscured the view of the water-pipe he'd brought back from Morocco the year before.

He put on his Business Face, the one he used at work and which I loved to slag him about. The Business Face basically meant that Bongo stopped grinning like a mischievous schoolboy, yet it did effect a radical transformation in the sort of person he *seemed* to be. Grinning Bongo, even in his suit, gave the impression that he'd just sobered up: his ruddy skin, his slicked-back hair starting to stick up again, made him look dotty and slightly camp, gave him a promise of fun.

Non-grinning Bongo was a Chap, the sort of fellow who, when not wearing a suit, wore rugby shirts with the collar turned up, who was a member of a sailing club and went to reunions of his boarding school: someone who always laughed a bit too loud, had a few M People albums, voted for the Party because his parents did and would eventually marry some squeaky blond girl called Tara or Sara, pronounced Sah-rah. Certainly this sort of individual would not be involved in any crime. Apart from something white-collar.

Even if he had been involved in a spot of insider trading, it didn't seem to me that the two detectives who walked in were experts in the stock market. They halted by the door and seemed reluctant to come any further, like shy teenagers at a party. There was also something incongruous about the two of them: the first was a huge bear of a man, perhaps in his mid-fifties, with unkempt curly hair and a large bushy moustache, obviously grown when *Magnum P.I.* was popular. He wore a tweed jacket, a white shirt not properly tucked into his grey Farah slacks and worn-down, muddy brogues. He kept putting his hands in and out of his pockets as if he was embarrassed about them.

'Howye, lads.'

West of Ireland accent.

'Did we get ye out of bed?'

Given that we were both fully clothed, it seemed as if his detecting skills needed a little work. We shook our heads.

'You're out the door to work then? Ah sure, we won't keep you long, so.'

The other man said nothing. He was much smaller than his companion, younger too, not much more than thirty. He was wiry, and stuffed into a buttoned-up cheap brown suit. His brow seemed permanently furrowed, as if he was working out some huge mathematical problem. He looked at us one by one with what seemed to me like raw hostility. He held a clipboard.

'Which one of youse is Dermot Mannion?'

Dublin accent. Northsider.

Bongo held up a hand. He looked like he was saluting.

'Right,' said young detective, as if this was what he had suspected all along. 'We don't need to talk to you, so you can go to work if you want to.' He pointed the clipboard at me. A tattoo in the shape of a dripping knife peeked out from underneath his shirt cuff.

'Simon Dillon?'

I nodded, for two reasons. First, because that is my name, and secondly, because at that moment I was rendered incapable of speech. It seemed impossible that it was *me* they wanted to speak to; and only afterwards did I wonder how they knew I was there in the first place.

'Yeah, yeah, yeah,' I finally said, addressing the words to Bongo by way of a question.

Bongo suddenly seemed very uncomfortable. He was obviously relieved that the gardai didn't want him, yet this now left him with the new problems of worrying about me and, much more importantly, moving from where he was in front of the water-pipe.

'Oh,' he said, rather stupidly. 'I see.'

Almost as if he could sense this difficulty and wanted to help, the older detective suddenly changed the subject.

'Jesus, you have a great view here,' he said, pointing at the window. 'Do you mind?'

He stomped over to the picture window and peered out, shaking his head in what seemed to be genuine amazement.

'God, you can see the whole city. Howth Head and the quays over there. Liberty Hall. The Spire. The Four Courts. I bet you have a telescope, what?'

'No,' said Bongo, warily.

'No telescope? Really? Ah sure, all the people in these high-rise apartments, they all have telescopes nowadays, you know. Everyone's looking all over the place, they're all watching each other. It's like that picture with your man, what's his name? The long stringy fella. Ah, what's his name? *Rear Window*, it was called.

'Anyway, that's what they are all at. It's the technology, you see, the internet and all that stuff. The Surveillance Age. I'd make sure to close my curtains at night if I was you.'

He nodded to himself and put his hands back in his pockets with a satisfied air, as if, once again, he'd managed to set a couple of citizens straight about the cruel realities of the Surveillance Age. His colleague remained beside the door, staring at his clipboard as if there was actually something interesting there.

Now obviously warmed up, Detective Magnum extracted a pipe from his jacket pocket and popped it into his mouth. He didn't light it.

'But that's the way it is nowadays. Things change so fast and it's hard to keep up. Especially for the old people. They get easily confused. That's what happens to their brains, you know. They atrophy. They just can't take the information in.'

He suddenly jerked his head back, once again childishly astonished by what he had just seen.

'Jesus, this is a grand big room. It's huge. I'd say you have lots of set dancing here.'

I was too exhausted to fully appreciate how surreal this situation had become. I was witnessing it from a dreamy distance, as if it had nothing to do with me; as if there weren't two lines of coke just waiting to be found on the coffee table, prompting a more extensive search and a long prison sentence. Bongo, however, was quickly becoming exasperated.

'Set dancing? Set dancing?' He turned to the younger detective. 'Look, we both have to get to work. Why are you here?'

The younger detective did open his mouth to reply, but the sound came from the other side of the room.

'Of course you have to get to work, and we won't hold ye up long. But that's the thing with today. It's all rush, rush, rush. Amn't

I right? People are running around like lunatics, and you know what: it's not healthy at all. All these microwaves and mobile phones and computers and all that. They all fry the brains, and you know scientists, scientists now in America, they've proved that rushing around will give you cancer, and it makes you less productive anyway. The more you rush, the less you get done, you know. And all these yokes that are supposed to save time, all these gizmos, they're just ways of getting money out of us. That's the other thing. Built-in obsolescence. Have you heard of that now?'

'Excuse me. Why are you here?' Bongo's face was flushed.

The moustached detective chortled and shook his head, amused by the impetuosity of his new friend.

'All right, all right,' he said, his palms extended outward in what he obviously considered a calming gesture. 'Don't you be getting yourself agitated at this hour of the morning. Bad for the blood pressure, even at your age, now.'

Bongo exhaled loudly.

'Right. Fine. Thanks for the advice.'

Magnum smiled broadly, oblivious to the sarcasm.

'So do you do much of the set dancing then?'

Bongo screwed his eyes shut.

'No. No set dancing. At all. Ever.'

'*Really?* I'm surprised. Because all that stuff is coming back, you know, it's all the fashion. The young people are mad into it. All that thump-thump stuff – sweaty vest music, I call it – that's all on the way out. I'm surprised now, two young fellas like you. I'd have thought now that ye would know all about that. And me an old fella telling you that.'

For a moment he sucked on his unlit pipe, silently marvelling that he, an old fella, would know about the demise of sweaty vest music. His partner, almost as if on a pre-arranged cue, started talking in a large, uninterruptable voice.

'Mr Dillon. Do you know a Mary Barton?'

'No,' I said.

'Have you ever heard of Mary Barton?'

'No.'

'So you don't know what happened to her last night?'

I shook my head, unaccountably ashamed of my ignorance.

'Two men shot her and her baby dead in O'Connell Street.'

'Jesus,' I said. The dreamy mist enveloping me was now starting to dissolve. Ugly, smelly reality was drifting back in. I felt sick.

The young detective nodded slowly. His colleague muttered, 'Shocking business. Shocking. Good-looking young girl. And a baby. Shocking.'

'Mr Dillon,' continued the young detective. He put a slight stress on the word *Mr*, as if he really didn't want to address me that way. 'Mr Dillon, do you know what a Pakhan is?'

'No.'

'Have you ever heard the word?'

'No.'

He bowed his head slightly and paused, as if considering what to say next.

I obviously looked bewildered, giving his partner an opportunity to favour me with the benefit of his accumulated wisdom.

'No need now to be alarmed. This is all very unpleasant, I know. It's a bad business. But we're only asking you the few questions because that's our job, just so we have all the facts. I'm sure now it's just all a bit of a mix-up. It's procedure. Your father would tell you that. How's he doing, your father? He's a great man, great man.'

People were always telling me my father was a great man. On this occasion, however, I didn't get a chance to come back with the usual *Oh yeah, he's fine*. The young detective obviously didn't appreciate the change of subject.

'Mr Dillon, we do have one problem. We found Mary Barton's mobile phone. The last call she made before she was killed was to your mobile. Can you explain that?'

I couldn't. I held my hands up, dumbfounded.

'And you say you don't know Mary Barton?'

'No.' I gestured towards Bongo, as if to confirm this. Bongo also shrugged.

'Maybe she misdialled. Maybe she phoned him up by mistake,' offered Detective Magnum. 'Them mobiles can be fierce tricky when it comes to dialling, especially them little ones. You can hardly get your fingers on the buttons. And that's what the companies want, so you have to dial a load of times, and of course that means more money for them. Sure the whole thing is a fix to get more money out of—'

'Yes, yes, yes,' his partner almost shouted. 'So you're saying you received no call from Mary Barton?'

'No. Well, it's been switched off for the last day or so.'

He arched an eyebrow, as if at last he had something on me.

'Why would you do that?'

'Because it's . . .' I didn't want to tell them the real reason: that I was avoiding calls from work. To my fogged brain, it seemed to be an incriminating admission. I looked at Bongo for help. Bongo sighed.

'Because he's been on the piss for the last two days. That's why.'

I hadn't really wanted to tell them that either.

The young detective, however, seemed satisfied with this. He took a quick look at the state of my clothes while a smirk curled its way around his face.

'Could you check for messages please?'

I took the phone out, turned it on and dialled the message service. The business of doing this calmed me down somewhat and gave me a chance to think, as much as I could, about what had just happened. The older cop was obviously tiptoeing around me because of my father.

The younger one extended a hand towards the phone.

'Can I listen?'

His face remained blank as he did so. Detective Magnum, meanwhile, was telling Bongo how he, in his younger days, would go on the piss for a week and hardly eat anything. He eventually had to give it up when he realized that alcohol didn't agree with him. Made him talk too much.

'No. Nothing there,' he said, handing me back the phone. His tone softened. 'Sorry to pry there, but just to be sure. You know.'

'That's OK,' I said, suddenly a great friend of law enforcement.

They started moving towards the door. The young one pointed at the phone again.

'Oh, you do have a few messages there. Angela is looking for you, and if I was you I'd get in contact with your work. They don't sound happy.'

I nodded, contrite.

'Just one more question,' he said, 'and this is procedure. You're not a suspect or anything. But where were you last night at about half seven?'

I couldn't be sure where I was at half seven. I tried narrowing it down: started in the Clarence Hotel, but that was in the afternoon. Left there after a couple, had one in the Thomas Read. It was rush hour by then: Dame Street was choked with traffic. We had a debate about whether to go to Brogan's or the Stag's Head; Brogan's won. Must have been there until eight o'clock.

'He was with me. In my hotel room.'

Odette Doherty appeared at the door, all brown skin and long legs, wrapped in a maddeningly tiny white towel.

The detectives gawked.

For a long time.

'Right. OK. Fine,' the younger one eventually said. 'That's fine. Sorry for bothering yeese.'

The older one said nothing. A stupid grin divided his face in two and he nodded his head like a toy dog in the back of a car. They shuffled off and slammed the door behind them.

'Christ,' said Bongo. He collapsed onto the sofa beside me. 'That's far more excitement than I need. What was that all about? And who the fuck is Mary Barton?'

'I don't know,' I said.

'Forget about it,' said Odette, as if this was an everyday occurrence.

Bongo squinted at her, suddenly suspicious.

'Why did you say you were with Simon yesterday evening? We didn't meet you until much later.'

She broke open her translucent smile. The children waved from behind the barbed wire.

'Really? Are you sure?'

Neither of us answered. It seemed foolish to be sure of anything.

'I must get dressed.'

She padded from the room, leaving her warm, wet footprints on the carpet.

three

'How do you know they were real police?' said Odette.

We had left the apartment and were aimlessly searching for a place to get breakfast on Haddington Road, a tree-lined sweep of large, confident Victorian houses, their big windows sparkling like eyes in the sunlight. I'd already bought a copy of the *Star*:

SLAUGHTER OF THE INNOCENT
Brutal Killers Call for Beer
after Mother and Baby Murdered

'Of course they were.'

She arched a graceful eyebrow at me, strangely unconvinced by my compelling argument.

For some minutes after the detectives left, Bongo and I had fuelled our mutual puzzlement with an avalanche of questions about what had just happened, none of which we were capable of answering. We hadn't, however, managed to come up with this one.

While she dressed – and I having finally snorted my coke – we had reserved much of our speculation for Odette: who was she? Why was she so willing to provide me with an alibi? (In the process giving herself one.) As for Mary Barton, Bongo suggested that I had slept with her once but was so drunk I couldn't remember. I was keen to think that it might have something to do with Brian Blennerhassett. He was rather quick to leave the apartment, and someone had told the gardai I was there. With the Charley doing its insidious work in my bloodstream, any one of these ideas seemed plausible and in the next instant, ridiculous. We seemed foolish, and somehow not entitled to be discussing murders and police and mysterious women; we were like pretentious teenagers.

After a shower, a shave, a new shirt and a suit doused with after-shave, I felt more level: the most likely explanation was still that this was all some strange coincidence. This new idea, that the gardai weren't really gardai, was paranoid.

'That's a bit paranoid,' I said, surprised with myself for saying it out loud. 'And – why? Why would anyone pretend to be a cop and go looking for me? What's the point of doing that?'

'I don't know. Perhaps you can tell me.'

I started laughing. The cocaine had made me a bit chatty, but it was also the way she said it: *perhapz yoou can tella meee*. She should have added, *Meester Bond*.

I put a (friendly) arm around her and we started walking again. Her hand brushed mine. Her black hair flopped over her face and she folded it back. She seemed suddenly girlish.

'Please, just believe me. You're not long in the country. That big bogman, did you see him? They couldn't be anything but Guards.'

'Well, they were not very good police.' She stopped walking. The girlishness evaporated. 'No, no. I don't believe it.' She held

42

the newspaper up to me. 'Did you read this? Do you know who this Mary Barton is?'

I had bought the paper, but only looked at the headline. I didn't want to know any more about how this woman had died; how her little girl had been shot to death. I wanted to get back to the nuts and bolts of my own life: I wanted to see my daughter, though I knew I wouldn't try. It wasn't my allocated day. Angela allowed me access two nights a week, and it would involve listening to a recitation of all my other faults as a parent to ask for an exception to this arrangement. It was Tuesdays and Saturdays. I'd turn up at eight, be nodded at by her, wildly hugged by Emily. I'd bring Emily to bed with her books: *Maisy's Bus*, *Maisy Goes to Play-school*, *Maisy's Bedtime*. As we would settle in to read, the front door would slam; just loud enough for me to hear.

Emily would look up at me and roll her enormous brown eyes.

'Where's Mama gone?'

'To get poison for Daddy.'

'Okaaay.'

Every word a song, every sentence a small pageant: we'd yawn when Maisy did, giggle and point at her cartoon bum when she put on her 'jamas, make the sound the owl makes, and then say good night: to Maisy, Teddy, Mama, Dadda.

Odette pointed at a paragraph in the paper and shoved it in front of my nose.

Last night the dead woman was named as Mary Barton, 33, from Bayside in Dublin. She was the wife of James Barton, currently serving an eight-year sentence in Mountjoy for the importation of heroin. James Barton is believed to have strong connections with the largest criminal gang in the city, headed by the so-called Drummer. This has prompted speculation that the killing could be the result of a gangland feud.

'This dead woman is married to a big drug dealer and she calls you. But you say you do not know her and the police just say, "That is OK, we believe you, Simon." Is that not strange?'

A fair point. But Odette didn't know my father. Mathew Dillon was, until a couple of years before this, probably the best-known High Court judge in the country, partly for his propensity for wearing trilbies and carrying a cane, but also because he liked to dispense crowd-pleasing novelty sentences: if a guy was up before him for repeatedly stealing cars, my old man wouldn't send him away but order him to work for a year with the gardai on car-theft prevention; a bloke who owned a shirt factory was done for cheating his taxes, so my father ordered him to clean toilets for two years, in his own factory.

That particular case turned him into a legal pin-up. For days afterwards all the papers ran gushing profiles: his compassion, his wit, how he was raising two sons by himself after the tragic death of his wife, yet still found time to indulge in his two great passions, the works of James Joyce and playing the fiddle every Thursday night with a group of doddery old diddley-ey merchants in Dalkey.

All complete crap, of course. But I'll tell you about that later.

I gave Odette the basic details, just enough for her to realize that any detective in the city would know my father and so be rather keen to believe the word of his elder son.

But this information seemed to bolster her argument rather than mine.

'If he knows your father, this does not mean he is real police. Criminals will know your father also.'

This had become annoying. Not because she didn't agree with me; it was something in her manner: there was a coolness, a rock-hard certainty that started to make me doubt what I was saying, even though I knew it was true. I began to wonder whether Odette, for some reason of her own, was trying to fuck with my head. I shivered; the way you do on a sunny day when clouds suddenly roll in, turning it cold and dark. She seemed strangely *comfortable* with all this.

'Just listen,' she said. 'Did they show identification?'

I shrugged.

'I dunno. Maybe they showed it to Bongo.'

'So, no ID.'

'Yes, but that doesn't mean—'

'Wait, please. When I said I was with you last night, they did not even ask me my name. They just said OK. My father is not a magistrate. They do not know me. I am not even Irish.

'And also: they wait until they are going before they ask you where you were last night. Real police do not do that. Only police in the movies.' She stressed the word movies with a dismissive flick of her fingers, as if cinema-going was somehow a degenerate pastime.

She seemed to prefer to believe in some black conspiracy, rather than what was obvious. I began to wonder if Odette was entirely stable. She had come to Ireland by herself, gone to a nightclub alone and started chatting to a complete stranger, then agreed to go back to an apartment with him and two other men she didn't know. That was a bit weird, even for a French person.

I considered changing the subject, though I was rather interested in how she knew so much about how Real Police should act. Then again, maybe I didn't want to know how she knew. I realized I was sweating.

'Odette, let's just go for breakfast. We'll probably never know either way.'

She ignored me. She was now staring over my right shoulder.

'Shit,' she said. *Sheet*.

'Hello again.'

Detective Magnum was standing right beside us, his face inches from mine. He was so close I took a step backwards. He followed.

'Isn't it a grand day?'

He slowly rotated his head and glared at Odette.

'Isn't it a grand day, love?'

He spat out the words, as if Odette's agreement on the state of the weather was the most important thing to him; as if all this sunshine would be meaningless unless she approved of it.

Some dull instinct made me look away. Des Conmee, a poet so spectacularly unsuccessful he had often borrowed money from me, was standing on the other side of Haddington Road. Not sure if I had noticed him, he waved timidly. I did nothing.

Odette, meanwhile, ignored Magnum and glanced up and down the street; a furtive animal.

'Ah now, love. I'd say you know better than that.'

He gripped her upper arm. He had dirty fingernails and hair on his knuckles. Beckoning with his other hand, he said:

'There's a couple of lads here want to have a chat with you.'

An old silver Mercedes had quietly pulled up to the kerb behind us. Beside it stood the other garda and a large swarthy man, bulging out of a dirty white raincoat. The smaller detective had loosened his tie and his brown jacket was pulled open. He rocked back and forth on his feet, like a child excited about going to the pictures.

'Hello again.'

He almost sang the words; suddenly a game-show host.

I would normally avoid Des Conmee: he was a bit of a bore, always bumming drink and money. But now I silently willed him to cross the road.

'Before we go any further,' continued the smaller detective, 'and just so there's no confusion here, let me introduce you to my two friends from Mother Russia.'

He pointed at the man beside him and another in the driving seat of the Merc.

'These two blokes are the most ruthless, cold-hearted fuckers I've ever come across. And they're as thick as pigshit. Isn't that right, Ivan?'

Ivan nodded and smiled politely.

'Doesn't understand a word I'm saying. Isn't that right?'

He nodded again.

I risked a look: Des Conmee had walked off.

'Now if you don't recognize them, let me tell you that these boys are already famous. These are the Beer Boys from Russia, and you may know them from such brutal murders as the slaying last night in cold blood of poor Mary Barton and her infant child. Plus several others you'll be hearing about over the next few days.'

He paused, to see did we share his delight in all this.

'So now that we're all clear that these men will drop you where you stand if I tell them to, let's all get in the car without any fuss so we can communicate with each other in an open and honest manner.'

In truth, life as most of us experience it is quite boring. Our days and what we talk to each other about are shaped by repetition: how did you get to work, what's for dinner, go and collect the kids. Perhaps we don't notice this, perhaps we don't want to because in reality there is little we can do to change it. In the average lifetime, there are only a handful of events which create any profound difference. Some of them we are aware of: doing the Leaving Cert, applying for jobs, getting married, having kids, coping with death. Others we do not realize the significance of until much later, or even not at all.

But there is also, sometimes, the unexpected: a single surprise which drops like a concrete block into a pool, disturbing every-thing, ramming into your face a single fact which you should have known all along: that even the most secure life is merely conjured up, a fragile mixture of water and air.

I know this because I've witnessed it. My father's life ran on shiny, well-greased rails, which was no more than he expected. His family were well-to-do, from Clontarf, with big Party connections. His father was also a barrister, and so, inevitably, the son went to Trinity (it being the big Prod college, you had to get special permission from the bishop in those days, but they had pull), where he too studied law. With a little help from his family, he built up his practice on the Dublin circuit, married a nice Kerry girl (also with Party connections), bought a large, ivy-covered house in Dalkey and produced two sons.

Her death, from a blood clot in the brain, was a blow of course, but not a devastating one. My mother was, after all, only one of the many elements my father felt entitled to fill his life with: still left were his promising career, his pristine reputation, his chummy lunches in the Shelbourne, the late-night visits from government ministers, the books, the fiddle, the two bewildered young boys, ready to be wheeled out before the world if the need arose.

His surprise came much later, in the form of a small, apologetic man called Michael Keogh.

Michael Keogh was born and lived most of his life in Crumlin. People there knew him as the Lash Keogh, mainly because he was notoriously lazy. Ask the Lash to do you a favour and the answer invariably was 'Of course. But I just have to lash down to the bookie's first. I'll see you in an hour.' The Lash spent a lot of time in the bookie's.

Curiously, my father and the Lash had quite a lot in common: they were about the same age, both had two sons and both were widowed early. They didn't meet until their early forties, though both of them, when younger, had spent considerable time in court, my father acting for the accused and the Lash acting as the accused. The Lash's court appearances, however, were less impressive than my father's; he was an unsuccessful criminal.

Mostly petty stuff: robbing from shops, bogus compo claims, drunkenness. He was never violent and by the time he got married and had his first child, the Lash had given up crime altogether, although he still had some dodgy friends.

He got a Corporation house in Perrystown and an HGV licence, and despite the death of his wife spent the next fifteen years driving a truck for Tayto and looking after his sons. Until the day two gardai stopped him on the Kinnegad bypass, searched the truck and in a box of Worcester Sauce-flavour crisps found enough heroin to put the Lash away for ten years.

The Lash, naturally, denied it, claiming it was planted there by people trying to get rid of him. Why, he wouldn't say.

My father was only a circuit court judge by then and so had nothing to do with the drugs case. But he did preside at the hearing at which the Lash's sons, then in their early teens, were taken into care. I can still remember him telling me about that hearing; well, telling a room full of people of whom I was one.

The Lash was hardly what you'd call a hard man, he was far too small for that, and had the sort of disposition where he felt a constant need to agree with everyone. I imagine that when he was a young lad he ran around with a gang of much tougher boys, who only tolerated him because he didn't mind the odd bit of bullying and would constantly act as a sort of Greek chorus to their violence: *Jesus, Wacker, you hit him a good hard one there. Stevo, that was a massive kick, that was brilliant.*

I'm telling you this just so you understand that pride and the maintenance of dignity were not big priorities with the Lash; he was all about survival, and so saw nothing wrong with pleading or grovelling to get himself out of a scrape. At his trial he tried to change his plea several times, in accordance with how he thought the case was going. He told a series of blatant lies in his evidence, even tried feigning various ailments to get the jury on his side: a limp for the first few days, then narcolepsy, so he could pretend to fall asleep when asked a difficult question.

None of it worked, of course, and in the end the Lash accepted the verdict and sentence with the sort of fatalism common to men with his background. Once he got to that courtroom, he knew he couldn't win. He just couldn't help trying to cheat it.

In front of my father though, he was radically different: pale and quiet. He never interrupted the proceedings, and when he gave his evidence he was monosyllabic. For the hour and a half it took to take his children from him, he sobbed in his chair. At the end he tried to hug his boys and had to be dragged away from them. He squealed like a wounded animal and, most unusually for the Lash, struggled with the gardai in the courtroom. He pointed a shaking finger at my father and screamed:

'Youse is a dirty fucker.'

My father grinned back.

'*Of course*, I had great sympathy for the young boys,' he later told us, his eyes watery from his third Scotch, his whiskered, walrus face shining red. 'But their interests would not be served by remaining close to that man or any other member of his family. An unsavoury lot.

'You should have heard him screech on the way out, when the penny finally dropped. He roared at me: "Youse is a fucker." Which I believe is ungrammatical, even for him.'

Just over seven years later, my father was standing in the driveway of our house putting his golf clubs into the boot of his silver Mercedes (a marque obviously favoured by both sides of the legal divide), when the Lash marched up to him and jabbed a sawn-off shotgun in his face.

Although myself and my brother never had much interest in sport, our father was always a large and vigorous individual. In his young days he played rugby for Leinster, and for years went swimming a couple of times a week at the forty-foot. If he was an American, my father would be called a jock.

Add to this years of congealed legal arrogance, and you have an individual who is difficult to intimidate, even with a gun. Quite calmly, he peered down at his assailant, whom he had completely forgotten ever meeting before, and knew that this man was nervous. Without a word, he deftly reached into the still-open boot, whipped out a titanium 3 wood and set about demonstrating why his long game was the envy of most men his age.

But the Lash was not so easily put off. He lunged up at my father, anchoring himself around his neck with one arm while trying awkwardly to pistol-whip him with the shotgun. There was something of a height difference between them, so for some minutes my father staggered around our front garden, the Lash attached to him; a crazed dwarf attacking a giant.

The struggle came to an abrupt halt when the gun went off, finally alerting the dozy detective parked around the corner. Within twenty-four hours of being released from Mountjoy (he had got out early for good behaviour), the Lash Keogh was back inside again.

My father was rushed to hospital, having sustained what turned out to be a relatively inconsequential injury: a series of pellet grazes to his left buttock. Nonetheless, there was the predictable media slobberfest.

He held a bedside press conference, wearing his trilby, for fuck's sake, and looked suitably suave while the reporters asked how outraged was he at being shot.

'Angry? No, not at all. Considering that this chap was aiming at my head but only managed to hit me in the backside, I'm rather pleased.'

But as it turned out, he wasn't pleased at all. I don't know when the actual moment was: when the Lash turned up with the gun, or perhaps at the press conference afterwards, when the journalists kept ramming it home to him: *But sir, you could have been killed; you were within inches of your own death.* Somewhere in there, there was a moment when a series of synapses fired in my father's brain and suddenly his indestructible existence melted before him. For the first time in his life, he became afraid.

He resigned from the bench – he called it retirement – before he even left the hospital. When he went home he changed all the locks and had most of the windows at the back of the house boarded up. He stopped playing golf and swimming, and for months at a time wouldn't leave the house, refusing to visit anyone or pick up the phone. He has remained this way for the past two years, and I doubt now that he will revert back to what he was before. He has grown thin and dark-rimmed through lack of sleep, and spends most of his time in his study, reading his way through a pile of daily newspapers, ringing all the crime stories with a thick red marker. Unless I or someone else visits and cooks, he lives on tea and toast, angrily munching as he glares out from behind his curtains at the black, malevolent world which has him cornered.

There are some friends of his who still visit, but precious few and not that often. Among his fears my father now counts silence, so he talks compulsively, reciting as if by rote all the ills of the modern world which he sees around him; a world of which I am the chief representative. By his logic, my world murdered his, so he's not always that happy to see me.

Mostly his sisters look after him, and I visit, briefly, once a week. At their insistence we have kept the whole thing quiet, though in the early days I did bring out a psychiatrist to see him. My father chased him off with a golf club. He keeps golf clubs all over the house.

One violent surprise devastated my father, and now it seemed the same thing was about to happen to me. The only difference was that, in this instance, I could see it coming, and perversely this did give me some comfort. I was surprised at how calm I was as Magnum herded us into the car: myself, Odette and a Russian squeezed into the back, the other Russian at the wheel. Magnum disappeared. The smaller detective got in the front seat.

Well, obviously not a detective. There was even a sliver of relief in this: at least it meant Odette wasn't mad. As if to acknowledge this, I said:

'You're not really a Guard, are you?'

He turned and stared at me, to verify that I had actually come out with these words. He barked with laughter. The Beer Boys, apparently keen to be mirthful at every available opportunity, raucously joined in until they were coughing and snotty.

I felt Odette's hand on my knee. She put a finger to her lips. She had a budding bruise on her arm from where Magnum had grabbed her. That was the last thing I saw.

I was seized by the hair and a black plastic bag was shoved over my head. I heard the screech of sticky tape being pulled out and then something was wrapped tightly around my neck. In such unexpected circumstances, what little serenity you have retained easily dissolves.

In such circumstances, your first reflex is the wrong one. As your eyes search for whatever fuzzy light there is penetrating the bag, you instinctively take in a large gobful of air. The air goes in, but so too does the plastic: it sticks to your face, instantly creating a tight mask of suffocation. So you blow out the air, wasting it, but already your head is dripping in sweat, and whatever oxygen is left has become warm and thin. You quickly become terrified to breathe and terrified not to, your head baking in a black vacuum, the tape around your neck seeming to tighten with every bump in the road.

I panicked. I grabbed at the bag to try to tear a hole in it and got a stinging slap for my efforts. My wrists were pressed into my lap. I remember thinking that of all the ways to die, suffocation would be my last choice; as if, were I to point this out, these men would apologize and decide to shoot me instead. I felt rivulets of sweat trickling down the back of my head and collecting inside the sticky tape at my neck. It made me itchy, while the skin on my face felt like it was being peeled off with paint stripper.

To my left I could hear Odette mumbling. I thought I heard my name so I leaned towards her. A terrific crack of light flashed before me, together with a jolt to the side of my head, which for a second I feared had snapped my neck in two. The sparse illumination inside the bag became even more blurry. I tried to cough, but couldn't. My mouth was dry and sandy and I couldn't produce any spit. It felt as if I had swallowed a large ball which had lodged in my throat. The ball was expanding, making it impossible to breathe or swallow. I panicked again. I tried struggling, but could barely move my arms. I pointlessly waved my head about and tried to shout, but no sound came. Another enormous jolt, this time to my forehead, crashed me back against the seat. There was a clang of metal and bone.

I slumped there, all the energy expelled from me, like a punctured football. In a fuzzy, detached way, I knew there was blood trickling down from my forehead and over my nose. I put out my tongue to taste it. I thought of New Hampshire. I was there once, years ago. Small towns with familiar names, tucked into the sides of mountains. Mount Monadnock. Wooden houses with porches. Like *The Waltons*. Cherry pie. You're from Dublin? Really? *The* Dublin?

I don't remember anything else.

'Would you like a glass of water?'

The small detective was peering at me, shaking his head as if baffled by my foolish behaviour. I said nothing. I tried to, but my jaw was frozen.

'What did you have to get all hysterical for? Jesus, you're a bit of a big girl, aren't ya? Fainting and everything.' He pointed to my left.

'Your friend here didn't panic at all. Cool as a cucumber, this one. And she's all right.'

I turned to look at Odette, which was a mistake. The movement produced a crippling spike of pain through my skull. I moaned and put my hands to my head. I felt her slip a gentle arm over my shoulders.

'Ah, the poor baby,' said the detective. 'Have some of this water here and then we'll have our little chat.'

I accepted the glass and sipped. Although I desperately needed to drink, the coolness of the water hurt my head. I gulped and moaned, gulped and moaned.

The detective – I had nothing else to call him – sat rigid in a chair opposite us and sucked on a cigarette. His right leg jigged excitedly as he spoke. The Russians stood behind, like attentive butlers.

We were in some sort of an office, I've no idea where. The desks were grey, metallic and rusty, with yellowed computers flung on top of them. There were piles of newspapers everywhere and a whiteboard on which the single word, *Guests*, was scrawled in large red letters. On the desk beside me was a chewing gum dispenser, the kind you buy in novelty shops. It had a large blue button at the base, clear plastic in the middle and a lid made in the shape of Homer Simpson's head. To dispense the gum, his mouth was shaped into an O, as if someone had just pinched him. The machine, however, was empty.

The detective finished smoking and handed the still-lit butt to one of the Russians. The Russian held it daintily with two fingers and searched for somewhere to put it out.

'So, Simon,' said the detective. 'Simon, are you listening to me? Are you paying attention?'

I nodded, painfully.

'Good man. We're not going to hurt you, Simon. We just want to ask you a few questions and then we'll let you go. Do you understand?'

I nodded again. The pain was starting to subside somewhat, along with the tightness in my chest. With each large breath I took in, more and more of the fuzziness went. I felt I was coming back to the world. I was not dead. Not yet, anyway.

'Now, Simon, I don't want to make a big deal about this, all right? Mary Barton. What's the story?'

He held his two hands out towards me, as if offering an invisible present. Odette's hand started to stroke the back of my neck, as if she was trying to transmit through her fingertips the answer I should give. If she was, I didn't understand the message.

I swallowed, coughed and croaked.

'Look, I've nothing to do—'

'I know that, Simon. I know you've nothing to do with any of that business. You a respectable man and all that. Though you do like a few narcotics yourself, Simon, don't ya?

'Don't ya?'

'Yes. Yes.'

'Yeees, you do.'

He seemed to greatly enjoy wringing this admission from me, as if by doing so he convicted a whole generation of hypocrites.

'But do you know what? I don't care about the drugs. I know that when we called up to the flat there you were probably a bit nervous and that, probably thought we were the DS looking for your Charley or Whizz or whatever. Of course you're going to lie. I would have done the same, Simon. I respect that.

'But now that we're here and you know I'm not really a copper, you can be straight with me and then be on your way. We know for a fact you knew Mary Barton. We want to know how well you knew her.'

I swallowed.

'I hardly knew her at all.'

Odette's hand stopped stroking. I could feel her looking at me.

This, I realize, requires some explanation.

When the bogus detectives were in the apartment that morning, I hadn't really listened to what they were saying. I heard the words, but they didn't penetrate to that part of my brain which might have recognized what they meant. I was too deeply fogged with my hangover and far more concerned that they might discover the two lines of coke on the coffee table. I denied everything automatically, just to be rid of them.

They were long gone by the time my scrambled mind managed to throw up the possibility that it was *that* Mary Barton they were talking about, and even then I found it hard to believe. No: I didn't want to believe. Didn't want to read the paper. Didn't want to tell Bongo or Odette. Didn't want to even edge towards the thought. Thinking would make it real.

I knew Mary Barton through work. Not this work: one of my previous professional incarnations. A couple of years ago, not long after the Lash Keogh incident, my father hit upon what he, naturally, considered a terrific idea: that I become a court reporter. It was, he argued, the ideal career for me, for three reasons:

a) Deep inside me his brilliant legal genes must still be loitering.

b) I had probably picked up a lifetime of legal knowledge through osmosis from him.

c) I had once (foolishly) told him I had ambitions to write.

Perfect for you, with your legal background. You can write and you can sit on your lazy arse all day long. It took him one phone call to get me the job.

He didn't usually interfere in my life to this degree – in fact he usually showed no interest at all – but I think at the time he had some urge to tidy up unfinished work, and I was certainly unfinished. I should have told him to shove it, but I was broke and didn't have a better idea.

I had only been at it a few weeks and was still enthusiastic when I first met her. I covered a case where her husband Jimmy was up for assault, an experience not new for him. Even by the standards of Dublin criminals, he was regarded as excessively violent. Jimmy Barton was short, blocky, bald and would punch anything that annoyed him: his mother, his wife on several occasions; once even a judge, before whom he was up on a charge of assault.

This time was nothing special: he got a couple of months. The only reason I was sent to cover it was because Jimmy had gone to school with, and was now a trusted lieutenant of, Martin O'Connor, probably the biggest drug dealer in the city. O'Connor was known as the Drummer, but not because of any musical talents: apparently his stomach was so huge it looked like he was permanently carrying a bass drum around; the Apprentice Boy of the Dublin Underworld. He was also reputed to be a prodigious drinker and would spend days on end in some of the crimbo pubs in town. The story goes that at the start of a binge the Drummer would always heave his huge gut onto the bar, point at it and say:

'Right. Fill her up.'

At least, that's the story.

I was sent to Jimmy Barton's trial to report that the court was full of shifty underworld types, all of them wearing expensive suits and shades while nodding at each other in a sinister, Cosa Nostra-type manner. News editors do this: make up the story beforehand and then give you grief if you can't provide it. Which on this occasion I couldn't, and not because I was being lazy, but because, apart from a few drunks and car thieves, the court was empty and I was new to the job and enthusiastic and thought the truth of what happened should have some bearing on what went into the story.

It was because of this that I met Mary Barton. Desperate for some sort of copy, I approached her outside the court and asked her for an interview. She ignored me. She didn't seem to hear me. She was rooting through her handbag, muttering to herself, and only after I'd gone through my spiel and stood there like a gobshite for a few minutes more did she seem to notice I was beside her.

She asked me for a cigarette. I gave her a Benson & Hedges and went through the spiel again, and even the second time I wasn't sure if she took it in. She kept looking around, as if she was expecting someone to turn up. I suggested we go for a coffee in the Four Courts building. She didn't say anything, simply flicked the fag ash away and started walking.

There was no interview. After another couple of my cigarettes she seemed to come to her senses somewhat but had no interest in talking about her husband. She kept asking about me, where I was from, how I got to be a reporter. Eventually I got frustrated and asked her how she felt about being married to a drugs baron, but she didn't answer. She simply bowed her head, lit another of my cigarettes.

'I hate coming here,' she said. 'I'm lonely.'

She started crying.

She cried the way men do. Generally speaking, women succumb to their tears and are more graceful for it. Men, ashamed of what they are doing, try to fight it and end up spluttering and snotty and all the more pathetic.

Mary Barton was like this. She kept a hand welded to her shuddering face, even after she had finished crying, and only took it away because she was forced to wipe off the drops of mucus teetering on her chin. Her nose was red and her mascara had run slightly. She apologized for making a spectacle of herself. I said nothing. There was nothing I could say. Though I did want to: she was a small, pretty, overdressed woman; like a little girl wearing her mother's clothes, and in the small gestures of smoking compulsively and weeping behind her red hand, she seemed to tell me what her whole life had been like.

I ran into her a few times after that, mostly around the Four Courts when Jimmy's big drugs case came up. We would smile and nod, slightly uncomfortable. That was it.

All this I told to the small detective who listened without interrupting. When I had finished he silently lit up another cigarette and stared at me, as if by doing so he could divine how truthful my account had been. I felt myself shaking. I wanted to cry, and had a brief temptation to make something up, to say anything to break the silence. Odette began stroking my neck again. I stared at the chewing gum machine.

Eventually he handed the butt to one of the Russians, stood up and rubbed his hands together.

'That's a gas yoke,' he said, nodding towards Homer Simpson. 'The chewing gum comes out of his mouth. When you press the button it makes a noise, it says *Doh!* just like Homer does. Gas it is.'

He picked it up and pressed the button to demonstrate. Nothing happened.

'Batteries must be gone.'

He threw it into my lap.

'You have it, Simon. You keep it as a whatchacallit, *memento*.'

He sat down and flashed his yellow teeth.

'It's all right, man. You're off the hook. I believe you. Look at ya: you're shittin' yourself.'

I smiled, every bit the ingratiating coward.

He gestured to one of the Beer Boys, who left the room.

'We'll be letting you go now in a minute, but there's just one last thing you can do for us. Just a little message we want you to give your newspaper. Right?'

I nodded. To tell him that I didn't work for the paper any more didn't seem appropriate. His leg began jigging again.

'You tell them that there's a Pakhan in town. Remember I said that word to you before? Not a Pakkie. A Pakhan. What word is it?'

I repeated it, the good little boy at the front of class.

He stood up, pointed at Odette, who also said the word, but slowly, in an almost bored tone. She didn't seem scared. I felt a sudden rush of anger towards her, a brief temptation to point this out to the small detective: *I'm innocent because I'm shitting myself, but she's not scared. She's your problem.*

The door of the office opened and Magnum and one of the Russians walked in, hauling between them a tall thin man wearing a tee-shirt and faded black jeans, the horrible stone-washed ones that were popular in the 1980s. My kid brother Alan used to have a pair of those. I slagged the arse off him about it.

I don't know what this man looked like because he had a black plastic bag over his head, wrapped tightly at the bottom around his neck. The bag was quite large, so most of it fell to one side, making him look like an evil gnome. They stuffed him into the small detective's vacated chair. His tee-shirt was black and carried a picture of a badly drawn head wearing a bandanna or a bandage. Underneath the head were the words *Feet of Flames*. His breath was loud and raspy and his body tense; expecting to be hit.

'Now, Simon, we want you to deliver the message that the Pakhan is in town and he means business. Right? Who means business?'

'The Pakhan.'

'Good boy, Simon. All right, lads, take it away.'

The Beer Boys stood on either side of the seated man, like magicians ready to perform some astonishing trick. With a showbiz flourish, one of them leaned to the floor, picked up a baseball bat and, with a delicate twist of his body, smacked the captive man straight in the face. It made a deep, splatting sound. The man's head bounced back and then forward. From inside his plastic bag there was a faint *Doh!* and a rushed exhalation of breath. He sat still and slumped.

The Beer Boy placed the bat carefully back on the ground and picked up one of the man's hands, moulding it into a fist until only his index finger was protruding. While he was doing this the other Beer Boy reached into his coat pocket and produced a small pair of garden shears, the kind with the curly blades you'd use for pruning roses. There was a name for them; I couldn't think what it was.

Smiling, as if demonstrating a recipe on afternoon TV, one held the extended finger by the tip while the other carefully put the hooked blades around the base.

Silently they counted to three, and cut.

Secateurs, I thought. That's what they're called.

A thin, red stream shot out from the man's hand as it fell back into his twitching lap. Odette and I both yelled and jolted backwards. It wasn't just what they had done to him: it was the vivid colour of his blood and the way it seemed to be reaching towards us. I started shaking again, and crying.

The Russians, meanwhile, had also stepped back to avoid being splattered. They were laughing, like it was bubbling champagne at a wedding. One of them held the pale, disembodied finger, giggling as he did so. He wiggled it between his own fingers, and the more he did this the more hysterical his laughter became. He nearly dropped it, causing his partner to become breathless with consumptive-sounding giggles.

He swayed around to face us. He began to speak, then had to halt to compose himself.

'Pakhan,' he spluttered. The other Russian howled and slapped himself.

A pool of dark, thick blood had now formed around the unconscious man. Flowing from his open knuckle, it divided into rivulets over his jeans, wriggling their way down to the growing lake beneath him.

'Pakhan,' the Russian repeated. He staggered towards me until the finger was within inches of my face. I jerked my head to the side, but the finger followed me. I looked down and saw the erection pressing against the Russian's trousers. I tried to back away, but found I was against a wall. Tears blurred my vision, making me panic all the more. The small detective was saying something to me, but I couldn't hear it. I tried to stand up, but the Russian had already grabbed me by the throat.

'Pakhan. Pakhan.'

Slowly, he slipped the finger into the outside breast pocket of my jacket. It was still warm.

I started screaming then, though I could barely breathe, stretching my head to the right to get it as far away as possible from the warm leaking digit in my pocket. I must have fallen off the chair, because the last thing I remember is crashing against the floor and noticing that the carpet had *Dublin Corporation* embossed into it, which was a bit stupid seeing they didn't want me to know where I was. I thought I heard Odette shout something, and also the voice of Magnum; distant, as if on the other side of a roaring river:

'Ah Jesus, he's after getting sick everywhere.'

I wondered who he could be talking about.

four

I have no real memories of my mother. I have an idea she wore blue dresses, though this could have come from photographs. There was a period in my life, when I was about three or four, during which I kept peeing in public. I can remember, or think I do, being left by myself in a bottle-green Zephyr while she scuttled into the shops. I managed to crank down the window, drop my trousers and shoot a graceful arc of urine out onto the pavement, much to the screeching amusement of a clump of passing schoolgirls.

My mother was less entertained. Back at home, she heaved me up onto the wooden breakfast bar – the height of modernity at the time – and announced that we should have a little talk.

'Simon, I was upset with you for doing your widdle in front of people. Do you understand that?'

I nodded yes.

'Do you know why?'

I had no idea why. I looked around the room for a few seconds, then asked could I have some orange. She shook her head, but smiled and took one of my hands in hers.

'In future, Simon, you'll have to do your widdle in the toilet like Daddy and me. It's what the big boys do. It's what they do in National School.'

I didn't want to go to National School if that was what they did.

She seemed to sense this, and with an air of reluctance changed her angle of attack.

'Simon, when you were doing your widdle, did those girls laugh?'

I nodded vigorously.

'Yes, but they didn't laugh because it was funny. They laughed because they all do their widdle in the toilet. They think that because you don't, you are a baby.'

Baby: to a toddler, bent on growth, there is no crueller word. My fat little face puckered up, my eyes swam with tears. Knowing its effect, my mother tried to hug me, but I pushed her away and dashed into the back garden. I sat on the swing, but didn't swing it; my own motionless protest.

I stayed there for what seemed like months, though it was probably about twenty minutes. She came out with orange and a biscuit and laid them on the grass before me.

'I'm sorry,' she said.

An adult who could be sorry; who could admit to error. This was a wonder. She hugged me and told me she loved me. She smelt of hairspray and cotton. I never peed in public again. Well, not until I was a teenager.

But as I say, this probably never happened: it's a fiction I can conjure up to fill the arid spaces of my memory; so vivid to me that I often dream it.

She comes out of the kitchen, and I'm on the swing. She's wearing a blue dress and her auburn hair is scraped back into a bun. She's carrying something, but not the biscuit and orange. I can't make out the drink but there is a small, white plate and on it a large, black slab. It looks like hash, and I think: this is a strange thing for my mother to have. She tips her head to one side and says:

'Simon, this is your fault. You made this happen. Now don't be a baby.'

'Dillon, come on, boy. Wake up.'

I cracked open my eyelids. I could make out a yellow fuzz, little else, and it struck me that this was the third time that day that I had woken up in a strange place. I had been beaten, suffocated, interrogated and terrified; it probably wasn't even lunchtime. I felt a perverted swell of pride at how much abuse I could endure.

The fuzziness subsided, and I saw I was on a pavement, nose to nose with the plastic Homer Simpson, my hand clasped around him. Homer still looked surprised.

'What time is it?' I said.

'Why, do you have to get to the dole office?'

The Cork accent was familiar. I half turned onto my back to see Leo Broder crouched above me.

'Jesus, boy, you stink.'

I did stink. The smell of vomit pricked at my nostrils.

Leo Broder gingerly put a hand on my shoulder.

'Lie there now for a minute while this woman has a look at you.'

The paramedic's fingers investigated me. She asked did I hurt anywhere. Helpfully, I told her I hurt everywhere.

'Check out his arse,' said Broder. 'I'd say they couldn't resist giving him one before they let him go.' The paramedic tutted. Broder winked. Sodomy humour was his speciality.

Despite its growth in recent years, Dublin is still a relatively small town, so it's not uncommon to see familiar faces. But even by those standards, this was something of a coincidence. Leo

Broder was the only detective I knew, as well as being someone else acquainted with Mary Barton: a few months after his assault case, Jimmy Barton got fifteen years for possession of heroin with intent to supply. Leo Broder was the man who arrested him.

I had got to know Broder fairly well during my court reporter phase, though I had met him many times before that. Broder was that most unusual of individuals: a garda who didn't like country and western music. He had been a fan of the band I was in, and had come to a lot of our gigs in the earlier days. We'd often bump into him at parties or in the Sidebar; I'd even smoked a joint with him once. Hip Cop, we used to call him.

He was a couple of years older than me. His head was always shaven, and his wiry, Marlboro Man body always uniformed in jeans and black tee-shirts under a long leather jacket. But it was his face that was the most striking: he didn't look old so much as eroded, as if every drink and cigarette had been invited to leave its individual mark there. His eyes had disappeared into deep shadowed holes in his head, and his Cork accent was throaty. He looked like a man who'd seen a lot, but didn't like to speak of it.

That was what he looked like: Leo Broder was in truth a horny little schoolboy trapped in a moody cowboy's body; a stroke of luck he never got over. Women loved Hip Cop. This feeling, however, was not entirely reciprocated.

'So is he all right?' Broder asked impatiently. He had some reservations about women in the emergency services.

'Seems to be. A few big bruises. But we'll bring him in for observation. He may be concussed.'

'Arra, I don't know. Dillon, are you concussed?'

'Hip Cop,' I said, a few steps behind this conversation.

'Well, you still have a mouth on you anyway. Let's get you standing up.'

'No,' said the paramedic. 'We should put him on a stretcher.'

Broder ignored her and hauled me off the pavement. Verticality made my head swim. I staggered and they caught me. Slowly, the three images floating in front of my eyes coalesced into one. Ambulances, a fire engine, police cars strewn about, lights winking, doors open. People standing everywhere, cradling large cameras, chatting on phones, talking in groups. It was a wide main street but there was no sound of traffic. Just voices. Broder patted me.

'What's this?' He was pointing at Homer Simpson, still in my arms.

'Chewing gum machine,' I told him.

'I can fucking see that. What are you doing with it?'

'They gave it to me.'

'They gave it to you. Why?'

I shrugged. 'Present.'

'They gave you a present? They kidnap you, beat the shite out of you and give you a present. Jesus, you were fucking kidnapped by Santa.'

Broder called over a uniformed garda.

'Give it to him, Simon.'

'Why?' I asked, handing it over.

'Fingerprints, ya langer.'

'I think he's concussed,' said the paramedic.

'Ah, he is not,' said Broder, master of the quick diagnosis. 'I know him of old. He's always like this. I'll bring him across the street and get him a brandy. He'll be fine.'

'He really should come to hospital,' insisted the paramedic.

Broder took a long, relentless look at her. She was mousy-haired and dumpy. Although Hip Cop didn't like working with women, he would indulge their opinions. If they were good-looking. Unfortunately for the paramedic, she fell somewhat short of this criterion. Broder put an arm around me.

'We are going across the road here. *You* are going to fuck off. Is that clear?'

Her face washed purple. She rooted in her bag and roughly handed me some painkillers.

'I'm going to report this. This man could be seriously injured.'

She strode off. A smirking Broder watched her go.

'You do that,' he said. 'And while you're at it, join a gym.'

He shook his head, mystified by how unreasonable she had been.

'Jesus, Dillon, did you see the size of her hole? I wouldn't want you in an ambulance looking at a disgusting hole like that. You're sick enough as it is. And she could slip and accidentally smother you to death. She should have a licence for a hole like that. Fucking dangerous weapon.'

I paid no attention to the size of the paramedic's weapon. I was now looking about me, and finally starting to realize the extent of the devastation on this street. Behind us was what was left of the glass frontage of a bookie's office. A painted wooden sign, *Cunningham – Turf Accountant*, hung by a single wire from the top of the building and slowly spun around. The wide front window was gone, replaced by the back axle of the old silver Mercedes, as if the car had been carelessly tossed there by a thoughtless giant. Circular slivers of black tyre lay scattered on the pavement, mixed in with a million shimmering pieces of glass. There was a stench of scorched rubber.

The front windows of the shops on both sides of the bookie's had also been smashed, a Concern charity shop on one side, a butcher's on the other: in the display, a grinning plastic pig's head had a neat bullet hole between its eyes.

'You don't want to go in there,' said Broder, nodding towards the bookie's. 'Fucking horrible. Blood everywhere.'

I groaned, feeling sick again.

'Sorry, boy.'

'Where are we? What happened?'

'Not far from town. Stoneybatter. What happened? Fucking bedlam, man. Your Mercedes there came speeding down Manor Street and into Stoneybatter, but on the wrong side of the road. Five other cars crashed into each other, a man on the pavement over there had a heart attack and the Merc itself hit a fourteen-year-old girl.

'They stopped here. You and your friend were in the boot. They threw ye out and rammed the window. Then, cool as you like, out they got and let off a few dozen rounds. Automatic weapons. Everyone in there dead. Five of them. The man with the heart attack died in the ambulance and they don't have much hope for the young girl.'

He spat on the ground and popped a cigarette in his mouth. His lighter wouldn't work.

'Fuck.'

He threw the cigarette away. He dropped the tone of his voice until he was barely audible, as if what he was about to tell me wasn't obvious to everyone else.

'Dillon, these guys are fucking lunatics. We found two other bodies on the Coombe this morning and one on Fitzwilliam Square. Compared to them, the poor fuckers here died a peaceful death. The two guys in the Coombe were shot up the arsehole. Can you imagine how painful that is? You don't die at first, takes about twenty minutes. Everything bleeds out your hole. Fucking sadists.

'And the guy in Fitzwilliam Square? They cut his head off and stuck it on one of the railings. And birds were picking at it and everything. *Oh Jesus*. Fucking psychos. That's twelve people they've wasted in the last twenty-four hours. Twelve people. They're fucking serial killers. Jesus. The chief inspector, the minister, they're all going berserk.'

Another wave of nausea broke over me. I thought of the Beer Boys' cackling faces. I reached out an arm.

'I think I need to sit down.'

'No worries, boy,' said Broder. 'We'll get you over to the pub. Your chick is there. Wouldn't mind a chat with her as well.'

He slipped an arm around my back and guided me across the street, limping slightly as he did so: officially, the limp was due to a bad knee, the result of too many vigorous squash games. But the night we had smoked a joint, Broder told me he had the early stages of MS. That was, what, five years before? I didn't know if his condition had worsened or not. We never spoke of it again.

The pub was the standard suburban design, an indifferent 1970s wood effect: the kind of place that gets busy at the weekends, but never packed, where they have table service and most of the customers went to school with the publican. There was a dim-lit cosiness to it; an alcoholic womb.

This place, however, did have one unusual feature: a large, framed bus-shelter-size poster of Bertie Ahern, grinning outside the Mansion House. The picture was obviously taken long before he was Taoiseach: he was Lord Mayor of Dublin, and seemed impossibly young and chubby-cheeked, showing a row of battered teeth while his hair stood up in the wind. He wore his mayoral chain at a slovenly angle, and seemed like a schoolboy who had won the title by mistake and thought it all a bit of a laugh.

Odette sat beneath the grinning mayor and talked to a uniformed woman garda. Her black hair shimmered in the dim light and her baggy cardigan fell from one bare shoulder at a teasing angle. She looked up and smiled: as if we had arranged to meet there, as if this was a normal day where we'd go for lunch and a stroll around Grafton Street. There was something bouncy about her walk towards us; almost goofy.

'Nice chassis,' whispered Broder. 'Do you think there's any chance she's carrying drugs on her person?'

I didn't reply, save for a look of blank bafflement.

'Relax, boy. I wouldn't mind strip-searching her is all I meant. Jesus, your sense of humour is gone. You're going on like you've been through a traumatic experience or something.'

Odette hugged me, affording Broder the opportunity to visually devour her arse. I introduced them. He took one of her hands in both of his.

'Odette, Dillon has told me many times of how lovely you are. But now that I see you, I realize how much he needs to work on his vocabulary.'

She smiled.

'Thank you so much,' she said, mock-coy. 'We only met last night. But it is still lovely bullshit.' *Bullsheet*.

Broder laughed, the way he always did at attractive women's jokes, but still held onto her hand. I hugged her again, just because I could.

He brought us down to the Bertie Ahern corner and ordered coffee, sandwiches and brandy. I was instructed to drink the brandy first, and only after I had done so did I realize how much I needed it: my hands were shaking, and I could see in the reflection from the mirror behind the bar that my face was a chalky white. In that closed environment, the smell of puke from my clothes was also more pronounced. I took long, deep breaths to fight off dizzy spells. I ate and drank, and while I did so told Broder all I knew: waking up at Bongo's, the visit from the bogus detectives, even Odette's suspicions about them. The last bit I mentioned deliberately, more to alert Broder about my suspicions of Odette.

'Really, Odette. Now that was clever. Most people wouldn't spot stuff like that. Langer here obviously didn't,' he said. 'Don't tell me now you're in the police over there in Paris. Are ya?'

This was not so much cunning interrogation as straightforward chatting up.

'No, no. But I do deal with the police a little. It is not the same here exactly but I am an *avocate*. A lawyer.'

'Really? Ah sure, we've loads in common so. And what do you call it? An advocaat?'

'No. Advocaat is a drink made from eggs. I am a lawyer.'

We got more coffee and I told the rest of the story. The kidnap, Mary Barton, the torture. Broder said nothing and occasionally nodded, like he was listening to a story he'd heard before. He interrupted me only once; when I used the word Pakhan.

'Pakhan? You're sure that's what they said?'

When I finished he sighed loudly and lit a cigarette.

'You were lucky. I can tell you that for nothing. They obviously just wanted to scare the shite out of you.'

'Well, they did that.'

He looked thoughtfully at his fag.

'And you say they thought you were still a reporter?'

'Yeah.'

'I'd say that's what saved you. They wanted you to deliver the message about the Pakhan. They probably thought you'd need all your fingers for typing.'

'Ah fuck, Broder. That's not funny.' I had to take more deep breaths.

'Sorry, boy. Sorry. We found the finger in your pocket. The rest of him was down the road. What was left of him. They cut off *all* his fingers. We can't even find them. Then slit his wrists to be on the safe side. Bled to death. Fucking sickos.'

As I panted, Odette got to the point.

'Leo, do you know what is going on here?'

Leo shook his head. He gave a last huge suck on his cigarette and jabbed it out. He frowned, causing his eyes to sink even further behind his weathered cheekbones.

'Drugs and power, Odette. It's all got to do with drugs and evil men.'

He sat back in his chair and leaned in towards her. I had a brief flash of jealousy.

'In Dublin now there are seven criminal gangs who have the city carved up between them. On top of that there's a fair few Provos – you know, IRA – floating around the place.

'All the gangs control the drugs trade in their area, though nowadays it's about much more than drugs. It's protection money, robbery, smuggling cigarettes, stealing bits of computers and all the legitimate businesses they have for laundering the money; anything and everything really.

'Anyway, as you might know, there's been a fair amount of emigration into this country from Eastern Europe. Bosnians and Russians and all that. Now some of the boyos that came over with them have been a bit dodgy, all right. Connections with the Russian Mafia and that kind of stuff. But to be honest it wasn't that much of a problem. Credit card fraud, few bits and pieces like that. Nothing big though. But.'

He took out another cigarette and lit it, master of the smoky pause. Despite myself, I could see how people found him attractive.

'But,' he continued, 'in the last few weeks we've been hearing rumours that the Russian mob was going to move into Dublin big time. It seems someone has invited them over, but nobody knows who it is. The talk is that the Russians are sending over a Pakhan. That's like a Russian crime overlord or something. Apparently, in Russia, if a Pakhan arrives in town, all the local crimbos shit themselves and head for the hills.'

He touched Odette's arm.

'Pardon my French,' he said, immune from his own irony.

'So of course the gangs here and the Provos are all going spa. These two Russian blokes, these Beer Boys, have killed gangsters from all over town. Everyone is getting hit.'

He pointed out the door.

'That bookie's shop belongs to the Drummer, and now the Drummer's outfit is fucking huge. Big chunk of the northside, biggest gang in the city. Evil, clever bastard, he is. But the Drummer nor none of them can retaliate because they don't know who the fuck is attacking them.'

He laid an apologetic hand again on Odette's arm.

'That's OK,' she said. 'I have heard this kind of talk before. Don't forget, I am an advocaat.

'But Leo,' she went on, 'why do they want Simon?'

He shrugged. 'Haven't a clue. Dillon, you say she never rang you?'

'No.'

'When was the last time you saw her?'

Now I shrugged. 'Haven't a clue.'

'Well, maybe she tried to ring you and never got through. At the crime scene her bag and mobile were missing, all right. The lads probably took it to find out who she was talking to. Maybe she knew she was in trouble and tried contacting you because you were the only straight person she knew. Well, straighter than her, anyway.'

Given that Broder had put her husband in prison, he had a less than sympathetic opinion of Mary Barton.

A uniformed garda entered the pub and walked up to our table. He was carrying a neat pile of clothes.

'Dillon,' said Broder. 'I'm like your fucking mammy, I got you some clothes. Go in the jax there, change and go home.'

I looked at them. A pair of Levi's and a black tee-shirt. Broder's kind of clothes. The tee-shirt had a small black and white photograph of Bill Gates printed on the chest. My kind of guy.

'Where did these come from?'

'Courtesy of the taxpayer. Think of it as a rebate. Put them on and go home.'

But I didn't move. Emptied of energy, I stared at the clothes with bleary gratitude; like a tearful little boy on his birthday who hadn't expected any presents.

'I was going to go to work,' I said.

'Dillon, ya langer. You were fucking kidnapped by gangsters. They'll give you a few days off. I'll ring them, all right?'

I nodded and compliantly tramped over to the toilets, clutching my new clothes to my chest like a refugee. I could hear Broder telling Odette that the other guy they found was wearing stone-washed jeans, and you couldn't get them in Dublin any more. Did they sell stone-washed jeans in Paris?

The toilet was thick with the smell of disinfectant. I locked myself in a cubicle and cupped my head in my hands. Graffiti sprawled across the door. *Santry is a shithole. For a good blowjob ring Emer. You don't know nothing except yourself.*

You don't know nothing except yourself. There was a name for that. What was it? Solipsism. None of this is real: Bongo, Broder, Odette, the Beer Boys. Made the whole lot up. Just me in my imaginary jax. Nothing to fear, no hurt, no grinding work to do. No seething Angela. No little baby to point at me and say Dad-dee. That's what I seemed to want; to make my husk of a life safe by killing everyone else; too cowardly to kill myself.

The thought made me shiver. I felt like crying, but nothing came. My eyes and my insides were dry. I hugged myself, and felt pathetic for it. Now I wanted to get back outside, be with people; as if, should I stay here too long, everyone else would disappear. Awkwardly I pulled off my clothes.

Changing made me feel better. There's something optimistic about a stiff new pair of jeans. I emptied out the pockets of my trousers. Keys, wallet and £27.43, most of it in pound coins.

I used some of the pounds to buy a freshen-up kit from a coin machine. I scrubbed my face, brushed my teeth and told myself that it was just too incredible to believe that a bunch of Russians could come to Dublin and simply take over. It was ludicrous. There was a small bottle of aftershave, so I sprinkled it over my jacket which, remarkably, hadn't been hit by any blood or vomit. I put it on and inspected myself in the mirror. I looked like shit. But it was a vaguely healthier sort of shit. I looked around the toilet and absent-mindedly patted myself to ensure that I wasn't forgetting anything.

I still had Bongo's cocaine in my pocket.

You might think that someone in my position, who hours before had watched a man have his finger cut off because of drugs, would be less than keen to have anything to do with them. You might think that if you've never taken drugs. But fuck it: I'd been beaten stupid and scared shitless; I was cash-rich with excuses, and this, after all, is what people like me do in times of crisis. We buy the happiness we see advertised in brochures, pay for mechanics to fix what's broken down, take out home and contents insurance, go to see counsellors, homeopaths and a friend of a friend who'll do you a favour but isn't a dealer. This is my generation: clean and ballpoint neat, producing and consuming like factory hens. We're not rounded individuals; we're not individuals *at all*. Of all the people I grew up with, I can only remember a few clearly: the rest have coalesced into identikit couples, shopping in Brown Thomas. But shove a bit of white powder up our dreary, pale noses and suddenly we have the personality our lives have squeezed out, at least for a while.

This and many other thoughts scampered through my brain

after I had done a rather substantial line of Instant Personality. I thought of Angela, some time the year before, sitting cross-legged on the floor, surrounded by a huge fan of home decorating books. Fierce and almost tearful. *I have to do everything. Do you not care about making a home, Simon? I don't understand that. What do you care about?*

Good question.

I walked around the toilet for a while, splashed my face with water, took in healthy lungfuls of disinfectant. Yet still the weariness nibbled at my edges.

I did another line.

That did the trick. It did the trick a bit too much. I noticed I was talking to myself, striding up and down, that now, rather than a pale face, I appeared to have a tan. I was frantic for Broder and Odette not to know that I had taken any drugs. Why, I don't know. Neither of them would have been particularly shocked, though I suppose Broder wouldn't have been too pleased. I was like an anxious teenager.

Actually I wasn't. I was fourteen when my father first caught me smoking a spliff, and I didn't give a shit.

'Do you know what drugs can do to you?' he thundered.

'Yeah. That's why I take them.'

He slapped me across the head, which gave me a curious pleasure. I was made to throw the hash away and treated to a long lecture on the evils of drugs which he had witnessed. He was going to bring me down to court and make me sit there for a week, get a counsellor to talk to me, lock me in my room. But I knew none of that would happen, and it didn't.

After a brief fit of giggles I was ready to re-emerge from the toilet. I studied my bloodshot face one last time in the mirror, looked at Bill Gates peering out from my chest.

'You,' I announced to us both, 'are a failure.'

Outside, Broder was attempting to read Odette's palm, telling her that romance with an attractive Irishman was imminent. She winked at me.

'Perhaps you are right. And here comes an Irishman now.'

Broder threw me what he would call an arch look; his definition of arch being *you're going to have sex tonight, and I'm not*. He let go of her, picked up his mobile, keys and fags and stood up.

'You look much better,' he said.

I nodded, opting for silence as the best way to disguise my narcotic state.

'Right. Go home, go to bed. Stay there. Don't talk to anyone, especially reporters. I'll give you a bell this evening.' He rubbed his shaven head. 'Jesus, what a day. I have to go to a fucking funeral now in Glasnevin. Death is all around me.'

Broder patted me on the back, kissed Odette for slightly too long and then was gone. The other cops followed. Suddenly we were alone in the shadowed, stilly pub, chubby-faced Bertie Ahern grinning down at us like a vampire with a dental problem.

A barman appeared and began tidying up.

'Can I get you anything?' he said, in a tone that made it clear that he didn't want to get us anything.

'No, we're just going now.'

'You take your time. There's no rush. I just have to get ready for the lunches, you know.'

As we walked out the door I looked at my watch. Ten past twelve. Yet it seemed like weeks since this had all started. Odette felt like an old friend. She took my hand.

'What do you want to do?'

The police cars and ambulances had all gone. Traffic was snarling up and down Stoneybatter. The bookie's shop was already being boarded up: just a normal bit of building work in Dublin. You'd see it anywhere, except for the yellow tape which fenced off the front of it, forbidding access to the locals who stood about in anxious huddles. They glanced around them, unsettled by the idea that their home could have welcomed in such darkness.

It was still sunny, enough to make me squint, though a few clouds were now starting to creep across the sky.

'I don't want to go home,' I said. 'I'd feel cooped up. Let's go into Stephen's Green. We can go for lunch or a drink or something.'

I didn't really fancy lunch. But I did feel like a drink. I felt like many drinks: Jesus, I deserved them. The danger was now past, my work was done, and if there was ever a genuine reason to go on the razz, this was it. I wanted to sit in a corner of the Bailey or Kehoe's or the Shelbourne bar, anywhere, and talk about this; analyse it until it could fit into my head.

We started hailing taxies. I really wanted to chat.

'I must say I feel so much better now. I feel better than I did when I woke up this morning. I was wrecked this morning.

'You know what is strange though. Those blokes went to all the trouble of going up to Bongo's apartment and pretending they were Guards when they could have just waited for us outside. Why did they do that? What was the point of that?'

'Maybe they didn't know what you looked like,' suggested Odette. 'Maybe they wanted to check first to see if you had guns.'

'Guns? Guns? Why should they possibly think that we would have guns?'

She never answered the question. A taxi swooped in beside us, and even in my heightened state I knew it was sensible to keep this conversation private.

The driver had the radio on.

'Sorry, now. Do you mind if I listen to this for a minute?'

He turned it up without waiting for a response. It was a news report on the killings. The driver shook his head in disgust.

'That's shocking, isn't it? That must be the place it happened. Yeah, that's definitely it,' he said, pointing to the wrong bookie's shop.

'Really?' said Odette. She had quite the line in Gallic irony.

'Oh yes, love. Full of criminals, that place. Never go in there.'

The news report went to the crime correspondent, who explained the background. While Broder had been telling us about the budding gang war I had experienced a slight shiver of delight at being in on all this secret information. He might just as well have been repeating what he heard on the radio. Except for a mention of me, it was all there: how many dead, what gangs they were from, the Russians, the Beer Boys, the arrival of the Pakhan. Another body had been found in Tallaght, its legs and arms severed and stuffed into nearby dustbins. There were to be questions in the Dáil, calls for calm, a review of immigration policy, a huge manhunt, a diversion of resources: a bureaucratic response to horror.

The driver tut-tutted. He eyed Odette.

'I detect a bit of an accent. Where are you from, love?'

'I'm French.'

'Aw well, then you'd know what it's like. Don't youse have loads of the blacks over there?'

He pronounced it *de bleeks*, like he could only say it through gritted teeth. Odette hmmed in response.

'We've some of the blacks here as well, but I'll tell ya, love, they're not as bad as the bloody Eastern Europeans. All this killing, I could have told you years ago this was going to happen. Never should have let them in. Them Russians are a dirty lot. Sure they still can't run their own country. And them Romanians? They're knackers – they're worse than knackers. Puking in the taxi, fighting. Whenever they get in here I know I'll be up to the guards with them because they won't pay.

'I tell you this, I'd rather have one of the blacks in this taxi than one of them Eastern Europeans. Would ya believe that now?'

'Astonishing,' said Odette.

I tried looking out the window, grumpy at not being allowed to talk by this living cliché. But I couldn't concentrate. I looked back, and noticed that a good portion of the driver's head was swathed in an enormous black eyepatch. I couldn't get my interruption out fast enough.

'I hope you don't mind me asking, but I couldn't help seeing you have an eyepatch there. Did you have a bit of an accident?'

The driver fixed me in the rear-view mirror with his one functioning pupil; for so long that I began to worry about him not watching the road.

'Sorry,' I said, embarrassed. 'Sorry for asking. I was just wondering . . .'

'No, it's all right,' he said, his gaze finally reverting to the front. He pulled up at a set of traffic lights and wearily cracked up the handbrake. He drummed his fingers on the steering wheel. Odette threw me a puzzled look.

'You'll find it hard to believe, you know, when I tell ya what happened.'

'You don't have to. I'm sorry for asking.'

'No. No. No,' he said, now aggressively insistent. 'Youse asked me a question and I've nothing to hide, not like a lot of fuckers around here, I can tell you.

'Anyway, me ma died a couple of years ago and left us the house. Not a big house, mind, but it had a big plot of land with it that we used to play football on. And this is, now, in the middle of a big estate, the Glenville Estate, do you know it? This would be worth a fortune now what with all the building and that. So when we get left the house, meself and the wife decide that we'll sell the house but build a new one on the plot of land and live in that, are ya wide?'

We made sounds and studiously nodded.

'The wife now is thrilled with this. Thrilled. Not with me ma dying, I mean, the ma and the wife got on well, but with getting the house. Bawling, she was, she was that happy. Women, wha'? 'Cos of the house prices and all that, sure all we could afford was a two-bedroomed kip in Marino. Three lads we have, stuck in the same room. Killing each other. So we were delighted.

'But can I get planning permission? Can I fuck? Now I know all the people on this estate, didn't I fucking grow up with them? None of them is objecting, but the Planning Department is coming out with all this: oh, there's a delay, delay, delay.

'A year goes by, and nothing. Until one day I go in and get chatting to this bloke who's, like, the head of the Planning or whatever and he's acting all shocked and going, "A year? You've been waiting a year? That's terrible, that is." So I turned around and I said to him, "What are you gonna do about it then?"

'But then he goes all cute, like, you know? And he's saying to me, it costs a lot to process all this, there's a lot of expenses. And he keeps saying *expenses, expenses, expenses*. Then the penny dropped.'

He was looking in the rear-view mirror and nodding at us, to see if the penny had dropped with us too.

'He wanted a bribe?' ventured Odette.

'I had to give the fucker five hundred pounds in cash. Got the planning permission the next week. Stuck in my fucking craw. Didn't want to build the house after that. I was sick. I mean like, I pay taxes and vote and all that. I was in the Labour Party for a while. I liked that Frank Cluskey. He was a good bloke.

'But fuck's sake, that was too much for me. I couldn't look at the place then. Didn't even sell the house. The windows got smashed in and there was druggies living there for a while and the wife was going spare but I wouldn't listen. I was . . . what is the word?'

He rubbed together his thumb and forefinger, to emphasize the intangibility of what he was looking for.

'You were disillusioned?' I said.

He thought about this.

'No,' he said eventually. 'Not that. I felt . . . weak. Do you know what I mean? Weak. I wanted to make a nice house for me family and that. The wife had it all planned out and I was mad into doing it for her and the kids. I was going to build it meself, you know? I spent years in the building game in Leeds. But after that, I wasn't able for it, you know?'

We were now on Stephen's Green, pulled up by the kerb at the top of Grafton Street. It was, as usual, heaving with moving bodies: teenagers trying to look cool, families dragging kids and shopping bags, puzzled tourists, tracksuits, designer suits, shades, belly tops. Young guys with guitars and long straggly hair singing Nirvana covers, mime artists, puppeteers, poetry readers, a group of Hare Krishnas. A tall, bony woman with a portable amp and microphone enthused about Jesus.

The taxi driver turned around to us. His eyepatch was disturbingly huge, as if the one he had chosen was a size too big. It was secured so tightly the straps from it dug into the sides of his face. It gave the impression that the top of his head was bulging with the pressure.

'But do you know what? I got over that. Eventually the wife sat me down and told me straight, "We can have a house there, the house we always wanted, and no matter how we got the planning permission, it's a bloody waste to throw that away. That's not fair on the kids." And she was right.'

'Yes, she was,' said Odette, now digging in her jeans pocket for money. 'I am glad it worked out OK. And now you have built the house?'

'Oh no,' said the driver, as if this was self-evident. 'She was doing it for the best and all that, but she wasn't right. I don't know, but there was always something *wrong* about it. Those fuckers in the Planning ruined it. A curse or something. Do you believe in that sort of thing?'

Neither of us answered. It was like he wasn't looking for an opinion, but the correct reply; as if this question had bothered him for years, and now at last we could provide the solution.

'I think it's shite meself,' he finally announced. 'But still.'

He turned and stared out the window at the tall preacher. She was jabbing her arms in the air, turning, shouting and stamping her foot like a demented ballet dancer. The passing crowds ignored her.

'Well, it was nice to talk to you,' said Odette, offering a twenty-pound note.

'I won't keep you. Just to finish,' he said. He kept looking out the window, as if he could see what he described.

'We had all the plans done and I started building the house. Four bedrooms and a big kitchen and all that. It was one of them new timber-frame jobs, you know, so I was able to put that up by meself. You get a kit, like, and instructions, and all you need is one of them nail guns. Fires in the nail with compressed air.

'I nearly had it up and one Saturday I was there with me youngest, he was six at the time, just doing a few small jobs and I said to him, "Don't touch that." But they don't listen at that age.

'He didn't mean to do it. He picked up the gun and fired one into me head. Went straight through me eye. Another little bit in and it would have killed me, the doc said. Or I would have been a vegetable. Lucky, I suppose.'

Again, we said nothing. Odette squeezed my hand. I looked over at the tidal movement of the crowds in and out of Stephen's Green, and suddenly I was aware of the noise around us: it poured into the car, rushing over the silence caused by this taxi driver and his lost eye. Unaware of his tragedy; almost mocking it.

'That is terrible,' said Odette.

He turned back to us.

'Yes, yes it is,' he said quietly. 'Didn't go on with it after that. Probably sell it.'

She stuffed the twenty-pound note into his hand and we left the car. He seemed unaware of us, hazard lights blinking, watching an invisible rerun of his life turning to ash.

'My God,' said Odette, looking back at him. 'Poor man.'

I didn't want to look back. I pointed, and we began walking along the Green in the direction of Baggot Street. A dark-eyed woman in a shawl touched my arm and parroted a mantra:

'Money for children. Money for children.'

I ignored her. We walked a little faster.

I glanced at Odette. She smiled in return, and suddenly all my doubts about her crowded back like greedy bargain hunters at the winter sales: you'd think she'd want to go back to her hotel room and rest, or ring her family or the French embassy or something. *Complain.* She was a tourist, and in her first twenty-four hours here she's kidnapped by gangsters; could have been killed.

Why was she still with me? Someone she hardly knew?

Why was I still with her? Why didn't I go home or ring someone?

I didn't want to. I didn't want to leave Odette; I was too scared. Like my father and that taxi driver, I had just witnessed how the invisible frame of my life was all but rotted away; one good belt was all it needed to bring it down. I saw threat everywhere: it stalked behind the sunlight, crouched in the glare, just out of sight. It was literally a disaster waiting to happen, and Odette seemed the only person capable of dealing with this chaos. Yes, I was coked and paranoid, but given the day I'd already had, I think it was more than that. I stayed with Odette because she felt like my only friend in the world. Bongo was at work, and I knew how Angela or my father would react if I contacted them: they wouldn't be able to resist the conclusion that somehow this was all my own fault.

Dilly Golding, a journalist who I had drunkenly snogged many years before, slunk towards us. More recently, she had been appointed social diarist with one of the Sunday newspapers, a position she mistook for one of immense power. She folded the sides of her tiny leather jacket across herself when she saw me. Her smile seemed to pain her, as if she feared yet another humiliating scene where I would beg to be included in her column. I nodded curtly. She walked on.

I took Odette's hand, and brought us to a halt. Red-faced couples stumbled out of Habitat, slumped in their furnishing inadequacy.

'Let's have some lunch,' I said. 'There's some stuff about Mary Barton I should tell you. I hope you won't be annoyed.'

five

After I had told her, Odette nipped at a glass of water and said:

'But why would I be angry about this?'

'Because of this morning. I lied.'

She smiled, almost as if she had known this all along. She picked up my hand and kissed it. It seemed impossible for me to piss this woman off.

I had brought her to a place off Dawson Street called Browning's. I'd been going there for years; it was a bit of a bands' hangout. Meeting musicians was not something I particularly strove to do, that part of my life being well over, but I liked the restaurant. It had dark panelled walls and stiff white tablecloths. On a cursory glance it looked quite expensive, which successfully put off most tourists. It actually only did burgers, though they were the juicy kind you get in New York bars: with pencil fries and a token bit of lettuce. The only drinks were freezing Coke and bottles of beer.

It was popular with musicians because above the panelling were pictures of just about every band to come out of the city. My old group was there, along with a few dozen other next-U2ers. On the corridor to the toilet. *Funny.* It had an American feel because the guy who owned it was from Noo Yawk, though he'd been here so long you'd hardly notice: his accent had flattened into an Irish-American hybrid, and now he sounded more like a guy from Carlow who had watched a bit too much *NYPD Blue*.

His name was Pete Clancy, though he claimed he had no Irish blood in him, and before he opened Browning's – he called it that simply because he thought it sounded classy – he appeared to make his living from hanging around with bands. The first whiff of a deal and Pete would materialize, buying drinks, giving advice, getting you drugs. He also wrote a few band biographies and photo journals. However he did it, he made enough money to open Browning's, and now the bands came to him.

He was a parasite, but a pleasant one. Every time I went into his restaurant he would extend a hand and move me to a table as far away from the toilet as possible. He'd say, 'The usual?' and get me a cheeseburger and a Rolling Rock. He'd make some chat about who was coming up, who'd gone off the boil, but never bitchily. He'd always ask, 'Simon, you playing at all?' and I'd always shrug and shake my head. He'd make a sad face. 'I tell ya, best rhythm section in Dublin, man.' And off he'd go.

Saying it now, it sounds a bit pathetic that I would acquiesce to engaging in this ritual. Other than Bongo, I'd lost contact with the rest of the band. I didn't play any more, had no intention to and didn't really want to talk about it. Only with Pete Clancy would I allow that scab to be gently picked at. I don't know why; perhaps it was therapeutic. In Dublin, both success and failure are treated cruelly. You're an arrogant bastard if you make it, you're a joke if you don't. Pete knew this, yet despite all his years here he never became infected with this attitude, as if he had some secret knowledge that one day everyone would get what they deserved, and that everyone deserved what they wanted. He was as cute as a rat's arse, yet he was innocent. Funny mixture.

So when we went in that day, Pete and I did our usual little dance, all of which seemed to impress Odette. Pete wanted to show her the picture of the band, but didn't push it, knowing I wasn't keen. And anyway, by then I'd become a bit agitated: my hangover/beating/trauma had again begun to catch up with me, along with a certain amount of anxiety over what I had to tell her. I considered doing another line before I started, but decided against it. Perhaps I should have: the story I told rambled about like a drunk in a maze, and she kept having to interrupt me to clarify what I was saying. I felt childish and embarrassed.

What I told her concerned Mary Barton. I hadn't revealed everything to Odette before, which is why I haven't told you. I'm not trying to deceive or hold anything back; just to describe the events as they happened. My first instinct had been to say nothing and hope it would all go away. But meeting that taxi driver, along with a woolly weariness on my part, suddenly had me craving to simplify my life, purge it of duplicity and complication. Not that it turned out that way.

My original description of meeting Mary Barton was largely truthful. I did attempt to interview her, and she was distraught and distracted. In the coffee shop it quickly became apparent to me that I was going to get nothing from her, and I really didn't fancy having to ring up the paper to say this was the case.

So I sat there for perhaps two hours, alternately feeling sorry for her and for myself, and looking for any excuse not to make that call. Eventually, she provided one.

'Do you want to go for a drink? I feel like a drink.'

This, I know, is hardly a legitimate excuse for bunking off work, but to my skewed thinking it was enough: I was trying to get a story out of her, and if this required alcohol, then that's what I'd have to do. Professional to the last, that's me.

Strangely enough (since I was sober when we went there), I can't remember the pub. I can recall what it looked like, but not what it was called or where exactly it was located. Somewhere behind the Four Courts, not far. I've asked people about it, even tried to find it once, but never could. As if it never existed.

It was a local, but not like the Bertie Ahern shrine Odette and I were in earlier: this was empty, small and dimly lit, with worn red-leather seats bolted into the wall. There were a few trophies behind the bar, a torn sign advertising a pub quiz and a Dublin football jersey. We parked ourselves on stools. The barman greeted Mary by name and gave me a long look: I half expected him to say he didn't serve my type. She introduced me – I was amazed she remembered my name – and he nodded, satisfied, as if he hadn't heard anything bad about Simon Dillon.

'Are you drinking?'

This, you might think, was a bit of a daft question to ask someone who had just walked into a bar. But there's going for drink and Drinking.

Mary nodded. The barman – whose name was Tom, I later learned; married with four kids; used to drink but gave it up because he kept getting in trouble; did a year for GBH when he was in his twenties; born around the corner; worked here for fourteen years; nice guy – produced two bottles of Carlsberg and two shots of tequila. Mary Barton threw back hers like it was water. They both looked at me as if I had already committed some awful faux pas.

'Cheers,' I said, and downed the tequila.

They started laughing.

'Cheers, dahling,' said Mary Barton, reaching for her beer.

Coming into this place, I had experienced a not inconsiderable degree of unease. Mary Barton, after all, was married to a drug dealer with violent tendencies, so this was likely to be some sort of crimbos' hangout. But after a few more shots of tequila, all of which arrived unasked for and, as far as I could tell, unpaid for – I offered money, but each time it was shushed away – the disquiet that came in with me had discreetly slipped out of the pub.

The three of us sat and talked in low voices, about families mostly. Tom talked about his kids, Mary about her parents and I about my brother and father, my mother's relations in Kerry. No-one pressed for information, there was no need: as if, for just that afternoon, there was a confessional pact between us, and afterwards all our small family tragedies would be safely tucked away. We carefully examined one another's stories, and studied the past as if finally safe from it. It was a perfect pub afternoon, the sort you always strive for but in reality only experience a few times in your life.

I can't remember other people coming in, just that I looked around and suddenly the place was full. Tom shrugged, marking the end of our conversation. From that point on we called and paid for drinks in the traditional manner, as if nothing had happened.

After that, my memory is patchy. I remember eating fish and chips at the bar, and then afterwards moving to one of the red leather seats to take part in a pub quiz. Our team – no thanks to Mary or me – nearly won, but we were stumped on the tie-breaker. Something about the French revolution. Our runners-up prize was a bottle of whiskey.

The place seemed to empty out after that. Mary went to the toilet and I went outside for a breath of air. I was surprised by the darkness and the attack of cold. I leaned awkwardly against a wall and told myself I was seriously drunk and should take it easy. I smoked half a joint I found in my pocket.

When I went back in she'd taken off her jacket, and only then did I notice her in any physical sense. She was wearing a neat, white blouse, the standard gotowork (or gotocourt) variety, except in Mary's case it seemed to be several sizes too small. Mary Barton was short, slim and had substantial breasts: a touch of a young Dolly Parton without all the plastic. Her blouse threatened imminent eruption.

With that much drink taken, I was incapable of subtlety, and Mary was incapable of appreciating it. I whooped about the blouse, pronounced that she had brilliant tits. She slapped me on the arm and told me I was a naughty boy. Encouraged by my naughtiness, I grew even more suave: I dropped fifty-pence pieces into her cleavage and offered to retrieve them.

She rejected my chivalrous offer, but at some point not too long after I had insinuated my hand beneath the blouse and was rubbing her back; and then we were mouthing each other like two hungry dogs. There's a Dublin word for a kiss: a *ware*, and that's what this was; wolfish and erosive and the sort of thing that never happened to me. In the band the others would slag Bongo and me with *Going out with Pam again?* meaning the palms of our hands. He was the drummer, I was the bass player; it was expected of us.

The taxi to her place I have no memory of, and the sex I can only recall in flashes, like still photographs taken with a hidden camera. It probably didn't last long, but it was energetic.

The following afternoon I woke up surprisingly free of pain, but with a mouth as dry as sandpaper. Mary was perched on the bed beside me, swathed in something frilly. On her lap was a tray supporting a huge fry-up and a pot of tea.

'Howya, lover,' she said.

I wanted to evacuate the premises right then: fling on my clothes, leave the country and change my name. But I didn't. I couldn't. She watched me as I ate my breakfast, shy and delighted, her creamy face free of make-up and the twitching tension that had spasmed it the day before; like a little girl with a new pet. I ate like a condemned man.

This was one of the rare moments in my life when I had the clarity to realize how much I had just fucked up. At the time Angela and I had effected yet another reconciliation: this one was just six weeks fresh. I was making an effort to be responsible, following a sustained period in which I had spectacularly failed to be. The week before she had told me she was pregnant.

I should have told Mary Barton all this straight away. Declared it a tragic, heartbreaking mistake and left. But I didn't. It was cowardice, but also Mary Barton herself, her awful frilly nightgown, her chintzy house: a horrid mock-Georgian barn in Castleknock, decorated top to bottom out of an Argos catalogue. It was surgically clean and obviously unlived in, as if she'd been keeping it in plastic for years, waiting for someone like me to turn up, anyone who would be half-nice to her and not spend most of his time in prison. I felt I was being crueller to her than I was to Angela.

'I like your house,' I said.

Mary Barton was not stupid.

'Ya do in your fuck. Posh fella like you from Dalkey. This would be too – what is it? – vulgar for you.'

She smirked at me. I smirked back.

'How do you feel?' I ventured.

'Fine,' she said, deliberately missing my insinuation. 'How about you?'

'Aw, I dunno.'

She took the tray off the bed and sat down beside me. A stretch of white thigh peeked out from under her nightgown. Despite myself, I got an erection. I say despite myself because, apart from the fact we were both cheating on our spouses (and her spouse might slit my throat for it), I would not normally – soberly – have found a woman like Mary attractive: too short for me, too much make-up, the wrong clothes, nothing in common.

Bullshit.

She was working class, and I wasn't. There was a fear of the unknown, a nagging instinct that the two of us being together wasn't natural. I was majorly horny and minorly disgusted at the same time; one fuelling the other.

She lit a cigarette, offered me one. I refused.

'All right, so I'm married. I've a baby. You married?'

'Yes.'

'Kids?'

'One on the way.'

'There you go. That makes us equal.'

I took a cigarette. I had no good answer to this. We *were* equal. The sharpness of her logic surprised me. My erection wouldn't go away.

She smiled again. It was cheeky.

'You don't remember? I didn't think so.'

I shrugged, flummoxed again.

'You told me all that last night, ya dipstick, about what's her name? Angela. She's at home and you don't want to go there, because you don't know if you love her and you feel guilty 'cos there's a baby coming. So, Simon, you don't have to give me any shit about you taking advantage of me or whatever. We got drunk and came back here. We're both grown-ups. My old man's in the 'Joy and I don't think I like him anyway. I took a shine to you. That's all there is to it. That's why you're here.'

'OK, OK,' I said, hoping this conversation had finished.

'God love ya,' she said, stroking my face. 'You look terrified. Sorry. That's just the way I am. Say what I think. That's what being married to that bastard has done to me. I hardly ever saw him, you know, that's why this place is so spotless. Thought he had to be on the move all the time. I don't like to stay here on me own.

'And when he got arrested this time I made a decision. I'm in me thirties now, I've a baby, and I know if I tried to leave him he'd kill me. My life hasn't worked out the way I wanted it, so I'm not going to waste what I've got left. No time for bullshit any more, do you know what I'm saying?'

I nodded. I knew exactly what she was saying. I just couldn't put it into practice.

'Good for you,' I said. 'I'm just a little uncomfortable, that's all.'

'And do you think I'm not? Jesus, when I woke up this morning with you snoring in the bed I was morto.'

We smiled at each other. She patted my arm.

'It's just that I haven't done anything like this before,' I said. 'Been unfaithful, you know.'

'Me neither.'

We both knew we were lying.

Not completely without bullshit, then.

As I left she gave me her mobile number, pecked me on the cheek and said it was up to me to ring her. No pressure. I nodded and made a mental note to throw the number away as soon as I could. I rang her two days later.

We met maybe once a fortnight after that. In a hotel, usually the Clarence or the Merrion; somewhere expensive. She liked to spend money. We'd order up room service, get drunk, take drugs and have sex until we were sore.

I'd make up excuses for Angela about having to cover stories down the country. I didn't want her to find out, and even then I didn't indulge in the illusion that this was to shield her from hurt: I simply didn't want to endure any recriminations, face up to the bitter twist of her mouth. There was no guilt; only my lurid obsession with Mary Barton and how far she was prepared to go.

Once inside the hotel room it was a holiday from the rules of our real lives. There was nothing of the woman I didn't have, no part of her that I didn't relieve myself into. She was a dirty bitch and I told her so, told her because she encouraged me to, begged me to use her as a silken, fleshy bag for whatever we could imagine. The faintest threat of boredom from me would rip from her an urgent tumble of new suggestions, whispered like a needy junkie in my ear. I was there and not there, a spectator at a blood-filled execution, marvelling at how much she was prepared to give to please me; until the day I looked up and coldly saw her: blind-folded and mouth open, strapped to a chair.

'Come on, Simon.'

Her breasts were pendulous, her milky limbs bulging from pathetic leather pants; a sad, middle-aged parody of dark sex.

'Come on, come on. Do it, Simon. Please. *Please.*'

I didn't want to look at her any more.

I ended it, and she took the news with a certain grace. As she had said, no pressure. In a curious way it was the healthiest relationship I've ever had with a woman. There were no bitter residues afterwards. We still liked each other, still met for coffee or phoned to catch up. I'd seen her a fortnight before she was killed.

Most of this I told to Odette at a corner table in Browning's. She picked at her chips as she listened.

'You must be very upset,' she said.

I wasn't, but this didn't surprise me about myself. I have a way of holding bad news at arm's length.

'A bit,' I said. 'I don't think it's sunk in yet, what with everything else.'

She stroked my hand. 'You have a complicated life, I'm discovering.'

We smiled.

'Everything OK?'

Pete Clancy appeared by our table to make his usual post-prandial check. He eyed Odette's nearly full plate with concern. Despite my lack of hunger and the story I had to tell, I had eaten everything.

We both nodded.

'You sure?' he said to Odette.

She gestured towards me.

'I was listening.'

'Simon was talking it up, was he? Hey, that don't happen every day.' He winked at me. 'Say, all this stuff going on in town, all these gangsters and killing. It's bad news. Dublin's getting to be a dangerous place. I tell ya, in town today . . . it's kinda edgy. Think I'll go back to New York for a bit of peace and quiet. Simon, ain't your old man a judge? What's he say about all this?'

'Nothing I listen to,' I said. I looked at Odette. Sensing an atmosphere, Pete padded off.

'Is he American?' asked Odette.

'Yeah, but been here for years.'

'He doesn't sound American.'

For a woman just twenty-four hours in the country, Odette had a good ear for accents.

'Now,' she said, suddenly businesslike. 'Who else knows about you and Mary?'

'No-one.'

'Bongo?'

'No. Never told him. He likes Angela.'

'What about your friend Leo? He is a policeman.'

'He knows I met her, interviewed her. That's all.'

'Are you sure?'

I looked towards the window and the soundless crowds beyond, trying to think of any indication that Broder might have known. When it came to women he was as subtle as a riot; he wouldn't have been able to resist asking about it. Yet this wouldn't have been just another shag to him. She was Jimmy Barton's wife.

'No. If he had known, he definitely would have said something.'

'But you cannot be sure?'

'No.'

'And if you cannot be sure of Leo, you cannot be sure of anyone else. Those men this morning wanted to know how well you knew Mary.'

'So?'

She spread out her hands, as if showing me a poker hand.

'They had some reason to kill her. They killed her, not her husband. I'm sure they could have got him if they wanted. He is in prison? Easy in there, to kill someone. Mary Barton must have done something they did not like, and they want to know who else was involved. Simon, I do not like to tell you this, but if they find out about the affair, and they will, you will be in danger. You *are* in danger.'

She was like a doctor, giving me bad news. The diagnosis was definite and final.

'No,' I said, always keen to face up to reality.

'Yes,' she whispered, squeezing my hand.

I looked around, as if the solution I sought might be at one of the other tables. It was mostly small groups of guys, slugging beer and nodding their heads to each other. The only other couple there appeared to be arguing, their heads low, speaking in aggressive stage whispers.

'OK,' I said. 'I'll ring Broder. Tell him about it. I should have anyway. I just . . . I dunno why I didn't.'

'No.'

'No?'

'We do not know what Mary Barton was doing. It could look bad for you with the police as well. Her husband sold drugs, yes?'

'Yes . . . no,' I said, like a whiny child who has been told it's time to go to bed. This was ridiculous. I smiled, with the sole intention of trying to get her to do the same. She refused.

'Isn't this a little paranoid?'

'That's what you said to me this morning.'

QED. So far, she had been right about everything, and she knew it. She leaned forward to press her advantage. 'Perhaps I am wrong about this, but is it worth taking the risk? Simon, people are getting killed. You must be careful.'

I slumped in my chair, and felt tears prick at my eyes. I nodded agreement. The whispers from the arguing couple had become more urgent, bordering on shouts. I looked at Odette's uneaten food, and got a sudden flash of my mother, her green eyes wide with congratulation. *Good boy! You've eaten up all your carrots!* My imagined childhood.

'Excuse me,' I said, and headed for the toilet. I felt suddenly faint, and for a moment thought my burger might be making an unplanned comeback. In the corridor to the jax I had to pause for breath, and found myself staring at the last thing I wanted to see: myself, hair longer and spiky, wearing a black leather biker's jacket I'd always wanted to buy. I was standing at the back of the photograph; a huge, stupid smile strapped to my face, as if being in this band picture was all I'd ever hoped for. I looked impossibly young and dangerously optimistic, an arm draped around John Artifoni, our leader. The one who had made it all work, for a while.

But I'll tell you about that later.

I headed for a cubicle, straddled it backwards and with a minimum of preparation did two lumpy lines in quick succession. It made me sneeze violently, so I did another short one, just to be sure. I was more annoyed than scared: Odette seemed to have a mission to make everything black. For a few whispered minutes I fired abuse at her, the filthy French psycho bitch. Then I stopped, and knew she was right.

I just wanted to get drunk. But I couldn't, and I knew that even if I tried, I wouldn't enjoy it. I cleaned myself up and marched back to the table. Odette looked apologetic.

'I'm sorry.'

'No,' I interrupted, a bit too loudly. 'You've been right so far today. Probably right this time too.'

'Yes, I think I am.'

The arguing couple were preparing to leave, putting on jackets in silence while avoiding each other's gaze. *Yes, I think I am.* Odette was pretty sure of herself. How could she be? She'd just arrived here, how did she know what I should do? Why was this stranger so keen to help me? Why was I so keen to take her word? This, after all, had started with her, and it was she who seemed so keen for it to continue.

'We need to do a little investigating,' she said.

'Oh, for fuck's sake,' I blurted out. Much too loudly.

The arguing couple, now by the front door, turned to stare at me. Odette sat back in her chair, as if physically thrown there by the force of my words. I felt like a skinny kid who had just thumped the school bully, trapped between fear and exhilaration; liberated by the knowledge that there was nothing else to lose.

She looked at her hands, then peeked up at me from under her fringe.

'Simon.'

'Why are you doing this?'

'Simon . . .'

'No, no, you listen. I'm fucking sick of this shit. I've had fuckers kidnapping me and there's people being killed everywhere and this is nothing to do with me. Nothing. I'm going home. I don't – I don't want any more to do with this, and I don't know who you are, but I know I don't want anything to do with you. Leave me alone.'

'Simon, please listen to me.'

But I'd already stood up and stomped out of the restaurant.

six

I looked at my watch three times as I stumbled up Dawson Street, wheeling around the slow stampede of oncoming shoppers. Each time, it was twenty past one. Running: it made me think of my brother Alan. We would race to the drooping lemon tree at the bottom of the garden. He would always lose, but never became frustrated. *I like running.* Never understood that.

Finally, I hobbled to a halt by Stephen's Green, lines of salty sweat streaking my face, and wondered at what I had just done. The carnivorous anger I had blasted at Odette was vaporized, along with everything else inside me; I was a panting animal, startled by the sounds of drilling and the clatter of footsteps. I didn't know where I was running to, or what from. I felt dislocated from my surroundings, as if I had just arrived into my life, and now had to recount the facts so far. *Your name is Simon Dillon. You are in Dublin. It is twenty past one.*

I have experienced this sensation many times before, even when I haven't taken drugs; particularly one student summer I spent in

New York (where I bought my first bass guitar and decided I was going to be the next Jaco Pastorius). I would look up at the cliff face of skyscrapers and feel the sheer strangeness of having existence, of not knowing what to do about it.

But what to do now?

I decided I didn't know, and so, in the absence of that knowledge, I would do nothing. Or at least, I would slouch on a bench in the Green, smoke a cigarette and see what occurred to me.

It being lunchtime and sunny, all of the benches were already occupied, so I opted instead to rest on a bright stretch of grass, near the lake and the twee bandstand. Odette caught up just as I was about to sit down, her bag slung over her shoulders like a mountain climber, nostrils slightly flared from the effort of running. I shook my head like a weary pontiff, refusing any more discussion.

She kicked me in the arse.

Not hard, but with enough force to send me tottering forwards, to flay off the image of tired dignity I was trying to project. She pointed at the grass.

'Sit.'

I sat.

'You stupid fucker.' *Fuckeer.*

She kicked at the grass in irritation. Pellets of mud flew into my lap. She jammed her eyes shut, then flopped down beside me.

'I'm sorry. I did not mean that.'

I took out a cigarette and lit it while Odette looked about her, lips pursed.

'This is difficult,' she said, to no-one in particular. She turned to face me and put a hand on my knee, then took it off so she could disentangle herself from her bag. She returned the hand to my leg, but gingerly, as if scared of being burnt. Somehow the gesture reminded me of Angela. She used to love to touch my face, but would have to stretch to do so: mismatched in height as well as personality. *You're my best friend, Simon.*

'OK, OK. You have been honest with me, so I will try to be honest with you. OK?'

'All right.'

'But first, Simon, please believe that I am trying to be your friend. Please. I only want to keep you safe, because you do not realize the danger you are in. That is all.'

I said nothing.

'First,' sighed Odette, 'about me.'

'Simon! Jesus! I'm fucking knackered. The night I had.'

Kevin Egan lit a cigarette and towered above us. He kept glancing around him like a fearful fugitive, which is what he always did. Kevin Egan never said hello or goodbye, as if such greetings were a scandalous waste of time and words. Instead he would fire off a breathless monologue on what had just happened to him. He wouldn't think interrupting a private conversation was any sort of imposition; he probably didn't even notice.

'Christ, the amount of drugs I took. You weren't at the U2 thing last night? Just a small thing. Played some new stuff for a few friends. Crap, actually. Sub-Joy Division. But I said it to Bono. I always say these things to him and he takes it from me, he's OK like that.

'Then we were down to the Dinner Hall, you know, the new place off Merrion Square? Not great really and fuck expensive. Impossible to get into but I know one of the guys who own it. Half the government was in there with their secretaries, all pissed, you know what I mean? I was chatting to loads of them. *Bastards.* But didn't I also get talking to your man Dignam, big top cop in Store Street? Pissed of course, and he tells me all about this Russian Mafia thing. They're gonna take over. All the Dublin criminals are fucked and there's not a thing the cops can do about it. Big fucking war coming.

'Ended up with him giving me a lift home. Limo with a motor-bike escort. That was cool.'

He stopped talking, placed a hand on his hip as if posing for a photograph, and took a long pull on his cigarette.

'Wow,' said Odette.

Kevin Egan nodded, accepting the compliment.

I said nothing. I wasn't expected to. Even though he hadn't looked at her once, it was all for Odette's benefit. She had been impressed. That was all he wanted.

I knew Kevin from one of my previous careers or, more precisely, one of those periods in my life when I did the first thing that came along. Kevin would say he was a marketing director or some crap like that, but in fact he was a salesman: he sold advertising space on *Building Contractor*, the Irish construction industry's leading organ. Don't get me wrong: by saying he was a salesman I'm not trying to demean what he did, just be more accurate. I tried to do the same and couldn't sell to save my life. Kevin, however, was a genius at it.

I didn't know that much about him, or at least not that much which I could be sure was true. He was from some place in the midlands, Offaly, I think. Big GAA fan, though too chubby and soft-skinned to be good at sport himself. Not handsome either: he was too pale and red-haired and wore shabby suits; there was always a slovenly shirt-tail hanging out of his trousers. Kevin Egan also had an enormous inferiority complex, which I assume is what turned him into a pathological liar.

Salesmen, the good ones, always have a problem, *always*: alcohol, drugs, gambling, fraud. (In Kevin's case it was a little bit of everything.) The problem usually keeps them out of the office for the first three days of the week, until they run out of money. They show up on Thursday looking like shit and spitting out the usual excuses as to where they've been: I was sick; I was beaten up;

my aunt died. Kevin Egan, however, couldn't be content with any-thing so pedestrian: he would have been in Chicago at the opening night of *Riverdance*, or was a crucial witness in a murder case and had spent the last three days at a secret location giving evidence.

The stories would be indulged and never challenged to his face, because then Kevin would sit at a phone and sell thousands of pounds' worth of advertising. The office was a dreary, damp base-ment, yet if you closed your eyes and listened, you could easily be convinced that he was phoning from his plush, glass-fronted complex in the Financial Services Centre. And for the two days he was in, Kevin would believe it too.

We would go for the odd pint after work. When we were alone he was a quiet, almost shy man. He would peer up at me from under his eyelids, as if constantly questioning whether I wanted to be there, with the likes of him. He would tell me lies, but with nothing like the gusto with which he did it at work; he was trying them out, practising for other occasions. Sometimes I simply laughed at what he came out with, and he laughed too. Just so long as I never used the words *you are lying*, he seemed content. And it seemed cruel to do otherwise.

He did what he did for money, naturally, but for something else too: as if through will and imagination he might be able to invent a life for himself he didn't really deserve. There's something in that I admire.

Satisfied that he had induced the desired reaction from Odette, Kevin Egan said that we must meet for a drink some time, I nodded and off he went.

Odette stared after him and, with some suspicion in her voice, asked:

'Who is he?'

I didn't want to tell her he was just a sad salesman who spins lies, that he probably spent last night in front of the TV with a can of Heineken and a Marks & Spencer's instant dinner. Not out of sympathy for him, but for myself. As he talked it had struck me that, when we were stripped down to the bare bones of our respective lives, I was no better than him. Worse, even: I didn't have his imagination.

'Just a guy I know.'

'Oh.'

She nodded slowly, as if fascinated with this mundane piece of information. The moment for Odette's Big Revelation had been stolen from her by Kevin Egan, and she seemed graceless about it: darting black looks after him and peering at me for the nourishing encouragement she needed to re-embark on her story.

I didn't give it to her. I suddenly didn't care what she had to say. I was exhausted and cranky again, annoyed at how Kevin Egan had made me feel.

She produced a packet of Gauloises, gave me one, lit them. I never noticed she smoked before.

We sucked on our cigarettes in silence.

Finally, she said:

'What is that?'

On the bandstand a group of men wearing stripy jackets and straw boaters read aloud from books. They sang out the words and gestured in a campy way, much to their own amusement.

At first I didn't know what this was, until I again glanced at my watch and realized that it was 16 June: Bloomsday, when a few literary types and herds of tourists process around the city, re-creating scenes from a book describing a Dublin which hasn't existed for a hundred years.

Up until his attack, my father would have been one of those people. He loved Bloomsday. It was good for publicity – *Judge with Sense of Fun* – an excuse for him to drink all day, and a way of convincing himself that the Dublin he grew up in wasn't entirely cold in the ground. Here, dressed in their silly clothes, were people just like him, keen to share in his mirage of an idyllic youth, when people were honest and everyone subscribed to the ould decency. It made the city a middle-class place; more than that, a particular sort of tweed-wearing, literary, well-spoken middle class, where the sheen of gentility and the well-chosen word were favoured above all else.

It was Dublin as Mathew Dillon wanted it to be, and all springing from a myth, or so I'd been told: the action of *Ulysses* is set on 16 June, because, the story goes, this was the date when James Joyce first stepped out with his future wife Nora Barnacle. One night one of my father's professor mates drunkenly claimed to me that this isn't actually true. Joyce had been out with her a few times before that: 16 June was when she first gave him a hand-job.

That's more like the Dublin I know.

I related this, or most of this, to Odette; I left out the bit about the hand-job.

'I have not read it. Is it good?'

'Maybe. I dunno. I've only read bits of it, and most of that I didn't get. You need to read two other books to understand it.'

I had a mental flash of watching my father reading *Ulysses* aloud to a group of people who laughed at jokes I didn't understand. I thought of my mother's funeral. I was six, my brother was three. Auntie Marion from Kerry, our mother's sister, was in charge. She was a hugely fat and normally jolly woman married to a skinny and morose woodwork teacher from Westmeath.

The teacher (so our family logic went) had failed to provide her with any children, so she spoiled us instead. Not just with sweets and toys, but with lavish amounts of attention: pillow fights, ridiculous bedtime stories, football; Marion was better at being a child than we were.

But when faced with death, Marion reverted to religious type. She draped herself in a black mantilla and stuffed us into stiff collars and ties which sawed at our young necks. Alan and I were made to stand in a corner of the kitchen – we were considered too young to see the body – while he cried because he knew Mammy was in the living room and couldn't understand why he wasn't allowed to see her. Alan was a feisty kid, he wouldn't stop screaming:

'Amma, Amma!'

I held his hand and told him Mammy had gone to heaven, but this only made him cry more because he wanted Mammy to come back from heaven and give him Liga. Mashed up with milk. The way he liked it.

'Ega, Ega!'

I started to cry too. Marion, her face already swollen from tears, was perched precariously on one of the breakfast bar stools. She reached out to pat me on the head, but couldn't stretch that far. Her hand dangled in the air, impotent in grief.

In the midst of all this wailing, my father strode in, his hat on, a bottle in his hand: a fierce, thick-necked giant dressed in black. He stopped and curled a lip at our aunt.

'Marion, *please*.' He pointed at us. 'Will you do something about *that*.'

I was only six, but I knew he meant Alan and me. I knew that for some reason he was mad at us, and for the first time I realized that he always seemed that way.

Odette stubbed out her cigarette in the grass, more times than was strictly necessary.

'OK, Simon. Now I'm ready. You are not making this easy for me. But you should hear this.'

I nodded, too tired to get up and walk away; but planning to as soon as I could.

'Firstly, my background.'

My mobile phone rang.

'Shit!' *Sheet.*

As I fumbled the phone out of my pocket, I smiled at her, but grimly. This latest interruption was life taking the piss out of both of us. It frustrated her storytelling, but it was probably my employers preparing to have me fired. I should have turned it off.

'Simon. How are you?'

It wasn't a voice I recognized.

'Fine. Who's that?'

'What? You forgot me already? Ah, I'm hurt now.'

'Who is this?'

'Well, in fairness, I didn't give you me name, but we did have a long chat this morning. I gave you a present and all: that Homer Simpson yokey. Do you remember?'

'Oh.'

'Yes, Simon. Ohhhh.'

I looked at Odette, pointed at the phone and mouthed the words *the guy from this morning*. She mouthed back: *what?*

'Here's the thing, now: we want to have another little chat with you. There's one or two other facts that have come to light that we'd like to run past ya.'

The guy from this morning.

What?

'Now we are otherwise engaged at the moment, but we'd like to meet up with you in a couple of hours. What I propose is that I ring you in an hour and a half and tell you where to show up. By yourself this time, please.'

THE GUY FROM THIS MORNING.

She mouthed an oh of understanding.

'I'd say you might not be keen to meet up with us again, what with your nervous disposition and all. I'd say you'd be thinking of making yourself scarce. So this is what we've done, Simon. We are now in possession of your baby daughter Emily. She's fine, being looked after and all that. But if you don't meet us, we'll chop off her legs and send them to your wife. I'll ring you back in ninety minutes.'

I dropped the phone and looked at my watch again. It was ten past two.

seven

I scooped up the phone, but it dribbled from my hands again, suddenly transformed into mercury. I scrabbled after it on the ground while Odette nagged at me:

'What did he say? What did he say?'

I didn't answer. My throat had contracted so tightly there was barely enough room to heave air into my burning lungs, certainly not enough to make any noise. I pinned the slippery mobile phone to the grass and jabbed in Angela's number.

'Hello. This is Angela and Emily's house. There's no-one here . . .'

She was at work. *Of course* she was at work; she was always at fucking work. *I like my job, Simon. Why does that threaten you so much?* But it was more than that: the work was work, the house was work, the child was work, our marriage was work. No time off. *Angela and Emily's house.* She changed the message the day after I moved out.

I succumbed to a surge of hatred towards my wife, as if changing that message was what had caused all this.

'Siren Software. How can I help you?'

'Could I—'

I couldn't finish the sentence, and not because my voice box had been squeezed into redundancy. I couldn't ring the mother of my child and tell her that that child had been kidnapped by monsters in human form; that they were prepared to laughingly mutilate and kill our baby because I, fucking worthless I, had nothing better to do than gorge on some dangerous sex to take my mind off my own inanity.

The phone fell to the grass again, but I continued to stare at the spot it had occupied on my hand. Soon tears obscured my vision, so much that I could not even make this out, just melting colours and shapes which shook as I did, the smell of Odette as she stretched out her arms and pulled me onto her lap, whispering, hush, baby, hush. It will be all right. We will fix it. Rest now. 'Night, Maisy, 'night, Teddy, 'night, Mama, 'night, Dadda.

We'd been like all new parents, full of rigid conviction not to repeat the mistakes visited upon us. I was especially strident, motivated by love of my daughter and the chance to spite my father: raising her properly a way to point up his deficiencies. I could have been like her, if it wasn't for you.

Stupid really: years of trying to provoke him rarely showed any results. He ignored Alan and me. More than that; he went to lengths to avoid us. Every summer we'd be bussed to Kerry and Auntie Marion, while during the rest of the year his work was enough to keep him far from the house. Even at weekends there was always golf or swimming or some conference he had to attend. If he was at home, he was locked in his study: a remote, musty place where we were not welcome. He'd be gone in the mornings when we got up and would stay away until it was our bedtime. He would often ring the house to tell the nanny to put us to bed, because he was coming home early.

We went through a lot of nannies. Maybe a dozen, I'm not sure. They were mostly OK, though the only distinct memory I have of them is of their variety. For some reason our father had a policy that each new nanny would be as different as possible from the previous one. If the old minder was fat and in her fifties, he'd hire a skinny twenty-year-old. We had a part-time model, an ex-prison officer, an ex-nun; even, for a short time, a black woman from Zimbabwe: an extraordinary sight for Dalkey in those days.

None of them ever resigned: he'd always sack them first. After a period of time he would become impatient and suspicious, accusing them of non-specific yet dubious motives in that way he had; he could make the most innocent of pastimes sound grubby. He would say it in a tart, vaguely disgusted tone:

'So you took them to the *park*, did you?'

Any reaction on their part – and one would inevitably come – was a de facto admission of guilt. *How dare you love my children.*

I sniffed, gouged the tears from my eye sockets.

'No,' I said. 'She's at the crèche. They're fucking lying. She's at the crèche. They wouldn't just give her away.'

I sat up and grabbed the phone again.

'They have your daughter?'

'No, they *say* they have her. But that's crazy.'

'My God, Simon. They do.'

I realized I didn't have the number for the crèche. I wanted to dial directory enquiries but couldn't think of the number for that either.

'You know who I'm just after meeting?'

Kevin Egan was standing before us again.

'Fuck off,' I screamed.

'Simon,' said Odette.

Kevin Egan's body stiffened, unsure of how to deal with this rebuff. He lit a cigarette.

'What's the number for directory enquiries?'

'Simon, listen,' repeated Odette.

I dialled the operator.

Without a word, Kevin Egan walked away.

Odette pinched me on the hand. Hard.

'Jesus!'

I dropped the phone.

'Simon, if they say they have taken your daughter, believe me, they have. Simon, I know these people.'

I know these people. A shudder ran through me.

'How do you know them?'

She closed her eyes.

'I just do.'

'I'm going to ring the crèche anyway.'

'You ring the crèche and they will ring the police. If the police get involved, your daughter is dead.'

'Leo then.'

'Simon, he *is* the police.'

I flung the mobile at the ground. It bounced away from me. I screamed.

'Fuck it, this is my daughter! I've got to do something!'

She cautiously placed a hand on my shoulder.

'I know. What do they want from you?'

'To meet me. In two hours. They're going to ring back with a location.'

She nodded to herself, then got up, picked up the mobile and offered it to me.

'That gives us two hours to find out something about what Mary

Barton was up to. For your sake and your daughter's sake we have to do that.'

I took the phone from her and studied it, as if the answer to our problem could be found in this small rectangle of moulded plastic. There was nothing else I could do, and I didn't want to spend the next two hours thinking about Emily, about what could be happening to her. I knew I should ring Angela, but I was far too craven for that. Emily wouldn't have raised a word of protest about going off with complete strangers. *She's like you. Talk to anyone. Go off with anyone.* Angela had come to hate that in our daughter. *Where the fuck have you been until now? Don't tell me: you got talking. Sick of this, Simon. Sick of it.* All my fault. I nodded at Odette.

'Mary had a brother. I know where he works.'

'Will he talk to you?'

'No, he hates my guts. But I think I know how to make him talk.'

It was now 2:25. An hour and three-quarters to go.

Exactly three minutes later we were in another taxi, listening to another driver spin a theory as to why Dublin was suddenly littered with fresh corpses. It was the parents he blamed. We hmmed and didn't really listen.

Despite the urgent logic of going to see him, I didn't savour the prospect of meeting Mary's brother. Tommy Menton had expressed a desire, if the opportunity ever arose, to beat me to death. I didn't know if he was capable of such an action, but I could see that his reasons were sound enough. He and Mary had been close, so she had let him in on our little secret. Tommy – known as Ajax to his friends for reasons I am unaware of – had made it plain he didn't approve. He thought it far too dangerous for Mary to be cheating on her husband, and simply didn't like the look of me: I was a poof from Dalkey having a bit of rough on the side, and sooner or later I'd dump Mary and scuttle back to the southside. Which is what I did.

On the three or four occasions we had met, Ajax always staunchly refrained from looking at or speaking to me; until Mary went to the toilet or left to make a cup of tea, and then he would be straight over, his wild piggy eyes so close to mine they would coalesce into one huge green orb in the middle of his forehead. When he spoke there was a waft of tobacco and the soft patter of spittle on my face. He would thump my chest with a chubby fist.

'Don't think I don't know your game, fucker. You're putting her life in danger, you snobby poof. Fuck off outta here or I'll kill you. I can have you dead anywhere, any time.'

I never answered him, the first couple of times out of shock and also because I wasn't sure if Ajax was serious or not. The delivery of the threat was so emphatic, so *rehearsed*, that I suspected he was simply trying to wind me up. I had visions of him at home in front of the mirror, with one of those flick-knives that are really combs, breathing out the words so his mother downstairs wouldn't hear.

But he kept it up, and on the final occasion I thought he was going to produce his flick-knife comb, or perhaps a real knife, only Mary walked back into the room and fucked him out of it. The fact that she knew he was threatening me, and that she seemed to take it seriously, changed my mind about Ajax's intentions.

Afterwards she told me he was harmless and not to take him seriously, but I remained obviously unconvinced. So she told me something to back up her claim, a piece of information I now intended to use against him. If Ajax did intend to slit my throat, today would be the day.

Going to his work also felt unwise. I had been in it once, or at least peeked in the door, and wasn't struck by the convivial atmosphere. Ajax claimed to have a vague managerial role in a snooker club on Capel Street which gloried in the name of Hot

Rods. The patrons were almost exclusively bikers, meaning that they were hairy, leather-clad and usually middle-aged blokes sitting in sinister clumps and smoking huge spliffs while bobbing their heads to the collected canon of Guns n' Roses; actually owning a motorbike wasn't that important. In the lore of Dublin nightlife, Hot Rods was also reputed to be popular among prostitutes and smack dealers: other than the lights over the snooker tables, the place did its suspect business in almost total darkness.

Inside the taxi, I explained this to Odette. She waved a hand, as if it was irrelevant. The softness in her had gone again.

'You wait outside. I will go in and get this Ajax.'

The taxi pulled up outside the building, and the driver eyed it in the way you would a convicted killer on the television. The sound of power chords leaked onto the street. He threw us a quizzical look, and was about to say something but was cut short by Odette, who paid for the journey; I had no money left. I felt pathetic.

We walked around the corner and found a place for me to stand where I would be out of sight.

'Ajax,' she said. 'What does he look like?'

I shrugged.

'Small, black hair, pigtail, goatee. He'll be wearing some sort of black heavy metal tee-shirt. Stuff around his wrists.'

'Simon, everyone in there will look like that.' Her lips gave the promise of a smile. 'I'll find him, don't worry.'

She turned to go.

'Odette, be careful. This guy wants to kill me. This is a really dodgy place you're going into. It's *dangerous*.'

My voice squeaked, like a complaining child. She turned back and looked at me; no, studied me, as if to fully take in how broken and scared I was. She took one of my hands and put it on her face, but not in a gentle way. The gentleness had retreated back inside her; this gesture was almost a threat. It had a precise aggression, like spiteful sex with someone you don't like but still enjoy fucking: sensuality and pain both craved and given.

She whispered, 'Simon. I'm dangerous too.' She took my hand from her face and swooped it down to her breast, squeezing it there. Her nipple was hard and pugnacious. She dropped my hand, winked and walked into the building.

I leaned flat against a wall, trying to mesh myself into it. Each breath was painful, like I'd been inhaling car fumes. I wanted to run off. I kept getting mental flashes of Emily, of a naked Odette. I felt sick with myself. People passed by, but didn't look in my direction. Groups of loud children, mothers with bags and babies, all stepped carefully around me as if they feared what I was about to do and at all costs wished to avoid infection from my suicidal virus. A group of bovine-looking tourists obediently traipsed after a tour guide, his head bedecked with a Joycean boater. He spoke at them in short, excited bursts.

'Now just up ahead here is Little Britain Street, the site of Barney Kiernan's pub. Not there any more. But it was a real pub. In Joyce's day. This is where the Cyclops episode of *Ulysses* takes place. Inside, we meet the Citizen, a bigot of Irish nationalism.'

The tourists oohed, as if a visit to the site of Barney Kiernan's pub was all they had ever hoped for.

My mobile rang.

I literally jumped with fright. I tried to drag the phone out of my jeans pocket but the aerial got stuck, forcing me to struggle dementedly with my groin like a drunken flasher. I eventually got the phone free, but then dropped it on the road. I retrieved it, now covered with oily mud. Remarkably, it still worked.

'Simon?' said Bongo. 'What was that?'

I couldn't talk. My lungs felt flattened of air. I made a noise.

'Simon, are you all right? Simon?'

'Minute, just a minute,' I managed to splutter out. I hunkered on the pavement and took deep breaths. I thought I was going to be sick, but eventually the nausea passed. The day was now really hitting me, especially the drugs I'd taken: my heart felt as if it had to struggle to keep me alive. I was as fragile as a stick, ready to be blown into nothingness by any random gust of air.

I held the phone to my ear.

'Sorry, Bongo,' I said. 'It's been a bit of a day and I think it's catching up with me.'

'I know. Hip Cop rang me. He wants a statement about the blokes in the apartment. They fucking kidnapped you? I can't believe it.'

'Well, they did,' I confirmed, bereft of anything better to say. What is interesting about the most dramatic moments of our lives is that the more dramatic they are, the less there is to say about them. They have happened. They have been so vivid, describing them is pointless. All that is left are exclamations and platitudes.

'I can't believe it,' repeated Bongo.

'Yeah, yeah,' I said.

'Well, are you OK? How come you're not at home? Broder said you'd gone home.'

'Just didn't fancy it. Bit claustrophobic, you know.'

'So where are you now? What are you doing?'

I never told Bongo about Mary Barton, mostly because it would confirm his long-held and often expressed belief that I was far too immature to marry anyone, never mind father a child. More lies.

'Went for lunch with Odette to Browning's,' I said, making a mental promise that I'd tell him everything next time we met. 'I'm just outside now waiting for her. She's in the loo.'

'The French woman is still hanging around? Jesus, she must be gagging for it. Or you are.'

'Bongo. Please, not now.'

'Sorry. Sorry. Look, you go home. You must be wrecked.'

'I am.'

'Go home, get some sleep. I have to stay here. We have some fucking Germans coming in this afternoon that I have to bullshit. But come round to my place this evening. We'll have a drink. OK?'

'OK,' I said, really meaning it.

'You're really going to go home now? Don't stay in town anyway. All these murders. It's fucking scary, I tell ya. My old dear was already on the blower begging me not to go out for the next few nights. Don't think I will, either.'

'She's probably right. Look, I'm going to go straight home now and get a kip. I promise. I'll see you later.'

'OK, man,' he said, his voice soft. 'Take care.'

I clicked off and realized that the tightness in my chest had eased somewhat. I wiped the mud from the phone with a discarded crisp bag and was subsumed by a desire to do just as Bongo had said. Go home. It was a cramped, untidy flat that was anything but homely, yet now it was the place I craved most in the world to be. There, warm and asleep, and afterwards down to Bongo's for a few quiet drinks, nothing excessive. Back to work tomorrow. Visit Emily. Go out to Dalkey at the weekend and see the old man. Whatever normality I had in my life, I craved it now like a withdrawn junkie.

'That bleedin' poof? That's what this is about?'

Odette and Ajax were standing several yards away. His words had come out rich with the usual poison, but his face was open with puzzlement. Odette pointed at my head.

'What happened to you?' she said, in an I-can't-leave-you-alone-for-two-minutes tone of voice.

I put a hand to my cheek. The muddy phone had left a long scrape of inky filth on my face.

'Phone. Dropped it. Mud,' I said, employing a dazzling economy of words.

'Bollocks,' said Ajax.

This seemed a strangely inappropriate thing to say, as if Ajax didn't believe my explanation, as if he suspected some other, darker reason for the mud. And I noticed then that he had delivered his judgement with a certain lack of conviction, that it was nothing more than a Pavlovian response to a hostile situation: swearing as a form of verbal jostling; a human hedgehog, sticking out its spikes. Ajax, I realized, was scared. The piggy eyes were watery and dull, and his partly open mouth led the eye to his weak and vulnerable chin. He plunged his hands into his jeans pockets and half turned from me, as if to go back into the club, yet didn't have the conviction to go through with it: too scared even to run away.

'You didn't tell me he was here,' he said to Odette. She stared at him. Barbed wire, but without the children. Ajax looked at the pavement, idly kicking it with a weathered Nike.

'Fucking poof,' he muttered.

I stood up. With as much force as he could muster, Ajax looked towards me and roared.

'Ya fucking bastard, she's dead. Are you happy now? Are ya? Are ya?'

Yet there was no power in this; more pathos than anything. His eyes had filled with tears, his face contorted into a parody of crying. Ajax hadn't expected to see me, and the encounter had only brought home to him again the death of his sister. She had been right: he was harmless. My fear evaporated; I felt pity for Ajax, and guilt at having come here. I wanted to make some gesture to indicate that I sympathized, but I knew he wouldn't believe it. Why should he?

Curiously, I had always envied his closeness to Mary Barton. Not for her, but for my own family. Unlike me, my brother had decided not to resist my father's indifference. He adopted a pose of Zen-like quiet during his teenage years, and as soon as he could had emigrated to Australia, where he now runs a catering firm. He rarely visits.

The only other family I keep in contact with is Auntie Marion, who loathes my father, though she has spent years denying it. My mother's people never liked him, forcing my mother to delicately defend him against what was never said out loud: he was too Dublin, too rugby club, too cosy with that wing of the Party where anything could be bought. You know the guys I mean; you've read about them: the foreign accounts, the dodgy planning decisions, the bundles of weathered cash, the open-faced denials. A ring of greedy dogs, sniffing one another's backsides; my father was one of those. Friends you choose. Family is foisted upon you: loving them is a miracle.

'Odette,' I groaned, 'let him go back in.'

She ignored me.

'Why was your sister killed?'

Odette was like a brittle headmistress grilling a weepy schoolboy: there was a dash of contempt in her tone, the certainty that she could X-ray every pathetic lie he mustered.

'Don't know,' said Ajax, as if he had been asked this question a dozen times before.

'Where was she going on the bus?'

'Don't know.'

Odette closed one eye, like a dog who hears the distant rustle of a rabbit in the grass. There was something different between the two answers.

'Where was she going on the bus?'

Ajax said nothing, his head still bowed towards the pavement. But his eyes were darting, looking for an escape. He sniffed hugely and puffed out his chest, the rattle of snot through his tubes sounding like the aggressive cackle of an exotic bird. Suddenly his head was up. With a tepid defiance he glared at us.

'I'm not telling you bastards anything.'

He stumbled over the word *bastards*, realizing too late that this was not an appropriate insult for a woman. The grammar of abuse. Odette remained stony-still, and for a moment I admired Ajax's useless bravery.

'I think you should,' she said, as if this was a self-evident fact.

But Ajax was more confident now, probably relieved that his defiance hadn't resulted in a beating or a bullet.

'No,' he said to me. 'I don't fucking have to tell *you* anything.'

Odette's gaze moved slowly to where I stood. I knew what she wanted, and I knew I would give it to her. There were two grown men here, yet without touching us, producing a weapon or even saying much, she had us both terrified. The fact that I had been touching her breast minutes before only increased this sensation. I moved the fingers that had been there, as if to check that I still had a hand.

'Simon, why does he have to tell us?'

I didn't have to say anything. The metallic rasp of her voice was what made him look first at her, then at me, and realize what it was I knew. I watched the reaction spread across his face: a squint of puzzlement around the eyes, an open mouth of disbelief, a brief grimace of anger with his sister, then an even larger one at the reminder of her death, and finally an open, pathetic slackness, as if all his face muscles suddenly ceased to function. Tears made busy squiggles down his cheeks as he fought for breath.

He nodded his head as a sign of defeat, not shocked now. This was what he would have expected of me. He jabbed out a finger.

'You . . . fucking . . . cunt.'

The usual insult now had no currency. Ajax made a habit of accusing other people of being poofs for the usual reason: because he was one himself. Despite his devotion to the whole metal/biker thing, on week nights he also liked to slip along to the Phoenix

Park or some of the cheesier clubs in town where a chat-up line consisted of a look and a nod towards the toilets. According to Mary, Ajax didn't consider himself gay, simply that he had an addiction for anonymous sex with other men. He didn't even like gays, but then there aren't many gay bikers. Other than the band.

She told me ostensibly so I wouldn't be worried by his threats, but I think also because she wanted to confide in me, to make me feel that I had a trusted place in her life; a place I didn't want.

He covered his eyes with a hand and slowly slid down the wall until he was crouched on the pavement. Passers-by made wide detours around him, assuming drink or drugs. I looked away, feeling tears stab at my own eyes. Behind me I could hear Ajax mumbling tearfully and Odette driving in her questions like metal rods. I had to get away, but to where? And how would that help Emily? I was sick and weak, too much so to go on, too much so to run. My mind seemed to be whirling around, too quickly for me to pluck any single thought from it. I didn't know why I was so scared of Odette, or why I had trusted her before: *why* now seemed to be the most ridiculous question I could ask myself. There was no *why*.

Ajax was walking briskly away and towards Capel Street, rubbing an arm against his snotty face. Odette watched him go, a sudden cast of sadness over her features. She offered me a smile; the one she had revealed at Bongo's flat, full of waving, curly-haired children asking only to be bundled into friendly arms.

'That was not nice. Poor boy,' she said.

She wiped her face, and appeared to be close to tears. She didn't attempt to come near me.

'You think I am a bitch.'

'No,' I said. Truthfully, for a change: I'd been thinking more along the lines of nutter.

'I had to do it, Simon.'

She flopped back against the wall, rummaged in her bag for a cigarette. Her eyes were glassy. Her hand shook as she produced her lighter.

'I don't know what to say,' I said.

She nodded. She sucked on her cigarette while I looked about me, awkward and heavy from doubt piled on counter-doubt. There was, after all, nothing she could possibly want from me. I had no information or money or contacts. I was a victim in all this; that was obvious. And if that was obvious, why was she helping me? I knew I didn't have the courage to ask her.

Odette flicked away the cigarette, stood up straight, patted her face, extracted a tissue and daintily blew her nose. She took out another, walked over to me and delicately wiped the mud from my face. I had a brief flash of my mother. A worn blue hankie, spit and a stern rub.

'Have you a car?' she asked absently.

'Yes,' I said without thinking, grateful for a change of subject. 'It's not far from here. I parked it yesterday because I was going on the piss.'

'Good. We have to drive to Maynooth. That is how much, twenty kilometres away?'

She was all business again. She took my hand.

'Let's go to Maynooth.'

I looked at my watch. We had an hour and twenty minutes left.

'Why Maynooth?'

'To see a bishop.'

eight

All I knew about Gavin McCabe was what I had read in the news-papers; and I didn't read newspapers that much. He appeared on TV and radio a fair bit, I knew that; like many others in this city he pursued the hallowed mantle of Controversy. He was a bishop, but not the usual flaccid-skinned, slightly apologetic variety. A Tridentine, about which I also knew little, other than that they were some sort of Catholic breakaway sect who preferred the Latin rite. They were supposed to be ultra-conservative, though any time they appeared in the media it was for ordaining women and having married priests. All bums on seats, I suppose.

One of the few fortunate aspects of my childhood was that we didn't get exposed to much religiosity. We made our communion (£103 in presents from relations and neighbours) and confir-mation (£217), but that was for the sake of form. Judge Dillon was and still is a discreet but card-carrying atheist, so our exposure to mass was at best occasional: funerals, anything political; anything where there might be a few photographers present so he could throw his hands around our shivering shoulders and look the Brave Widower. Only on visits to Kerry would we be forced to go, and even there its function seemed to be more social than spiritual: a way of showing the neighbours that you weren't dead and could still afford a good suit. Apart from a brief period in college when I wore black and read a lot of Hermann Hesse, religion has remained a tedious mystery to me: an observance maintained by my woolly-backed ancestors to stave off their fear of the sun.

Gavin McCabe, anyway: what I didn't know about him was far more interesting. He was a small, hardy Scotsman in his mid-fifties who came to Ireland about twenty years back, though he was not known as Gavin; then he was Tom McCabe, a slightly notorious Glasgow gangster who came to Dublin not for the scenery or the rich cultural life, but because the long arm of Her Majesty's law couldn't stretch this far. By all accounts his intention was to turn over a new leaf and lead a blameless life: meaning that whatever new crimes he committed, he didn't intend to take the blame for them. It was a successful strategy for a short time, until he was finally done for credit card fraud and sentenced to eighteen months by none other than Judge Mathew Dillon, who, in a typically brilliant piece of crowd-pleasing hypocrisy, declared McCabe a wicked man and advised him to read the Bible during his incarceration.

McCabe took my father at his word. Six months after his release he changed his name to Gavin and was ordained a Tridentine priest. Two years later he was made a bishop, and declared that his parish would consist of the most marginalized group in Irish society: his former colleagues in the criminal world.

From petty thieves to hitmen, all the gangs, the Provos and even the Drummer, Bishop McCabe knew them all and made no secret of the fact that he married them, baptized their children and, when the need arose (which, presumably, was often) administered the last rites. There were even rumours he said secret Christmas and Easter masses for the Dublin criminal community. Must have been interesting when the collection basket went around.

This, naturally enough, made the bishop a national figure, with regular appearances on talk shows where he would defend his parishioners (but not what they did), and blame poverty, inequality and greed for the growth of crime in the cities. Any big case and he was there, as a sort of padre to the criminal troops, advising the accused to make his peace with God. Sometimes he claimed people were innocent, sometimes he 'sponsored' crimbos who he maintained were retired and should be left alone by the police.

Opinion on him was predictably divided: he was a genuinely Pauline figure, working with the sorts of people Christ would go to see if he was here, or he was a conman who had come up with a great angle for selling religion to gangsters. There was no hard evidence one way or another, though Bishop McCabe certainly had the humble cleric's lifestyle: as a mischievous gesture to the mainstream church, he lived in a caravan in Maynooth, the world headquarters of conservative Irish Catholicism. He had no phone or car and was never found in any compromising situations. He was also a charming man, with a sandy, sing-song voice, slitted, sparkling eyes and an endearing chuckle. He had a teddybearish quality, with just a hint of the roughness from his former career. Most people who met him believed he was the real thing.

But as I say, Odette and I knew none of this at the time. All she had extracted from Ajax was an admission that although his sister had been on a bus for Sligo, she had intended to get out at Maynooth and visit the bishop. Apparently, everyone there knew him; he'd be easy to find.

Odette let me drive, which is a curious thing to say given it was my car, but that's the way it felt. I kept checking my watch. An hour and twenty minutes to drive to Maynooth, talk to this bishop and get back into the city was cutting it fine, and we both knew it. It filled my rattling old BMW with a stiff tension. I could feel her looking at me as we moved down the quays. She asked about various buildings as we passed them: Dublin Corporation, Guinness's, Heuston Station, Kilmainham Jail. I gave clipped, efficient answers.

'We will get back in time. I promise,' she said.

I tried smiling. It came out as a grimace. We gave up talking.

The silence in the car built up like a snowdrift, and I found myself sweating. I clicked on the radio: a news bulletin about another gangland slaying, this time in Clontarf. The man's stomach had been slashed open, his entrails tied around his neck. I thumped the radio off, sucked in air to calm my still-intact stomach.

Odette sighed loudly, like a girl on a date disappointed because her boyfriend is too shy to make a move. She looked back in her bag, rooted around, slammed it shut.

'Pull over,' she said.

The instruction was like a slap across the face. I had a sudden need to swallow, but couldn't. I wanted something sweet. Coke, Fanta. No: Cidona. A bottle, with a striped straw and a bag of cheese and onion Tayto. In Auntie Marion's bar in Kerry. Millions of miles away. I didn't want to pull over; it would waste time. I didn't want to go to Maynooth at all, but didn't know what else to do.

My chronic ambivalence annoyed me as much as her, and it was obviously annoying her. *Pull over*: she had said it with a dark, muscular finality; as if she had had enough, and was now going to put an end to this nonsense.

'Pull over?'

'Yes.'

'What, here?'

'Anywhere, I don't care. Just pull over.'

My breath would only come in short, tantalizing bursts, always just short of a lungful.

'Right,' I said, not knowing if I was actually going to obey her instruction, fearing the outcome if I didn't. I knew I was being illogical, but I couldn't resist the panic rushing through me. All I could think of was Cidona.

'I'm thirsty,' I said.

'We will get drinks then.'

I almost overturned the car to screech into a Statoil station, and made a slow deliberate path through the petrol pumps. I wrenched the handbrake and, with what little control I had left, turned to look at her.

But she was smiling. The barbed wire was gone, giving a clear view of the people beyond: sitting at a long kitchen table drinking wine, throwing crumbs to a lazy dog while they watched their children gallop around an untidy back garden.

'I'm sorry,' she said. 'I got a little annoyed because . . . I am frustrated too. I know we have little time. I do not blame you.' She put a hand on my moist and shaking arm. Hers brown, still and cool.

'We will do whatever you want to do, OK?'

I nodded.

'OK,' she whispered. 'Now I must go for a minute. I have to have a *poo*.'

She seemed to have a gift for choosing words that sounded adorably silly in a French accent; also for saying and doing what I least expected. In my thirty-five-year life, I have never before had a woman tell me she was going to take a crap, especially when I had been half expecting her to pull a gun. Despite all sense, I smiled back. There was even a faint tingling in my groin, which made me wonder did I possess some sexual taste I had previously been unaware of.

'Bye-bye,' she said, and left the car.

I watched her walk off, unhurried, her bag slung over her shoulder like a student on a weekend skite. She turned the corner, and I was alone. I looked around the car, half convinced that this was some sort of trick, that she was hiding in the back seat pointing a huge pistol at my head. There was nothing but accumulated car debris: flattened cigarette packets, empty Coke cans, my crumpled jacket, a strap from the long-gone baby seat which I couldn't unbuckle. I quickly looked away.

The road was in front of me, flat and open, waiting to take me along. All trace of Odette had suddenly disappeared from my life, and to keep it that way all I had to do was twist a flat, sweaty key and gently depress the accelerator.

Yet I couldn't; I was frozen. She had said *bye-bye*. For the first time that day her intention had been plain. I could go if I wanted to. Like Mary Barton: no pressure.

I missed her then. I had an urge to run around and interrupt her in the middle of her *poo* and grovel for being so craven when she was the only person trying to help me. Tell her that this time, for a change, I wouldn't let her down. Whatever her big secret, she was the only friend I had.

Slumped in my seat, I lit a cigarette, but it was too hot and left me light-headed. I was exhausted from all this, and parched. Felt like a nap. Maybe get Odette to drive the rest of the way, get some drinks. Cidona. She'd probably never had it before. I told myself I would do all this, but it was merely a way of teasing; a curtain to be raised, revealing what my true thought had been. Bongo's coke. I whipped up my jacket and headed for the toilet.

There was still no sign of Odette when I returned (now a new, energized, sweat-free person), so I smartly double-backed to find her, grinning to myself with the thought that perhaps she was constipated. I found this observation so astonishingly hilarious I was almost laughing out loud when I bumped into her. She had changed into a tight, black tee-shirt.

'You had to change your top. That must have been some poo.'

For me this was a comic observation of such brilliance I let all pretence at sobriety slip and sniggered like a stoned schoolboy; which was pretty much what I was. Odette quietly watched me, her bag clutched to her breast, a half-smile curled around her face.

A lack of breath finally brought my giggling fit to an end. I stretched an apologetic hand to her and staggered slightly.

'Sorry, sorry,' I said, fighting back residual laughs, 'don't know what's wrong with me. I'm half-hysterical.'

She smiled again.

'Simon, it is difficult to figure you out.'

'You too.'

I had to fold my mouth around itself to restrain another explosion of sniggers. Odette playfully slapped me on the arse, then threaded an arm through mine. We walked back to the car, I started it up, and off we drove, Cidona and rest forgotten.

Odette lit two cigarettes and slipped one between my lips.

'OK,' she said. 'Tell me about your band.'

'Not much to tell,' I said. But I did anyway.

John Artifoni was the one who brought us together. He had everything we didn't: looks, songs, talent, a marketing plan; even a name.

Moon Palace. He told us that's what we were to be called, and we accepted it gratefully. We had no idea what it meant, and he never told us. Ever. Not that it mattered; in Dublin, a band name is useful only if it can be abbreviated. Within a fortnight of our birth, we were known as the Moonies.

By the time I left college (a degree in English and History; easy to pass, comfortingly impossible to get a job with), I had already been in half a dozen failed musical ventures. Yet still I had no interest in anything else. Much of my time was taken up with fending off parental bluster about my lack of a career, going to gigs, drinking and dreaming about being famous. I would spin huge pillars of mistruth about courses I was investigating, interviews I was going for, when in fact I worked with Bongo as a caretaker in a twenty-four-hour car park; a job where we were paid to get stoned and watch television. It was difficult to imagine any profession as rewarding as this.

We met Artifoni after a gig at the Baggot Inn, though we'd seen him around. He was a striking guy; the sort who could stand by himself in a bar and make everyone else feel they were missing something. He had deeply Italian, almost Arabic features, stone-black eyes and starkly angled cheekbones. There was a definite touch of the Lord Byron about him; scary and attractive in equal measure.

Can't remember who was playing, but the gig was crap. We met Artifoni at the door, attempting to get his money back on the basis that the poster had billed the terrible band as *Dublin's New Musical Gods*; a case, he argued, of fraudulent advertising.

The bouncer, however, had a more laissez-faire view of advertising practices, and was just about to express his belief in the free market with his fists when we stumbled into the altercation, claimed Artifoni as our lifelong but stupidly drunken friend and dragged him down Baggot Street. We brought him to the canal, sat on a wet bench, smoked a joint, and became united in outrage at the appalling gig we had just witnessed. Luckily for Bongo and me, the rhythm section had been particularly awful, giving us the opportunity to display some knowledge of our respective crafts. In truth, we were probably no better than they were, but at least we had some idea of how bad we didn't want to be.

We smoked three more joints, all the hash we had left, convinced Bongo not to jump into the canal and decided to form a band. Simple as that.

Simple because from that point on, we did everything Artifoni told us. He brought in the Smith brothers, Bill and Jimmy, skinny silent twins from Galway who listened to Artifoni with messianic reverence and respectively played keyboards and rhythm guitar. John was lead vocals, harmonica, our manager and a strategist with a brutally cynical view of the music business. *Everyone* was a bastard: the more we relied on other people, the more vulnerable we were. Our success would lie in the slog of gigging, for a year or two or maybe even five; long enough to build up a fanatical core audience and force the major labels to take us on our terms, or not at all.

We believed him too, because whatever John Artifoni lacked in vocal range, he made up for in sheer unadulterated balls. With him in front it felt like an invisible shield was thrown around the rest of us; on our first night at a real gig, I can't remember a trace of nerves. We were fucking brilliant. John told us so.

The audience, however, were a little tougher to convince. He had – he claimed deliberately – got us a gig at a barn of a pub in Leitrim: the logic being that if we could turn these punters, we could turn anyone. They ignored us. The following night they ignored us again. Two weeks later in Offaly the crowd did turn, but it was to watch a boxing match on the TV beside the bar. I'd love to say that there was one occasion that stands out in my mind, one magical night when suddenly we had the audience by the throat, but it didn't happen that way. It was a slow, denuding process, where we played and played, safe behind the Artifoni barrier, barely aware that no-one was listening. What was important was doing it, doing it, doing it, in any sort of a shithole in any part of the country until one of our riffs wiggled its way into someone's brain and stayed there like a nagging headache. No promotion, no hype, no airplay. Just nagnagnagnagnag.

I don't remember a magical gig, but I do remember a day about eighteen months later when Alan and I were required to attend the funeral of some Party crony. On the way out of the church a fifteen-year-old girl pointed at me and loudly announced:

'You're in the Moonies, aren't ya?'

My father was pleasingly horrified by this assertion, even more so when I explained that Moon Palace was a band, quite a good band, and I now intended to give up the job he'd acquired for me in the Irish Permanent Building Society to become a full-time musician. He told me I could waste my life if I wanted to, but not under his roof; which I knew he'd say. I had already paid the deposit on a flat. He said my mother would be appalled. I hated him for bringing her up, but then felt a rush of satisfaction: the cruelty of it betrayed his desperation.

This was how I finished my story to Odette, though not because that was the end of the story. We had arrived in Maynooth, got directions to Gavin McCabe's caravan and were now pulling into a threadbare, muddy field infested with rusty car husks. The cars' innards, exhaust pipes, steering wheels, windscreens, dashboards, tyres, were scattered about in random piles. At one end of the field about a dozen shabby caravans rested against one another in a tight semicircle, like they were expecting an attack by Indians.

'Oh shit,' I said.

It had never occurred to me that Gavin McCabe was co-existing with other caravan dwellers. I stopped the car.

'What's wrong?' she said.

I gestured towards the caravans.

'You know, er, travellers.'

She didn't know, of course, and I suddenly felt stupid at having to explain it. I didn't know what to explain. Knackers: they live in caravans, beg, steal, scam the dole, cut each other up with slash hooks. *What, all of them?* she'd say. *How do you know?*

'Travellers, Simon? What?'

'Ah, nothing.'

Odette patted my leg.

'Don't worry.'

We got out and gingerly made our way towards the semicircle. A skinny dog started barking, while a cloud of midges swirled around us. Yet there was no movement from the caravans, no doors opening, no twitch of curtains: nothing, as if they had been abandoned there, their occupants long since fled from some horror only we didn't know about. We knocked at a few dusty doors, but without a reply. We peered at each window in turn yet could see no evidence of life inside. We just stood there, Odette puzzled, me slightly relieved.

We had only fifty-five minutes left.

'What do yeese want?'

He emerged from around the back of the caravan we were standing outside, forcing me to wonder whether there were other caravans nearby that we didn't know about. Perhaps some caravans have back doors. I never knew that.

Odette shrugged at the man, not able to penetrate his accent.

'What do yeese want?' he repeated, without any effort to make himself clearer.

'We're looking for the bishop,' I said.

He stared at me, as if I had insulted him. He was about the same height as I was but hugely fat, stuffed into a white tee-shirt. In a faded script, the word *Tellybingo* straddled his chest. His curly hair was dyed an unconvincing shade of purple-black. He scratched his arm and looked thoughtfully into the middle distance.

'That one,' he finally said, pointing towards the last caravan of the semicircle. He turned on his heel and disappeared.

The door of the bishop's caravan was already open when we got there. He was waiting just inside, his hands in his pockets, squinting out at the sunlight.

'Hello,' he said. 'It's me you're looking for?'

I had an eerie feeling that somehow the *Tellybingo* man had already communicated this to Gavin McCabe. He brought us in and we stuffed ourselves around a Formica-covered table while he made tea. The caravan was surprisingly bright, but crammed with piles of newspapers, files and ring-binders. Yet still it was tidy; it had the austere, slightly grubby air of a man long used to living alone, who cleans because he has to. There was a large mahogany cross on the wall, along with a picture of the Pope, and a faint aroma of newly extinguished candles. As he filled his kettle the bishop studied us with a gentle curiosity.

'Do I know you?'

'No,' I said. 'No, you don't. But I knew Mary Barton.'

He put his hand to his chest, as if the words wounded him. He bowed his head for a moment, put down the kettle and sat opposite us. There was a slow grace about the way he moved, as if experience had taught him the right speed at which to operate.

'Excuse me, I don't mean to be rude, but who are you?'

We introduced ourselves, and he shook each of us by the hand.

'Simon Dillon. Anything to Judge Dillon?'

'My father.'

'Ah.'

He said it with a sad smile in his voice, like someone suddenly reminded of an old girlfriend.

'And you knew Mary Barton?'

'I was a court reporter for a while. Got to know her there.'

He nodded, but didn't seem to be listening. He gently chewed his bottom lip.

'Very sad about Mary. She was a lovely girl. I married her and Jimmy.'

We all fell silent for a moment while he stared at the table.

'But,' he finally said, 'that's what happens when you get mixed up in this sort of business. These Russians sound like maniacs. Mary was bright. She should have known better.'

'What sort of business?'

There was a slight edge to Odette's voice, so distinct that I actually turned to look at her. She ignored me and repeated the question. The bishop gazed at her steadily, his sad green eyes slightly glassy.

'Again, I don't want to be rude, but why do you want to know this?'

'Because she phoned me,' I said. 'Just before she was killed she tried to phone me and this morning these Russian guys kidnapped us and wanted to know how well I knew her.'

The bishop raised his eyebrows, as if indeed this was a shocking revelation. I knew I couldn't tell him about Emily: his concern, his worry, would only add to my own; it would be too much to bear. I glanced at the fake wooden clock on the back wall of the caravan. Fifty minutes left.

'She was obviously mixed up with something,' I ventured.

'Well, she was married to Jimmy Barton.'

'Yes, but it must have been something else.'

'But what has this got to do with you?'

'They might think I was involved with whatever it was.'

'These Russians, they let you go?'

'Yes.'

'Then obviously they believed you had nothing to do with it. Anyway, what has any of this got to do with me?'

'Because she was on her way to see you when she was killed.'

'Really?'

'Her brother told us.'

'You must have known Mary very well.'

I nodded. The look on his face told me he knew there were things I wasn't saying: he wouldn't be honest with me unless I was with him.

'Look, er, bishop.'

'Call me Gavin if you like.'

'Gavin, I know you married her, and I'm not proud of this, but I had a bit of an affair with Mary. It's just that the Russians didn't know that, and if they find out, they might think I was involved and fuck knows what they'd do to me then. Sorry about the language.'

I was suddenly close to a blubbing child, admitting my awful deeds. Given that I had managed to withhold this piece of information from the Russians, even when I was terrified for my life, it struck me as curious that I would reveal it so easily to Gavin McCabe. But as I say, there was something about the man, and telling him did bring some measure of relief. My memory flashed up an image of my first and only confession. Must have been seven. My father herding me into the dark box. It smelt of wax. He pointed to his watch and told me to be quick. Bless me, for I have sinned.

Gavin McCabe reached out a hand and patted mine.

'It's OK, OK.'

He sat back in his chair and gave us a sad smile.

'I'm glad you came, then.'

'But what is going on?' Odette was now almost annoyed.

The bishop held up a calming hand.

'Well, I'll tell you what I know. About a month ago, a rumour started going around that the Russian Mafia were moving into Dublin. Now at the time nobody believed it, but a fortnight later these two Russian fellas turn up in Ferndale.'

Ferndale was a part of Dublin most Dubliners wouldn't visit; a wretched shell of a place where the local pub looks like a bomb shelter and a big day out consists of a bus into the city centre to shoplift; we don't like to think about Ferndale.

'Now Ferndale is part of the Drummer's patch. In fact Jimmy Barton used to control it for the Drummer until he went inside. But these Russian blokeys go around telling everyone that it's theirs now, and that the local dealers have to come to them. They beat up the Drummer's lieutenant, so the Drummer sends down four heavies to deal with the Russians. The Russians shoot them all in the legs.' He made a shooting gesture, as if he was describing a film. 'So the Drummer sends over a dozen blokes – a small army – and the Russians do the same thing to them.

'Within a week everyone is too fucking scared to sell for the Drummer, and he's lost Ferndale.'

As I've told you, I haven't had that much exposure to religion, so perhaps it was genetic: but I trusted the bishop, and was genuinely shocked when he swore. This was a word I've been using and hearing all my life, yet from him it sounded genuinely dirty; like hearing your teenage sister talk about sex. Odette, however, was obviously far less sensitive than I.

'So who put the Russians up to this?'

'Well, that's the big question. Nobody knows. There's this rumour of a big Russian gang boss coming over, and that's causing a lot of panic. But nobody knows when, where or who. Basically, they're all shitting themselves.'

I squirmed in my sticky seat. I wished he'd stop swearing.

'The Provies, apparently, are talking about planting a bomb. As a show of strength. Who to? Some strength, blowing up a few old women. Oh aye, that'll sort out the problem.

'There's actually a big powwow tonight between some of the gang heads to talk about it. They are going to meet in town in that club – oh you know, that place all the pop stars go?'

'The Sidebar.'

My daughter is kidnapped, the city is ripping itself apart, and all I know is the name of a good club.

'The Sidebar. Well, they are all meeting there tonight to discuss their mutual problem. And believe me, these boys must be desperate to sit down and talk to each other.'

'But somebody here must have hired the Russians?' continued Odette.

'Yes. Somebody here did. Mary Barton.'

Odette threw a look at me as if this was something else I had known but hadn't told her. I gestured my innocence. Not that it particularly surprised me; halfway through the bishop's story I had a feeling it was going to arrive at this point. Mary was smart, tough and relentlessly realistic, and on a few occasions had even talked about going into the drugs business for herself, just for a year or so, to make a lot of money and then get out of the country. Said she'd take me with her and we'd live like kings. In a jokey way; or at least, that's what I preferred to believe.

'These boys were immigrants here, and Mary contacted them and hired them. Obviously her scheme was to scare the Drummer out of Ferndale and take it over. But then they turned against her and Mary is killed by the goons she hired in the first place. "Shot With His Own Gun", as the song says.'

Swearing, and now quoting Elvis Costello. This guy was full of surprises.

'Bastards,' I muttered.

'Indeed. But . . .'

He jabbed a finger at us, as if this was a question we might be able to answer.

'The question is: are these Russian blokeys operating all by themselves?'

'No,' I said. 'There were two Irish guys with them.'

'Hired muscle?'

'No: the Russians were working for the Irish, not the other way around.'

'That's interesting.' He shrugged. 'We just don't know.'

'*We* don't know?' jabbed Odette.

'Nobody knows,' replied the bishop with a self-correcting smile. He laid his hands palm down on the Formica table.

'That's all I can tell you.'

We sat in silence for a moment. I was surprised at how unsurprised I was at this information. I should have known all along: somewhere in my muddy, drug-sodden memory the clues for it had lain dormant. I fancied that if I sat quietly for long enough this information would work its way round to the front of my brain, provide a completion. I felt sad, and vaguely guilty.

'What about the cops?' I eventually said, just to fill the silence.

The bishop grinned, as if he had just been asked a childishly sweet question.

'They haven't a clue.'

'You know a lot,' said Odette.

The bishop nodded slowly. He formed his hands into a tepee.

'It's my parish.'

He smiled again, meshed his hands into a prayerful fist and put them in his lap.

My shoulders, I suddenly realized, were extremely stiff. I wanted to start giving myself a rub there and then. They had probably been stiff all day, but I only noticed it now because of the growing sense of ease which spread out around the back of my neck and head, like an injected liquid. It felt as if the thoughts I wanted to find were just about to arrive, that it would all connect up with what the bishop had told us. I felt I almost knew what these thoughts were; I certainly knew what the bishop was about to say.

This was, I observed of myself, a strange reaction, because I knew then that Bishop Gavin McCabe was swearing and quoting Elvis Costello because he didn't care about convincing us of his piety.

'Mary phoned and told me all about it. She was a nice girl, but a stupid bitch to try what she did.'

His hands came back on the table. He was holding a Beretta 9mm, though at the time it only registered as a large chrome gun, the sheen of its metal so perfect that for a moment I wondered whether the bishop had produced it simply to demonstrate the fine polishing job he had done. He pointed it at my chest.

'I think we should stay here for a wee bit while I make a phone call. I think there's a few people who would like a chat with you, Mr Dillon. You know more than you realize.'

The chemical swill had made its way all around my head by now, giving me a clear view back across the months I had known Mary Barton. It was laughably obvious: I had caused all this. There were forty minutes left to get back into Dublin. I knew then that Emily was dead, and I had killed her.

nine

Perhaps there's such a thing as fear fatigue. Perhaps you can reach a point where the shit has been scared out of you so much, there's no shit left.

Certainly as I stared across the table at twinkle-eyed Gavin McCabe, holding his gun like it was a surprise present, there was a curious lack of the debilitating panic which had visited me so regularly up until then.

The only distinct emotion I could identify was one of disappointment. I'm not claiming to be any great judge of character; like most people, I make up my mind about those I meet in the first ten minutes. After that, they sometimes surprise me. But mostly they don't.

Gavin McCabe though: I found it difficult to take in how wrong about him I had been. I had taken an instant liking to the man; freakishly, I still liked him, even as he pointed a gun at me and let the precious minutes tick by to the death of my daughter. I had a pacific sense of disappointment with the world, a world I already assumed was full of shits and charlatans. It just seemed so flagrantly *wrong*.

So I sat there, wedged into my plastic seat, a gun pointed at my chest, feeling disappointed and foolish. I didn't know it then, but many others had been taken in by the bishop, and most of them had far more reason to be suspicious than I. Gangsters are a surprisingly religious or, more specifically, superstitious bunch, and so automatically trusted McCabe, even to the point of letting him hear their confessions; not the murders or robberies, you understand, but what they considered sins: cheating on their wives or their fellow crimbos, the sort of thing that could get them killed. Especially if the wives found out.

The bishop never blackmailed them, but did charge royally to maintain the secrecy of the confessional, a principle he maintained strictly, unless he considered the information so juicy it might be worth a few bob to the Drummer. Turned out that the bishop made so much money from absolving consciences, he had a sprawling white villa on the Costa del Sol, along with a wife and three kids.

But, as I say, I knew none of this at the time, other than the fact that my judgement of him had been completely skewed. Yet Odette seemed to have suspected him all along. She could speak a language I didn't even know existed. Never before had someone blindfolded me so completely. (Except for John Artifoni. But I'll tell you about that later.)

I knew it wouldn't work, but I had to try.

'Please,' I said.

'Please?'

'There's something else you don't know.'

He cocked his head to one side. A shower of dandruff sprinkled his shoulders, snow on black ground.

'They have my daughter.'

Even saying this, I still felt nothing. I had to force a quiver into my voice.

'Who have?'

'The Russians. They took her from her crèche.'

He tutted, full of mock concern.

'That's terrible.'

'I'm not lying to you. I have to be back in town in the next half hour or they're going to chop her legs off.'

I didn't have to force the quiver now. My lips trembled.

'So you want me to let you go? Is that it?'

'She's two years old. She's a baby.'

Gavin McCabe said nothing. His face wore a slightly amused expression: he had greatly enjoyed my performance; even admired it.

'You're very good, I must say. Very good. Top quality bullshit.'

'I'm not lying to you. They're going to ring me in a few—'

'Shut up now.'

'Please, I'm begging you for my daughter's life.'

'*Shut up!*'

I did as he said. I was shaking so much I couldn't form words any more. I had a sudden, chronic desire to piss. I put my hands to my groin to hold it back. I felt like a child again. In Kerry, fidgeting until mass was over. Down there they were good: world-class bullshit. In Auntie Marion's bar, a dirty wooden hut with a field out the back that served as the toilet; the sort of place they now export to Japan in kit form. Alan and I thought constant filth (even the air was textured with dust) and having to urinate in fields were brilliant. So we spent a good portion of each day propping up the bar, drinking Cidona and guzzling Tayto. No matter what the time, there were always at least half a dozen people in there. Usually singing or talking an impenetrable Irish. We got to know most of them. Farmers would drift in during the afternoon, have a few pints, go off to finish their work, have their tea and come back again. They would always ask:

'Any news, boys?'

But there never was. We heard them endlessly recycle the same stories and songs, but on each occasion with some new nuance, as if they were trying to wring as much value as possible from an arid pool of material: just drag it out before death came.

With some coaching from Marion, we would observe them bitch to and about one another. There were no fights, yet there was always some friction between the customers, often over disputes which went back years. It was as subtle as breath. The intonation of a word, the phrasing of a question, the omission of a name, all of these were wielded as bare-faced insults, wrapped within a tone of simple chumminess.

None of the tourists who strayed in was aware of the aggressive subtext, but then a truce would usually be called whenever a stranger arrived. With one mind, they would all concentrate on the newcomers, on making them feel they had arrived in heaven. It was like watching a cult brainwashing new recruits. In turn they would shyly approach, all of them stressing how simple and poor they were in Kerry, not like you from a big place like Reading over there in England with your Ford Anglia. I've seen people walk in and be horrified by the grubbiness of the pub, only to end up staying for two days in the nearest B&B. I'm still not sure how they did it, but the locals in that pub were the best bull-shitters I have ever seen in my life. For people who never seemed to read a paper, they could talk on an astonishing range of subjects: politics all over the world, the English football league, history, geography, literature, all of it delivered to the other locals with a covert wink while the tourists would listen, en-thralled.

The pub is gone now, but Auntie Marion is still there. It was like home: they'd wrestle with us, rub our heads, marvel at Alan. *He's the image of his mother. Just like her too. A lovely nature.* I always meant to bring Emily down.

'Prick,' spat out Odette.

The bishop jabbed a finger up to her face.

'Don't you get fucking lippy, girl.'

He narrowed his eyes, bit his bottom lip.

'I know you. I'm sure I do.'

Odette said nothing.

'Just keep the lips buttoned, and no more dramatics from you, Mr Dillon. You should have kept your pecker in your strides.'

He laid a thick, brown hand palm up on the table. I caught a glimpse of dirty fingernails.

'Mobile phone,' he said to me.

'How do you know I have one?' I replied, surprised by my own defiance.

He waved the gun slightly.

'You yuppie fuckers always have one.'

I fished it out of my jacket and placed it in his hand. Lying there, it seemed small and delicate. He smirked, placed the phone on the table before him, then transferred the gun from his right hand to his left. There was a dull thud, like the sound of a football hitting the side of the caravan. Gavin McCabe dropped the gun and his head whirled around like it was suddenly in a zero-gravity environment. Odette was standing on the table, her arms pressed to the roof of the caravan. She supported herself with her left leg, while with her right she methodically kicked the bishop in the head. A spume of blood ejected from his ear, and he flopped sideways from my view.

Somehow I wasn't surprised that she'd done this; what taxed me more was how she'd been able to do it without me seeing.

'How did you do that?'

'I punched him.'

'I didn't see it,' I said, quite prepared to sit back and have a long detailed discussion of Odette's martial arts skills.

'He looked at the phone. You looked at the phone. It doesn't matter. We have to get out of here. There's no time. Emily, Simon, Emily.'

She swept up the gun, cocked the trigger.

'Later on, you may be asked. There was a struggle. The gun went off. OK?'

She placed the gun at McCabe's right temple and looked back at me.

'OK?'

I said nothing. The respective parts of my brain that understand and speak couldn't make a connection. It didn't make decisions like this; it couldn't.

'OK? Simon?'

'No,' I finally croaked. 'For God's sake. We can't start fucking killing people. You've beaten the shit out of him as it is. I don't understand this.'

'Simon,' she yelled like an exasperated schoolteacher. 'Who do you think he was ringing up? He was selling you out to one of the gangs, probably the Drummer. If the Drummer finds out about you and Mary Barton, you are dead. This bishop is the only one who knows, because you told him, and he will sell that information the first chance he gets. Even if we go to the police now and they lock you up in Fort Knox, sooner or later they will find you and kill you. Torture you and kill you. He dies or you die. There is no other way.'

'No,' I said. But I knew she was right.

Having the power of life or death over another human being is not something I'm used to. So I opted to react in the way any reasonable person would: I picked up my mobile, weakly repeated the word 'No' and staggered out of the caravan. Behind, I could feel Odette's annoyance glowing.

'Go to the car. Quickly,' she barked.

But quickly was beyond my abilities. I picked my way carefully through the clumpy field and waited for the pistol shot to jar every nerve in my body: a tart sting of sound which would change me into someone else, punctuate my life into before and after Gavin McCabe was executed.

I reached the car and leaned on the still-warm bonnet, and for a moment considered that perhaps Odette might have had second, less murderous thoughts and was now trussing the bishop up. But just for a moment: I'd seen the concrete look on her face, the complete acceptance that a dirty job had to be done and she was the one to do it. I had a good idea of what she was capable of, and knew she didn't need a gun to extinguish his life. I got on my knees and vomited magnificently. Beer and half-digested chips. The story of my life, in food form.

A waste, right until the end. Knowing that Mary Barton hired the Russians didn't explain why they killed her, why they kidnapped Emily and why now they would almost certainly kill me. *You know more than you think*. The only knowledge I had was of the grisly depth of my own ignorance, the squandering of my existence. I could have been of some use, if I'd been somebody else. Perhaps at the end, when they held the gun to my head, they might explain what this was all about, like the baddies in a James Bond film: reveal the secret sickness at the heart of my life; give a shape to the meaningless.

My phone rang. Bang on time.

'Simon. Can you talk now? Hope I didn't interrupt you at anything important.'

'I was puking,' I said, leaving it to him to decide on the importance or not of such an activity.

'Really? Oh.'

He seemed genuinely thrown by my reply; as if there was a strict verbal protocol for child hostage negotiations, and I had strayed scandalously far away from it.

'Anyway,' he continued, struggling to re-establish his previous tone of mannered irony. 'I'm just on, Simon, to give you the location for our rendezvous.' *Roundy Voo.*

I said nothing.

'Do you not want to know where it is, Simon?'

'I suppose so.'

'Now that's not very enthusiastic, Simon. Are you not keen to see your daughter again?'

'You've killed her already, haven't you?'

I heard a rushed inhalation of breath: a sigh of shock, or a laugh.

'Simon, how could you think such a thing? We are businessmen. We make deals. I have made a deal with you. If you keep your end of the deal, your daughter is fine.'

'Fuck you and your deal,' I said. But he didn't hear me. There was the muffled sound of the phone being handled, of whispers, then a high-pitched female voice over-enunciating each word: *Talk to your daddy, Emily!* Breath, childish squeaks of pleasure.

'Dadda.'

'Emily?'

'Dad-dee.'

More muffled sounds, more Emily chatting in her secret half-language. I knew what she was doing, she always did it. Give her the phone to talk to someone and she would press it to her ear for only a second or two; she would then hold it at arm's length and try to see the person inside, or show the receiver her dolls and books. My tears dribbled into my open mouth. The high-pitched voice again: *Thank you, Emily!* And he was back.

'Right, Simon. Half an hour. By the observation tower in Smithfield. By yourself. Don't be late.'

'Will Emily be there?'

'You turn up. We'll tell you where she is. Don't be late.'

He hung up.

The sound of Odette swearing caused me to look back towards the caravan. There seemed to be an almost inhuman strength to her, something animal, and for a moment this quality gave me a small rush of hope. So too did the fact that she had evidently changed her mind about Gavin McCabe: he was blindfolded, his arms pinned with sticky tape behind his back, but very obviously alive as Odette pushed and prodded him across the lumpy field.

'Hurry up, you shit.' *Sheet.*

I gave in to the notion that this would mean something; this would count in our favour. We had not taken a life, so one would be given back to us: Emily for the bishop.

Odette kicked him.

'Move it!'

No: there was no balance about this, no committee judging our deeds and awarding points. Emily would live if I turned up in Smithfield, and if they decided not to kill her. It was their whim.

Odette opened the boot of the car and shoved the bishop in.

'You didn't kill him,' I said, more as a question.

'Maybe later.'

She slapped him across the head.

'Now you keep your lip buttoned.'

She slammed the boot shut, put the gun in her bag.

'Did they ring?'

'Yes. The observation tower in Smithfield. Why is he in the boot?'

'He says he knows where they are holding your daughter.'

She took a step towards where I was still crouched. I quickly stood up, suddenly embarrassed by my recent regurgitation. My head swam. The more we learned, the less sense there was; we were like physicists unpicking the complicated equations that created the universe, only to discover that the universe shouldn't exist at all.

'What? How does he know?'

Odette joined her hands in mock prayer.

'It's my parish,' she said, displaying no talent for mimicry.

'He's lying, to save himself.'

'I don't think so. He knew about Smithfield.'

I looked at my watch. Twenty-five minutes left. I gestured helplessly. I didn't know what this new information meant, if it meant anything.

'We've got to get going,' I said.

'Yes. But what do you want to do, Simon?'

I didn't understand the question.

'If we go to Smithfield, they will almost certainly kill you, and there's a chance they will kill Emily anyway. The bishop says she's in Ballymont. There's a chance he is lying, and we won't have enough time to get over to Smithfield if he is. If she is there, there's a chance we may not be able to get her out. But if we can . . . Simon, we have to go to one place or the other. There isn't enough time to do both. Smithfield or Ballymont.'

'What do you think we should do?'

She strode to the driver's door and got in the car.

'I cannot decide that for you, Simon. It has to be up to you.'

Great. Fucking great.

ten

Making decisions was never something I excelled at.

I dunno: that was the singular phrase of my teenage years, the words always delivered with a slouching languidity, carefully designed to confirm that indeed I did not know. Or care.

Even as an adult, I have been like this; or at least, I have been able to manufacture huge levels of indifference at will, a gift I have sometimes used to swamp even the most enthusiastic company. Enthusiasm makes me uneasy. I find it suspect in other people, naive in myself. Sometimes I wish it were otherwise. Sometimes.

It's the way I am.

My only dalliance with anything approaching zeal was during my time in Moon Palace, and even then it was of a carefully diluted nature. It involved a lot of nodding and saying, *yeah, cool*: a neutral place I fancied to be equidistant between smug and ungrateful. By instinct I was careful, smelling the potential hatred from my peers: only a couple of years out of college and already a professional musician, in a band they all talked about, on the cusp (they all said) of a huge deal. A&R men bought us drinks. Artifoni took calls. We were interviewed by papers, TV and radio. We tried to be funny. We could go to the door of the Sidebar now and be recognized, now be whisked up to the VIP room. People I didn't know would point at me, would offer me drugs, would come up and tell me I was great. Of course I was great: I'd landed the Teenage Dream, and I didn't even have to try that hard.

Yet I was careful. I shrugged and smiled thinly. Said, *yeah, thanks*. Looked bored.

Perhaps that is why, when the dream began to disintegrate, I did nothing to stop it. I found myself incapable, or unwilling: if it required effort, I wasn't interested; it wouldn't be the same. I was a middle-class kid from Dalkey, and despite my lack of appreciation I still expected only good things to happen to me. Anything else didn't compute.

I haven't changed that much; except that now I'm aware of this failing. I knew I wouldn't be able to decide what to do about Emily, so I didn't. I let time and geography do it for me. Twenty-five minutes wasn't enough to get back into Smithfield. Ballymont was just off the M4 and therefore closer. So we went there. Odette seemed to know the way.

'Are you sure?' she asked.

I shook my head.

'I dunno.'

Ballymont was a part of Dublin I don't think I've ever been to before; certainly, I can't think of any good reason for having visited. Not the worst part of the city, though not exactly a tourist Mecca either. It was a working-class estate which at one time probably possessed a village charm, but this had long since been gobbled up, along with every millimetre of green space, by a huge ejaculation of gratified concrete. Like a bodybuilder who has taken too many steroids, Ballymont had spread grotesquely in all directions, shattering the frail skeleton it was built upon. There was no centre; just a grey labyrinth of tatty buildings, all equally miles from anywhere.

Odette drove slowly, scanning each corner for the painted-out street signs. She muttered to herself as she did so, like a desperate punter urging on the limping horse she has backed with her rent money.

'Bingo,' she finally announced. *Star of the Sea Flats. Nos 1–28.* Odette screeched to the right and gunned the car down the road, then swept it left into a stained concrete driveway. We crunched to a halt. She reached down in front of my legs, removed the gun from her bag and bolted out of the car.

The Star of the Sea building looked exhausted, dirty and slightly appalling; like a stotiously drunk old lady. The date *1950*, along with an illustration which I assume was the Star in question, appeared in mosaic high on one wall, minutely cemented there years ago by the men who had built this place; men who, at the time, may even have been proud of their work, who may have dreamed of living in somewhere like Star of the Sea Flats. The Star, however, had been rendered unrecognizable by young men who, for reasons of their own, considered stars a legitimate target for rock throwing.

Today the young men were elsewhere, had moved on to other targets. There were no people, except for two serious-faced children playing on a rusty swing. A woman in a wheelchair sat nearby. She smoked cigarettes, coughed and stared at the ground.

The building was three-storey, constructed of blackened red brick, and if it had had the good fortune to be located in another part of the city, might now be worth a great deal of money; would boast luxury apartments. It didn't deserve to be called ugly. The front doors of the flats opened onto a balcony, partially obscured by washing lines of worn clothes; bunting for a special guest who never arrived.

Yet this balcony could also have been a place where, on sunny days, neighbours would lean out and chat, where flower baskets would be hung; where, during winter, the lights over the front doors would provide a hint of the friendly intent inside. Like a star of the sea. Perhaps families had lived and died here and, despite all the grimy struggle, managed to store away a few nuggets of happiness; could look at the bubbling plaster on the wall and remember that sometimes they laughed; that the laughter passed into the air and became infused in the structure of the building, making it a benign place. I wanted to believe this. My daughter might be up there.

A thump at the window jerked me back to the cold present tense. Odette nodded that it was time to go. She held Gavin McCabe by the scruff of the neck. McCabe glared at me. I struggled with my seatbelt, and wished he wouldn't look.

'Sorry,' said Odette when I'd got out. 'I would leave you here, but your daughter will need to see you.'

'Of course,' I said, slightly offended that she could think I would want to stay behind.

'Where?' she said to McCabe.

He indicated with his head.

'Second floor.' He looked at me again. 'The two of yous are dead anyway, you know that, don't ya?'

'We'll see,' said Odette, and shoved him forward.

As we moved up the narrow stone stairs, I wondered why Gavin McCabe would have bothered telling us this: it seemed a pointless piece of information, and if it was true, it certainly had no bearing on what we were about to do. Perhaps it was simply bravado, or a way for McCabe to declare that he was still loyal to the half-seen forces who seemed hell bent on grinding up the remaining shards of my life. Whoever they were.

My phone rang.

Without thinking, I took it out and clicked the *OK* button, realizing too late that this was not an OK thing to do.

'Hello, Simon?'

His voice. I was late and they were in Smithfield, wondering where I was. Odette urgently mouthed a word at me. Gavin McCabe grinned, like he'd just won a bet. I turned off the phone.

'What did you do?' breathed Odette. '*Stall* them, Simon. I said to stall them.'

I didn't get a chance to ask why. She turned and started hustling the still-grinning McCabe up the steps. I followed two strides behind, both physically and mentally. If I didn't turn up, and Emily was here, they could ring the flat and tell them to kill her. We had run out of time.

On the second floor balcony, Odette wound McCabe's right arm behind his back. She hissed:

'What number, what number?'

Wincing only slightly, he used his free hand to point. Thirty-three.

'You'll have to let me go now,' he breathed. 'There's a peephole on the door. If they see anyone else, they'll know something is up.'

Odette smacked the Beretta across his head, then released her hold. She crouched, dragging me down with her, and aimed the gun at the bishop. She held it in two hands, just like they do on the cop shows.

McCabe smiled again, like we were two impetuous kids who wouldn't really do any harm. He turned and rapped on the door. From inside, a muffled voice answered. The bishop leaned in and shouted.

'Hector? You in there? It's Gavin McCabe.'

Hector made what seemed to be an affirmative sound.

'Is Helen in there with ya?'

The same sound came in response.

'Are ya no gonna let me in?'

A third sound, this time timid but interrogative.

'The big man sent me, Hector. Open the fucking door.'

There was a pause, then the sound of locks being rattled. The door squeaked open.

Gavin McCabe barged in, slamming it shut behind him. Odette stood and opened fire: one, two, three, four, five, six times; a hellish eternity of staccato screeches, erupting clouds of wood and glass into our hair and clothes until the noise was cutting my ears and I screamed at her to stop.

We had to flap through the dust and smoke to see. Everyone coughed, like warring armies taking a cigarette break. A baby started crying.

I gripped Odette's shoulder, and could feel blood thumping through a swollen vein. She put up her left hand to gesture me silent, then kicked the splintered door. It shuddered, glass tinkling from its small window, but miraculously remained intact. As if suddenly distracted, she momentarily studied a small junction box over the door, then ripped the phone line from it. Like an announcer at a sporting event, she called out:

'I'm going to count to five.'

No answer. I wondered was it wise to go into the flat after them, and suddenly felt like some sort of wretched spectator in all this. I felt sick.

'One.'

'Do you hear that?' shouted out Gavin McCabe.

'Two.'

'OKOKOKOK.'

She opened her mouth, then closed it.

'No more counting, please,' said McCabe, his voice rich with syrupy concern. 'You have us cornered in here. I admit that. Our phone is dead. There's nothing we can do. I'm just saying you've upset the wee girl. I don't think there should be any more shooting. Please. Someone in here might get hurt. And no-one wants that.'

Odette gestured to me again. We said nothing. Emily continued to cry. Underneath her wails, McCabe hissed incomprehensible instructions to the others in the flat.

'I tell you what,' he finally shouted again. 'You two just want the baby, and then you'll go. Isn't that right?'

Again, Odette ordered me to be silent. Emily's cries had reached the shuddering stage. She gulped for breath, while trying to express her fright and alarm in the half-dozen words at her disposal.

'You're not saying much, are ya?'

We said nothing.

'Ma-ha-meee,' finally managed my daughter.

'All right,' said McCabe. 'We're coming out with the baby. There's three of us. Don't shoot now.'

There were more whispered directions, the sound of bodies moving around each other, and finally what was left of the front door cracked open. Emily appeared first, but several feet off the ground, held aloft by an unidentified pair of hands. She had fallen silent, temporarily bemused by her weightless condition. She looked down and gently kicked her legs. As she slowly floated onto the balcony, a gun barrel appeared by her head. It was a twelve-gauge semi-automatic Huglu shotgun, and was held by a thin, ratty-looking man with a pock-marked face. He handled the gun uncomfortably, like it was too heavy for him. He didn't look at us, as if aiming the gun took up all of his available concentration. Behind him was Gavin McCabe, whose hands held Emily, along with a short-haired, white-faced woman sucking on a cigarette. She looked the other way, like she hadn't noticed what was going on and even if she had she wanted to make clear that it had nothing to do with her.

Odette stood stony still, legs slightly apart, her arms stiff in front of her; the Beretta pointed at the ratty man's head.

I looked at my daughter, and noticed the splatters of tomato ketchup on her blue dress; that one of her pigtails had unravelled and the hair there had become matted. I thought: Angela will give me a load of shit if she sees Emily like that. It was the only weapon she had which could pierce my indifference. *You don't care about your daughter at all. You don't care about anyone except yourself.* You don't care about me.

'Now,' said Gavin McCabe, 'here we all are.'

The words interrupted Emily's silent examination of her environment. The watery blue globes in her head moved around, and she took in the man holding her up, the smoking woman behind him, the other man holding a shotgun to her head. She looked the other way and saw the woman dressed in black, also pointing a gun, and behind her the bloodless, shaking man in the black jacket and blue jeans, still crouching for fear of being shot. Her chubby arms shot out like fearless pistons, her legs tried to walk on thin air.

'Da-deee!'

Gavin McCabe tried to hold her still, but nature has made toddlers slippery: her legs swung wildly, like a cartoon character who has run off the edge of a cliff. She jerked her body forward and twisted irritably, attempting to prise McCabe's stubby fingers from around her waist. She squealed, animal in her annoyance.

The man with the gun stepped back, trying to avoid Emily's flailing arms crashing into the weapon.

'Steady, Hector,' counselled the bishop.

But Hector wasn't steady. The shotgun, as if suddenly alive, began to vibrate in his hands. He glanced fearfully at us, then back at McCabe and the struggling Emily.

'Put her down,' said Odette.

'Da-deee!' screamed Emily, outraged that I didn't come to get her.

'Hector,' barked McCabe. 'Aim the gun.'

Hector moved the gun forward, then back, then forward, his arms locked into an indecisive cycle, his eyes darting between Odette and the howling child.

'Da-dee!' cried Emily.

'Put the gun down, Hector,' said Odette.

'Don't you fucking dare, Hector. You, Frenchie. You put the fucking gun down.'

The bishop stretched his arms out fully, took a step and swung Emily out over the edge of the balcony. I shot to my feet, then froze.

For a moment, everyone did. Suddenly, it didn't seem like us against them, but everyone against Gavin McCabe: it was a friendly argument which had gone too far, a game of Monopoly which had turned into a knife fight, and there was no way back from this. He had made it as absolute as the eternal.

Even Emily fell quiet. She slowly moved her arms and legs, wondering at the strange spatial relationships which made her unable to touch anything she saw.

'Hector,' said McCabe. 'Aim the fucking gun at them.'

Almost apologetically, Hector pointed the weapon vaguely in our direction. The smoking woman had slumped to the floor, her arms wrapped around her head like a bandage. Her elbows were bruised.

Odette ignored Hector. She aimed the Beretta at McCabe's head. He grimaced.

'Getting a bit tired now. She's a heavy wee lass. So, Frenchie, what we gonna do?'

Odette didn't reply.

'Trying to psych me out won't do any good now, girlie. When I get too tired, down goes the child, and I'd say your friend there won't be too happy about that.'

She still said nothing.

'This is a test of will, is it not? I have the will to drop this child. Perhaps you have the will to shoot me. And let's just say, for the sake of argument, that you're very fast and you manage to shoot both me and Hector here. What happens then? Nobody wins. Your pal there will be devastated, and I'd say not too keen to enjoy your protection any more.

'Any way you look at it, the people I know are going to get to Mr Dillon because they have the sheer will to do whatever they want.'

He looked directly at me.

'It's just that this way, the way Frenchie wants to play it, your daughter will die, Simon. And what's the point of that? I'd be happy to let her go. She's not going to be identifying anyone in a court of law.'

Odette didn't move.

I was shaking so much, I could barely get my tongue to function.

'Odette,' I whispered.

'Shut up, Simon,' she said.

'Odette.'

'Shut up, Simon!'

McCabe shook his head.

'Oh, she's proud. She's tough. She doesn't want to back down.'

Very deliberately, he looked back at Hector.

'When I drop the child, you shoot Frenchie. Are you ready?'

Hector nodded, but uncertainly, as you do when foreigners address you in their own language. I took a step backwards, my hands jammed to my ears; trying to push away the reality assaulting me.

'Odette,' I pleaded.

'He's not going to do it, Simon.'

'Oh, but I am.'

'He's not going to do it, Simon.'

Gavin McCabe sighed, and dropped Emily.

Her little blue dress billowed as she sailed away.

I screamed; or at least, I attempted to make some sound: as if to create an aural blanket under my falling daughter, something to bounce her safely back to me. But nothing emerged from my throat. My mouth, ears and eyes seemed stuffed, having received too much information from the physical world. It was immediate and distant at the same time; overwhelming, and I felt my system crash, my body fall gently to the powdery concrete. From a great distance, I saw Odette put three neat bullet holes into McCabe's right temple, saw him stagger back, then right himself, blood dribbling onto his crisp white collar. He sank to his knees and, like a supplicant in an old religious painting, rolled his eyes back towards heaven and fell forward into a puddle of urine no-one had bothered to wash off.

Hector watched all this, his facial muscles rigid with horror. His arms shook, like he was operating an invisible jack hammer. To Odette he said:

'No . . . I . . . I . . . He wasn't . . .'

The shotgun slipped from his fingers and clattered to the ground. Hector dragged the smoking woman to her feet and the two of them scrambled down the corridor.

Odette let them go. She took two steps forward, then turned back to look at me.

'Simon.'

I didn't answer. I didn't hear her. I could see nothing but Emily gliding downwards from my view, her face full of trust and wonder as she went, unaware of the cruelty which had been floating around her like gas fumes.

There was nothing left now. I could look back through the meandering path of my life and see that every thought and heart-beat had been a waste; nothing more than treading water before the inevitable. I wondered how my father would react when he heard that his grandchild was dead, that his eldest son was dead also: would he have any idea why, or would this simply add to his bafflement at a young man who had gone to so much trouble to antagonize him; who had refused to wash for months at a time just to get a reaction, had worn a *Fuck the Pope* tee-shirt when he knew a priest was calling to the house, who had spent secret hours searching his father's study, looking for clues of imagined corruption, clues of anything: of a life being lived, with a human being at its core.

The more difficult I got, the more remote he became. I drove him out of his own house, him unwilling to admit that he didn't know how to cope with me, me unwilling to provide any clues. Too late to change that now. One way or another, I have striven to make everyone in my life dead. I have no idea why.

Odette looked over the edge of the balcony, then back towards the shattered front door of the flat, then over to where I was slumped. Her movements were jerky and uncertain, as if suddenly she didn't know where she was.

'Simon.'

I looked up. Her eyes were watery. Perhaps I should have hated her then, but to what end? She had merely been the instrument of my self-destruction. I had eradicated all hate and love; created a black, flat universe.

'Simon,' she repeated. Like a delicate old woman, she slowly hunkered down on the concrete, unable to progress past the point-less repetition of my name. We looked at each other, and saw nothing.

Then we heard Emily crying.

eleven

Angela slapped me across the face. Or tried to. To her credit, she had never before attempted to hit me, though it was this lack of practice that ensured her failure. I was too tall, and her hand merely clipped my chin. In desperation, she grabbed a spotless ashtray and flung it in my direction, again missing the target. She collapsed in an exasperated lump behind her desk, suddenly aware of the faces on the other side of her glass-fronted office; all of them very much not looking.

She covered her forehead with one hand, pointed at the door with the other.

'Get out, Simon.'

She said it like someone who had just spat out a fly.

I didn't move, unsure if Angela had fully absorbed what we had told her, and we had told her as little as possible: men had attempted to kidnap Emily, but we had prevented this. It had something to do with a criminal I had interviewed years before; a case of mistaken identity which would soon be sorted out. But in the meantime it was best to be careful. She had sneered with disbelief.

'What have you done? This is something to do with drugs, isn't it?'

I looked out at Emily in the next office, both pigtails re-established, perched on a desk while a group of women gurned for her entertainment. Her little pink shoulders shuddered with delight.

'Angela,' said Odette. 'We will contact the police now, but to be safe, do not stay in your own house tonight. Do you understand this?'

Angela sat up straight, sliced a hand towards Odette but looked at me.

'Who is she?'

I said nothing, not knowing the answer. Odette still hadn't told me of her secret life: her admission that she knew our tormentors remained unexplained. Then again, we had been rather busy.

'A friend,' said Odette.

Angela snorted: a gesture of broken defiance in the face of the Other Woman. A sizzling irony: *Jesus, Simon, sometimes I wish you were having an affair. At least it would show you had some fucking gumption.*

'Just get out,' she said, not looking at either of us. She faced her computer, but her eyes were thick with tears. Without looking up, she pointed at me, forcing every gram of spite she possessed into her words.

'And you are not fit to be her father. You're *not* her father.'

'Angela.'

'No, Simon. I don't want to hear it.'

'Angela.'

'No, Simon.'

I left the office, having completed my role in the tedious ongoing drama of our dead marriage: a part I had learned by rote. I would pretend to be sorry, she would pretend to be disappointed. They were the only words we had for each other.

On the way out I kissed Emily goodbye: kissed her chubby cheeks, the grazed knees she had fallen upon, waved as I backed out the door, both of our lives saved by bad architecture.

The Star of the Sea Flats, unfortunately for its tenants but fortunately for us, was cursed with poor plumbing. In the mornings and evenings, the water pressure was such that the supply on the upper floors regularly slowed to a dribble, so the Corporation opted for the quick and cheap remedy of bolting additional water tanks onto the side of the building. Emily had landed on the flat, bitumen roof of one of these, just three feet below where Gavin McCabe had dropped her. She had sat there, shaking, clutching her scraped legs and screaming with indignation until I swooped her back onto the balcony. She had wrapped her podgy arms around my neck and sniffed away her tears. There was an oily smear on her dress, the only permanent damage, and for some reason this reminded me of a dress Angela had worn when she was pregnant; of a dinner party, can't remember where, but she was sitting with two other pregnant women and laughing hysterically, the three of them holding their swollen bellies as if they might burst with mirth. A long, long time ago.

Whether Gavin McCabe was aware of the existence of this water tank, I will never know. Whether Odette knew or not I could discover by means of a simple question; yet I couldn't bring myself to ask, and she volunteered no explanation. Back in the car we sat in silence; an elephant on the dashboard we both pretended not to notice. We smoked cigarettes.

Yet soon I found myself smiling. It had, after all, worked out: Emily was safe. Even if Odette hadn't known about the water tank, and had guessed wrongly about what Gavin McCabe was prepared to do, it didn't matter now. Emily was safe. Angela spewed venom at me, but she always did; she routinely told me I was an unfit father, slyly threatening to take away my access. This was my life as I had lived it for some months now, and to see the familiar angry road signs from my wife gave me a curious comfort.

'So,' I said, deliberately affecting as much jauntiness as possible. 'What do we do now? Bit of dinner and dancing?'

She glanced at me, suspicious of sarcasm.

'There's nothing else we can do but call the police. Do you have the number of your friend Leo?'

'Do I tell him about me and Mary?'

'You and Mary. Emily. Everything.'

I took out my phone. Something else occurred to me.

'How can we prove any of this?'

She patted my leg, and began peeling up her tee-shirt. An interesting tactic, if her intention was to take my mind off our current circumstances. However, it wasn't her body Odette wanted to show me, but a small minidisc recorder strapped to her stomach. She rummaged around and produced a tiny wire microphone.

'I have everything the bishop said to us. That was why I changed my tee-shirt. It wasn't because of my *poo*.'

She gave me a timid grin. I smiled in return. She rubbed the back of my neck.

'I know I am not what I appear to be.'

'You appear to be Bruce Lee's really tough sister.'

I felt her smile again.

'OK. I am not what I claim to be.'

'You're not a lawyer.'

'No.'

'What are you then?'

'Later, Simon. Ring Leo now.'

'Should I tell him you're not a lawyer?'

My phone rang.

'Where the fuck are you, boy? Why aren't you at home like I told you?'

It was Broder.

'I was just about to ring you. I'm in the car.'

'Why?'

'We went to see Gavin McCabe.'

'What? The fucking looper bishop? Dillon, what the fuck are you playing at? Four more people have got plugged. Little old ladies are scared to leave their houses. People are going home early from work. I'm fucking shagged out looking at dead bodies. You nearly got killed yourself this morning and now you're fucking jaunting around the countryside. Christ, are you fucking insane? The city is like Beirut and you go looking for gangsters to talk to. What the fuck are you doing, Dillon?'

Broder sounded a little stressed.

'Leo, listen to me.'

I rarely used his first name; it was enough to seize his attention.

'There's an awful lot of stuff I have to tell you. We went to see the bishop because Mary Barton was on her way to see him when she was killed.'

'How did you find that out?'

'Well, that's a long story, but . . . it's because I had an affair with Mary Barton.'

'What?'

'I had an affair with Mary Barton.'

'What? What?'

The conversation could have stalled on this point for some time.

'Broder, you heard me.'

'You were riding Mary Barton? Are you completely fucking in-fucking-sane?'

'Probably.'

In a perverse way, I was enjoying this.

'I don't believe it.'

He did though. I related what McCabe had told us about Mary Barton and the Russians. I told him about the kidnap of Emily and her lucky rescue, and how the bishop was somehow involved in this. I didn't mention Odette not being a lawyer. He sighed at each new detail.

'Where exactly are you now?'

'Lucan, just going past it.'

'You're not too far away then. Come straight to O'Connell Street. I'll meet you outside the Gresham. Jesus, if this thing about you and the Barton wan gets out, every gobshite in Dublin will be out to slit your throat. I'll have to put you into protective custody, you *stupid bollocks*.'

'OK. Good. Well, I think the news about me and Mary is out already, Broder.'

'Yes, I see. Of course,' he said, still grappling with all the new information. 'Look: when you get there, don't park anywhere else and walk up. Drive straight to the Gresham. If you don't see me, keep driving around until I arrive. Have you got that?'

'Yeah.'

'Jesus, Dillon, what kind of a fucking mess have you got yourself in? Be careful.' He hung up.

'So,' said Odette. 'What is his plan?'

I told her and she nodded approvingly, like a schoolteacher marking homework. She looked at her watch.

'How long?'

'Twenty minutes or so.'

I yawned. My body was catching up with me. The coke had vacated my system, and I started to feel weary and dehydrated again. I needed a week's sleep. I wanted a warm pub and a cold bottle of tequila. Neither seemed likely. Odette lit two cigarettes and passed one to me.

'This will be over soon,' she said.

I nodded noncommittally.

'And then I will tell you about myself. I promise.'

She smiled weakly, and again I saw the waving children, saw a softness close to weeping. Understandably, it felt like weeks since I first met her. I had seen her in the most extreme situations, yet still she had revealed little of herself. Perhaps a gentler, less certain version of Odette lurked inside. Perhaps not.

But I was glad that she wasn't ready yet to talk; I wasn't ready yet to listen. There were a couple of details I had also withheld, at first because of a dim sense of caution, now because of a certainty that there was an almost mathematical relationship between me revealing details of my past and strange men wanting to kill me. What I hadn't told Odette shouldn't make any difference, I reasoned. I was quite happy to wait until this was all over. Show her mine when she showed me hers. And Emily was safe.

My phone rang again. The display read: *Work*. Despite all that had happened, I still experienced a flash of panic at the prospect of speaking to my employers. I quickly trawled my mind for credible excuses, then realized that Broder had probably come good on his promise of earlier in the day and phoned them. They were simply calling to see how I was. Yet still I let the phone ring until it fell silent again. Odette glanced at me, but didn't ask why.

The traffic wasn't too bad, the majority of motorists being keen to get out of the city. We bulleted along the straight wide road into town and then were swept around the sharp incline that leads up to Heuston Station and the quays. Just there is a brief panorama of Dublin: the obelisk and the cross peeking out of the trees in the Phoenix Park, the ragbag architecture along the Liffey leading up to Liberty Hall, for years the tallest building: a shabby 1960s column of grimy glass, topped off by an undulating green roof; a bald man wearing a bad wig. I could make out the Millennium Spire, but not easily: it was evening now, but the lights around it had yet to be turned on. The city looked mucky and vulgar, a rich tourist who gets drunk and wakes up with a huge tattoo. *Dubh Linn*. The Black Pool. I have tried to leave it many times.

When the band exploded, I tried. Promised myself I'd never go back, like my brother. Went to London, then New York, then San Francisco. Eight months later I was drunk in the Bailey on Duke Street, claiming to everyone I met that I had never intended to leave for good. I gave up, but pretended I was still trying. I attempted to form another band, DJed for a while, wrote appalling jokes for a stand-up comedian, had a plan to set up an internet company, had a plan to go back to college, had a plan to write a novel, became a journalist, became a TV researcher. Fucked it all up.

Artifoni fucked it all up. Now, it's easy to see that he didn't want any of the prizes he had promised us. But back then, he was just being John: stalling and arguing with the record companies, finally choosing one; arguing with them over who should produce the album. He won that argument, but fought with the producer anyway.

Yet it was all benignly tolerated, the men with the money recognizing that Artifoni *was* Moon Palace. The rest of us knew it too, and at times secretly feared a Beatles-type scenario where one of us, or all of us, would be dropped. Then again, it would be difficult to imagine Artifoni making such a deal: if anything was constant about him, it was the degree to which he despised the people from the record company. Their indulgence gnawed at him, drove him on to greater tantrums. The very idea of the band succeeding seemed to infuriate him, as if we were all committing some huge collective sin; something we had all promised never, ever to do.

Appropriately, our first single was called 'Stroppy'. We played it live on a BBC2 music show, during which Artifoni dived into the crowd and appeared to have a fight with a member of the audience. The following Monday we were number twenty-three in the UK Top Forty, and we got the call. It was time to go on *Top of the Pops*. We giddily packed our bags.

John Artifoni ran away.

There are rules about these things, and they are simple. Not even rules: one rule. If they can't make money out of you, you're no good to them. You can be as rebellious as you like, as long as it shifts units out of the shops. But once you turn down an appearance in the shiniest of shop windows, you've broken the rule, and fatally. He didn't tell us to our faces; even in the welter of his self-obsession he knew the cruelty of this action, knew that in trying misguidedly to save his own dazed soul he was destroying ours. He wrote a short note and dropped it in Bongo's letterbox. It was full of neurotic self-justification and strangulated prose; it smacked of fear, or that's what we told ourselves. We made no attempt to contact him. Much later I heard that he went to Amsterdam, and as far as I know he's still there.

Even if we had gone out to find him, I don't know what we could have said or done; we were paralysed. The lives we dreamed for ourselves had shattered. Each of us was cocooned by our individual failure, stuck in Dublin, stymied by it. Defined by our past tense. There's the guy who used to be in that band. Thought he was fucking great, and look at him now.

Of course we had achieved something: we had toured, made an album; we had survived, for Christ's sake, for years: far more than most bands have done. I told myself this; at the start I did it every day, and not once did I believe it. It sounded anaemic and defeated, like the old men you sometimes meet in the Shelbourne bar, sitting there because this is the bar they have come to for the last thirty years; sitting by themselves because all their friends are dead and they've nowhere else to go: casualties of the temporal war, who still feel their toes despite having no legs.

I didn't want to be like them. I still don't. But the truth is I didn't know what else to do. I made my bet, lost it all and am still hanging around the race track, still going to the same pubs and clubs and meeting people who were once jealous of me, but now can sneer because the level of my failure has been greater than theirs. Every week I bump into dozens of people around town, and most of them I hate. Most of them hate me, most of them hate one another, yet we still meet and trade deft insults and slights. There is an addictive horror to it. It's a lifestyle, of sorts.

Travelling up the quays was a slow, nervy business. A lorry shed part of its load by the Ha'penny Bridge, prompting the usual cranky cacophony of horn blowing. Motorcycle gardai posed in their leather outfits and pointed theatrically at the traffic. With each frustrating halt, Odette scanned around us. She locked the doors, then smiled at the futility of the action. She plopped her bag on her lap, put her hand inside and left it there.

We didn't move much quicker up O'Connell Street. Every traffic light turned against us, as if part of a plot to spitefully slow our progress. Pedestrians crossing the road seemed to delay specifically in front of our car, deliberately turning their thin heads so they could squint in, their beady eyes glinting in the purple light.

The traffic edged down to the sprouting Millennium Spire. The stiletto in the ghetto: a skinny chrome spike shooting out of the city skyline. Dublin's major landmark, the centrepiece of Ireland's millennium celebrations, which due to a planning row wasn't built until two years after those celebrations had ended. A lot of people say it looks like a needle, but it never really struck me that way: I think of it more as a long metallic finger, pointing hopelessly towards something else; something better.

Broder was there, standing outside the Gresham Hotel, smoking a cigarette and darting his head around like an alarmed chicken. He saw us on the other side of the street and waved. I broke our final red light, did a U-turn by the taxi rank and parked, two wheels on the pavement, hazard lights winking.

He sighed and opened his arms as we walked towards him. I could see a gun tucked into a holster. He wasn't usually armed; he told me once he only carried a weapon if there was a 50/50 chance of him being shot, which, despite all his bullshit, wasn't that often. I shivered, and suddenly felt vulnerable to the delicate evening breeze dancing along O'Connell Street.

'All right?' said Broder. 'No problems? Fuck, Dillon. Fuck.'

There was sweat on his shaven head. He glanced about again, took us both by the arm.

'Sorry. We're going to have to wait here for another couple of minutes. Car should be here by now. Fuck.'

'I need to go to the toilet,' I said.

'Me too,' said Odette.

Broder looked at us as if we had both said something deeply tasteless. He eyed his watch.

'OK. I'll go with you, Dillon.'

They walked tight on either side of me. Assuming that body-guards were exclusively the province of celebrity, some of the tee-shirted tourists stopped to stare. The toilet, however, was empty. Broder checked all the cubicles, leaned against a sink and gestured like a host at a dinner party.

'Don't take too long.'

I chose the one furthest away from him, my needs being other than purely urinal. There was still a lot of coke left in Bongo's bag, and for the first time that day I felt a stab of guilt at taking so much of it. I'd pay him back, if I lived. If the other gardai didn't find it and put me in the cell next to the guys trying to kill me. I peed and chopped, snorted while the toilet flushed. If Broder suspected what I was up to, he gave no indication. He barely looked at me when I came out and splashed water on my face. I felt better, but not dramatically so: if time had allowed I would have gone back in and done some more. But he was looking at his watch again.

'Come on, Dillon. A bit of fucking water isn't going to make you look any better.'

Odette was waiting for us, and we strode back towards the front of the hotel. I was again sandwiched between them, like we were Siamese triplets.

'Simon, hi!'

Odette and Broder jerked with fright as Marcus Lynam appeared before us. Marcus, however, seemed unaware of the effect he had had: frightening people was hardly his forte, and at that moment he was more intent on wrestling with the yards of microphone wire tangled round his arms.

'Fucking thing,' said Marcus, his face reddening.

For years no-one had taken Marcus seriously. He was too small, too eager, too gawky with his large-framed glasses sliding down his nose. Like me, he had briefly held an impressive array of jobs on the outskirts of the media. He had even joined the Party, in the hope of making influential contacts. Unlike me, he did finally succeed in getting something he actually wanted: his own weekend radio show, in the process transforming himself from Gawk to Golden Boy.

'So,' he said, stuffing the wire into a satchel, 'what you up to?'

'Same old shit,' I said. 'You?'

I could feel Broder glaring at me. Gangsters are trying to kill him and he stops for a chat.

'I was just in here recording Bloomsday stuff. This guy reads extracts from *Ulysses* and takes his clothes off at the same time. Jesus. Californian, don't you know.'

Odette smiled. Broder looked at his watch.

'Dillon,' he said. 'Can we get a fucking move on here?'

'Sorry, sorry,' said Marcus, always the diplomat. 'Just before you go though: you know Brian Blennerhassett, don't you, Simon? Would you have his number? I need him for a thing on the show.'

'Er . . . no,' I said, as if he had suggested something far more appalling.

'Oh, OK. Sorry. Bye, bye.'

He quickly backed away from us and swooshed out the door. Broder shook his head.

'Who was that langer? Dillon, is there anyone in this town you don't fucking know? You're probably going to tell me you were riding him as well.'

This was aggressive; not inviting a reply. His phone rang. He whipped it out and had a terse conversation of grunts and OKs. He flipped it shut and attempted a smile. He had a relieved and slightly disgusted air, like a surgeon who's just performed a particularly messy operation.

'Here any second.'

He led us outside, produced a box of Major, offered them around. Odette refused.

'How can you smoke those? They are horrible.'

'What about them Gauloises? They're worse.'

Broder sucked on his cigarette and looked at me; as if he had never really noticed my face before.

'Dillon, I always meant to ask you. Whatever happened to your man Artifoni?'

'Went to Amsterdam, I think.'

'And what's he doing?'

'Don't know. We don't correspond.'

'Pity. He was some langer though, wasn't he? Fairly fucked up your life.'

I shrugged. He gave a twisted smile.

'I don't fucking get you, Dillon. All right, Artifoni left you in the lurch, but that was years ago now. All you've done since is go around blaming him. You're a talented guy. Educated. Your father's a fucking judge, man. You could have done loads of things.'

I shrugged again, puzzled this time.

'Well,' I said.

'You fucking Dublin southside boyos really get up my hole. You never had to work for anything, and when it's not handed to you on a plate, you go into a big huff and give up.

'Dillon, I like you, but you're a fucking eejit. You could have done anything. You could be like your mate Bongo pulling in loads of readies. But instead you go banging Mary Barton like you want to get killed. And you arrive here with half the gangsters in Dublin out for your balls and what do you do? Go into the jax to snort Charley. I'm not fucking stupid, you know.'

He was suddenly angry, like a little boy who has been teased to tearful frustration by the bigger kids.

'You don't know how things work, Dillon. And you've no fucking excuse for that because you should. Jesus, your father knows. There's only so much I can do. I can only protect you so much, but you've fucked it up now.'

He pointed at his head.

'I figured it out. It was you.'

He jabbed at the street.

'You fucking caused all this.'

I looked at where he pointed. Beyond the strolling couples and puzzled tourists stood the two Russians at the edge of the pavement, hands stuffed in the pockets of their grubby coats. One of them waved coquettishly, like a guest on a game show.

Even Odette was surprised. She looked at the Russians, at me, at Broder, and back at the Russians again. Broder looked at the ground, put his hand on my arm. Talked at my feet.

'Things are never simple in this fucking city, you know that. It's not just good guys and bad guys. Look: most of the time we try to catch them and put them away. But sometimes we have to negotiate with them, because that's the best we can do. Sometimes other people negotiate with them and I have to follow orders. I'm fucking stuck here, Dillon. Really fucking stuck.'

He looked at me for a response, but I said nothing. Not because I was outraged, shocked or disappointed. I simply didn't understand: this was too complicated to take in. I felt I shouldn't trust my senses, that what I saw or heard or tasted was of no value when it came to understanding the world around me. All I had were my own thoughts. The rest was accident; a victimless crime.

Misunderstanding my blank expression, Broder became even more angry, then desperate.

'I'm not taking money from these bastards,' he said, shaking his head. 'Look: there's nothing the likes of me can do about this. I'm just a fucking wanker with a popgun thinking he's the sheriff.'

He hurled his cigarette at the ground. The Russians took a step forward through the crowds. Broder motioned at them to stop, but fearfully; it was a request, not an order. They did so, causing everyone else to file around them; a pedestrian traffic jam. I watched all this, then looked back at Broder; my mouth open, trying to think of words to fill it with.

'Christ, Dillon, you got yourself into this mess. You did. No-one is innocent here.'

He paused, considering what he might say next.

'Do you remember the Lash Keogh?'

I still said nothing.

'The Lash Keogh? You know: the guy that attacked your old man. Got done for smack, your old man took his kids off him. He wasn't a smack dealer. He was going to give evidence against one of the Drummer's boys. The Drummer knew that the best way to hurt him was to have his kids taken off him, and he got your ould fella to do it. Everybody knew it. Your old man knew it. They're all in it up to their bollix.'

'What?'

This was the first and only thing I said, because now Odette had pushed her way in between me and Broder.

'Leo, you do not want to do this. You know you don't. Just take a step back and we will look after ourselves.'

Broder pushed back against her. His face was white and taut.

'It's too late, love, too late. They don't want you. You just fuck off.'

'I am not going to fuck off.'

The Russians started walking towards us; a stop-start progression through the slowly moving crowds.

'Leo, I do not want to hurt you.'

'Listen, love, I'm telling you. They are mad fucking killers. Just go.'

'Let him go, Leo, let him go.'

'I can't.'

Then the bomb went off.

twelve

Broder was correct: I did cause all this, but not in the way he thought. It wasn't greed. It was love, or something like it.

Still: he was smart to figure it out. Not so bright though when it came to second-guessing the Provos. Gavin McCabe had known they were threatening a spectacular and, as it transpired some weeks later, the Guards had known it too. The Millennium Spire was a pretty obvious target: the biggest landmark in Dublin, fairly thin (making it easy to blow up), and at the time it was swathed by a temporary hoarding (repair work after vandalism), thus limiting the possibility of detection and civilian deaths.

All of which was achieved with a German efficiency. The detonation itself didn't actually sound like one; certainly it had none of the gothic thunder I would have imagined an explosion to unleash: this was more a loud crack. There was almost a politeness to it, an awkward modesty, and in the split second it happened I don't think any of the people there thought it was a bomb; rather a crash or a car backfiring. It was the results that were far more noisy and destructive. The windows of the GPO and most of the shops nearby instantly disintegrated, causing a Christmas shower of glass to scatter about the street. Dozens of cars crunched into each other, and a lorry overturned, spilling out its cargo of chocolate-flavour Weetos, each pack with a free toy. There was a cascade of screams and a shuddering jumble of footsteps as people stampeded wherever they could, not knowing what to run from.

The hoarding around the spire had shot out in all directions. One panel slammed into a group of Italian tourists, another smashed through the darkened front window of the Ann Summers Sex Shop, while a third ricocheted off several cars, finally to embed itself high in the wall of McDowell's Happy Ring House, in the process enforcing separation upon the neon newlyweds who have grinned down upon the street for decades. The fourth piece of hoarding, however, caused the most damage. Like a perfectly skimmed stone, it bounced off the pavement and travelled north, slicing through trees, beheading the centenary statue of Matt Talbot, the Apostle of Temperance, to eventually crush a small plaster statue of the Sacred Heart of Jesus, his hands stretched out, as if he had always known this was coming. *I place all my trust in thee.*

Standing on the steps on the Gresham, we were sheltered from most of the destruction and felt little of the blast, though a few shards of glass were flung in our direction. We did, however, witness the pyrotechnic and civic benefits of the explosion: the spire snapped about four foot from the base and moved into the air like a massive Saturn Five rocket. Even now, people can remember where they were when it happened, along with a growing number who claim they witnessed the stiletto leave the ghetto for its maiden lunge at the heavens.

Well: not quite the heavens, which is where the civic benefit came in. It climbed about three hundred foot, but then began to twirl, baton-like. As if it was a dart fired by the avenging gods, the needle shot back down to earth and lanced the head of the Anna Livia Monument, known more familiarly as the Whore (pronounced in Dublinese as who-er) in the Sewer, without doubt the ugliest piece of street art ever constructed in the city. The monument exploded out in several directions. Water furiously glugged from it, flooding a large section of O'Connell Street and dissolving the Whore back to the rubble she was constructed from.

In the movies there is always an eerie silence just after an explosion. In real life there isn't. In real life the explosion itself is just an hors d'oeuvre of noise, a taster for a mammoth ragbag of disconnected sounds that stuff your ears to bursting. Screams, sirens, screeches, alarms, clanging, gushing, running: there was so much of it, it seemed to block out the very notion of sound itself. It was like watching a silent film on an extremely noisy projector; it was grating and relentless, bringing up the lump of panic you get in a strange room when the lights go out and for a few seconds you wonder if your eyes will ever adjust to the darkness.

We stood up from where we had crouched, or rather Odette stood and dragged me with her, my hands still over my ringing head. Broder remained down where he was: still too stunned to move, or at least giving that impression. The tourists in front of us were now horizontal on the pavement, waving and groaning as if they had all gone mad and elected to swim up O'Connell Street. The water from the Whore in the Sewer wriggled its way around them.

In the midst of this knelt one of the Russians, blood seeping between the fingers clasped to his neck. His companion was already on his feet, busily tearing strips of material from the coat of a screaming American woman. He smiled and nodded at her, causing her to scream even more.

Odette released the collar of my jacket and stomped down

towards him. When she was about three foot away she crouched slightly, bounced up off her left leg and whipped out her right towards his face: a balletic gesture. Except that in this case her right foot connected with his nose. The nose erupted, a mini-Vesuvius of blood. Even among all the din, I could hear the crunch. He put a hand to it and staggered back, tripping over the screaming American woman, now breathless with hysteria. Odette jammed a heel into his right thigh, causing him to buckle, and swung a vicious left hook at his windpipe. But the hand over his nose blocked this, and now he came back at her, a straight jab glancing off the side of her head. She wobbled but held her balance, dropped to one knee, jabbed him in the groin, then sprang up and head-butted him square in the forehead. The force of the blow knocked him back, but he managed to swing out a flat hand that caught her solidly on the ear. She crumpled with the blow, her head waving like it was no longer connected to her body, and fell to the pavement; a balloon with the air suddenly released. The Russian rested against a jack-knifed car and examined the blood on his hands. He smeared it on his coat and took a step back onto the pavement. But Odette was also on her feet again, this time running. Like a long-jumper, she slammed her right foot on the ground and launched herself at him, legs and arms spread like an attacking octopus. Her body clamped around his, leaving the Russian suddenly rigid and immobilized. Locked together, they staggered drunkenly into the road, splashing through the water. Odette lowered her head to beside his, as if she was going to whisper a secret. The man screamed. She spat out a chunk of his ear and jumped back off him. He slithered to the ground, blood streaming down his white coat.

Then she was beside me, dragging me down the steps and over the scattered bodies.

'Run, Simon. Do not think. Run.'

This was something I could do. The not thinking part anyway. Much to our mutual amazement, I managed the running as well, probably due to the considerable quantity of cocaine floating through my bloodstream. Mini-icebergs, seeking out my nerve endings. I even got a degree of pleasure from the exercise: falling into a rhythm, leaping over the prone bodies, dodging around the bloody walking wounded. Running felt like the most sensible thing I had done all day, and at last something I could do which would benefit me. I even took the lead, speeding up as we traversed the blackened site of the explosion. At either end of O'Connell Street, the damage, both physical and architectural, seemed slight enough: cuts, crashes, fright and smashed windows. Here, though, it had been fried into a stinking, volcanic landscape, the human limbs and metal fused to create new grotesque objects. Dozens of scorched body parts littered the roadway. I closed my eyes and ran even harder, to escape the smell.

Once over the bridge, we swung right at Aston Quay, past the Virgin Store and down to the alley beside the Ha'penny Bridge. Straight through the oblivious drunken Brits at Temple Bar, across Dame Street and into the tight warren of roads behind Grafton Street.

It was Odette who finally called a halt, grabbing me so roughly I spun to a stop. The street reeled and I crumpled onto the pavement, grabbing elusive gobfuls of breath. I was coated with sweat, heaving with exhaustion, but certain I could have run for hours more. She bent over, resting her hands on her knees.

'That was a good run, Simon. You are fit.'

I nodded my head in the negative, still unable to speak.

We were on the pavement outside Neary's pub, and everything was eerily normal. The ebbing sun peeked out from behind massing clouds. Girls in belly-tops and thick shoes walked carefully around us. The sirens still echoed from across the Liffey, but from this distance appeared just to be part of the city's aural mush.

Odette flicked back her hair, squatted and rubbed her forehead with her tee-shirt. Another flash of brown belly. The minidisc recorder still strapped there.

'Can you walk?'

I nodded. My leg muscles were throbbing. Slowly, I eased into the vertical.

'We need to get off the street for a little while. Do you know someplace we can go?'

I pointed at the pub.

Amazing it was, the schoolboyish joy I felt at finally gaining entry to a bar; as if Odette was my personal trainer and had denied me this fun until such time as I completed my five-mile jog. My life was paused; a commercial break in the relentless bombing and ear-biting. I sucked in the comforting stench of porter and smoke and grinned like a man at war for years who has finally returned home. I even had difficulty in deciding where we should sit, which is unusual for me because I have habits about such things. In a place like Neary's I would always sit at the bar, with my back to the cavernous extension slapped onto what was once a cosy maze of snugs and wooden stools. On this occasion, though, I opted for the seats by a wall, correctly guessing that after my recent exertions I would need as much lumbar support as possible. It even took me a second or two to choose what to drink, part of my reticence stemming from a vague sense that Odette would somehow disapprove (and refuse to buy) if I appeared too enthusiastic in my consumption. I decided on moderation and quietly asked for a whiskey and a pint of Guinness.

'I think I'll have the same,' she said. She might have been a psycho, but she was good to go drinking with.

As she ordered I flopped onto a chair, leaned back and studied the ceiling. It was yellow from smoke, the colour of bad teeth and of most pub ceilings in Dublin. Home. Funny what can give you comfort.

A trickle of sweat made its way down my nose and hung imminently. I wiped it off and looked around. The place was fairly empty, an early evening crowd. A drink after work before going home. What I might be doing, on another day. Except I probably wouldn't go home. They muttered in long, casual tones, still unaware of the nuclear devastation waiting for them just half a mile away. They ignored me, which I found strange: my trauma, I felt, should be writ large upon me, should make others uneasy. But this was normal life, and it swamps all. I was simply a sweaty man with his tee-shirt stuck to his tummy. It had all gone on without me, and suddenly I wished it hadn't, that I had been missed, that I would be welcomed back from the black places I had been flung into. I took out my phone and dialled.

'Angela?'

'What?'

'I'm just ringing to see if you're OK.'

'We'll be fine if you stay away from us, Simon. You just go off and have fun with your *friend* there, because I've had enough. That's it. Today was the last straw. I don't know what you've got yourself mixed up in, but I want no part of it and I don't want you anywhere near Emily. We're going away for a few days and when we come back I'm going to the solicitor for a divorce. And don't ring me any more. Is that clear?'

I didn't answer.

'Is that clear, Simon?'

I wanted to tell her that it was; that in truth it had been clear to me since we'd returned from Amsterdam: I was incapable of transforming into the grown-up man she had wanted me to be, that I had wanted her to make me into. I had tried, driven by the hope of escaping what I was. But each fresh attempt reeked of failure, a foreknowledge that my guilt about her would never be enough: what love there was had been easily burned away. I couldn't escape my genetic predisposition: I would always give it up and go drinking, too numbed to explain, to wonder why. Even now.

I hung up, tried Bongo. No answer.

Odette arrived with the drinks, her fingers hooked around the four glasses with admirable expertise.

'*Slainte*,' she said, and threw back the whiskey. I nodded and did the same. It burned and stuffed my dry throat, like I'd just swallowed a hot-water bottle. I slugged on my pint for relief, wiped my mouth, sat back and looked at Odette, who looked back at me.

There was a sudden shyness between us, but not the fearful discomfort of the car; this was like two workmates who by accident meet on the street and find there is nothing to talk about except the tiny machinations of their daily toil.

'Where did you learn to fight like that?' I eventually said.

'The army.'

'The French army?'

'Yes.'

'So you are really French?'

She laughed, but she knew what I meant.

'Yes.'

'But this isn't your first time in Ireland?'

'No.'

For some reason I hadn't expected her to be honest about this. I didn't know what to ask next. I stared at my pint, as if it might contain the answer. She stroked the back of my neck, then kissed my forehead, my cheeks. She felt my body stiffen and sat back.

'I'm sorry,' she said.

I nodded noncommittally, took a sip from my pint. The barman glared at us, displays of affection being strictly *verboten* in Dublin pubs. I took another sip, then finished it off.

'The thing is,' I said, not really knowing what the thing was. 'The thing is everything that's happened today. This is all new to me and I'm a bit freaked out. I have a right to be freaked out, I think. Jesus, I haven't done anything to anyone and I don't know what to think. It's like everything I hear is a lie. The lies are lies. It's . . . I don't know where to start. I'm innocent in all this. Well, OK, not entirely innocent, but I'm not killing anyone or anything. I'm, I'm . . .'

I'm talking complete shit was what I should have said, but even in my befuddled state I realized this was redundant. I pointed at my empty glass.

'I could do with another drink.'

Odette smirked. 'Of course.'

She stood up, then sat down again.

'We need to talk about what we have to do next, Simon. Who can we trust now? Leo: he was your friend.'

Leo was my friend, of sorts. Angela was my wife, and in the space of twenty minutes both of them had returned me to the shop, asking for their money back. I wasn't ready to think about this yet. I needed to drink, to create a warm placental barrier of alcohol around my hurt. But Odette was back to being a strict teacher, and I felt a sudden jag of anger, an urge to say: *why did we come into the pub, then?* as if she had let me in just as a form of torment, a literal taste of what I couldn't have. I was being childish. I really wanted to be childish.

She stood up. 'Same again?'

At least I was getting another whiskey. She paused before she moved off, as if considering whether she should go to the bar at all.

'Try to think is there anyone else we could go to.'

I opened my mouth, closed it, shrugged and smiled weakly.

She bent down and kissed me, this time flicking her tongue into my mouth like a small, cautious animal. The barman gave us another dirty look.

As she ordered the drinks, I tried briefly to think of anyone who could help. It was a short and ineffectual list. Bongo wouldn't be much use, though he could lend me a few bob if I needed it. My brother was too far away. My father was too mad to be of any help, and now, I found, also in thrall to some of the people who wanted to kill me.

Auntie Marion wouldn't be surprised by that news. But I found I was. I had spent years telling myself I suspected his honesty: this was why I had searched his study so many times. Yet now it struck me that I had been searching for something else entirely.

I attempted to put some shape on my thoughts, which, in no order of importance, were the following:

a) I wanted to get drunk.

b) I wanted to go back to the aimless life I had before.

c) I knew I never could go back, but equally I had no idea where I could go to.

d) I missed my daughter. I wanted to hug her.

e) I was shocked that Angela wanted a divorce.

f) I was relieved that Angela wanted a divorce.

g) I wanted to shag the arse off Odette.

h) I was scared of Odette.

i) I was terrified I was going to be killed.

j) I was too exhausted and scared to do anything about any of the above.

This, as they say, was enough to be going on with.

'Did you think of anyone?' said Odette as she sat down and positioned the glasses on the table. She was matching me drink for drink.

'No.'

'What about your father?'

I didn't hear her say this, because suddenly I was on my feet. Confused as I was, I couldn't shake off the ghosts of my earlier ideas: that there was something else going on here, some other theme woven into the day's events for others to divine and me to miss, some other drama being played out just a millisecond beyond my perception. To put it more crudely, I wanted someone to blame, and he had been delivered to me. With delectable timing, he had hurried from Bongo's apartment that morning just before the mock cops had arrived. And now there he stood in his prissy black suit, his preposterous shades shadowing his acned, hooked chin as he scanned the place for someone to buy him a drink.

Brian Blennerhassett seemed surprised but not alarmed to see me, though I like to think that his eyes – if anyone could have seen them – registered copious amounts of alarm as I grabbed him by the throat and began yelling *cuntcuntcunt* in a voice so aggressive I barely recognized it as my own. His reaction was to drop his trendy leatherette bag and seize up like a frightened insect, his skinny arms crossed against his chest as he vainly tried to prise my hands away from his jugular. His legs must also have buckled, as the more I squeezed the smaller he seemed to get. I could feel the sweat from his chin trickle over my hands, while the scattering of spots on his ill-shaven chin seemed to grow redder.

'Did you tell them to come? Did you? Did you? Speak, you fucking little shitfuck!'

Despite my eloquence, Brian Blennerhassett said nothing. I was, I must admit, momentarily taken aback by his silent bravery, though I realized later that his lack of speech was due to the fact that I had such a grip on his windpipe, he was unable to make any sound.

'Simon, please, let go of him!'

Odette was trying to lodge herself between us, but not in the manner I had seen her do earlier. Now she was a girl like any other, ineffectually trying to stop her drunken boyfriend from delivering or receiving yet another bloody nose. I let go. She hugged me and made soothing noises while Brian Blennerhassett launched into a symphony of coughs and splutters. The barman, still behind the bar, shoved a warning finger in the direction of my face.

'You. You going to calm down now?'

'He will, he will,' said Odette, a natural at the part of the long-suffering mot.

'Sit down so,' said the barman, and turned back to his work. Snogging, as I have said, is not accepted in most Dublin pubs. But fighting is treated with a degree of latitude. Brian Blennerhassett continued emitting a range of disturbing guttural noises, but the barman ignored this. Perhaps he knew him.

Odette pointed me back towards my seat. Exhausted by my outburst, I obeyed. I watched as she placed a hand on Brian Blennerhassett's gagging form and with a gentle voice coaxed him back to normal breathing. While he was bent double that way, I could easily have walked back over and kicked him cleanly in the head. But I didn't. Instead I went to the toilet and did another couple of lines.

When I returned he was sitting at our table, wearing what seemed to be a hurt expression on what could be seen of his face. He sipped whiskey and Coke.

'I hope you're not going to resort to more fisticuffs,' he purred. Odette threw me a warning look, correctly assuming that a statement like that was best answered with action. I said nothing, and huffily turned my attention to the fresh drinks on the table.

'We have had a strange day,' said Odette. 'Simon is upset.'

'I can see that,' replied Brian Blennerhassett, his annoying voice box now back in full working order. 'But I understand. Bongo informed me of all your adventures today. Kidnapped by hoodlums? How remarkable. This, I take it, has some connection with all these murders I have been hearing about on the radio? Some people are now too scared to come into town. Imagine.

'And did something just happen in O'Connell Street? Judging from the noise, there appears to be some huge kerfuffle over there.'

Neither of us answered. The conversation level in the bar, however, had noticeably increased, had transformed in tone to one of itchy concern. Hands were being placed on shaking foreheads, mobile phones were being produced, drinks quickly finished up. The news had arrived.

'You are in good fettle, given these recent traumas,' he told Odette. He looked at me and said nothing.

'So you don't know anything about this?' I finally spat out.

He looked at me like I had gone mad.

'You left this morning and two minutes later those guys turned up. Bit of a coincidence, Brian.'

He sat up straight, shoving his hooked nose imperiously into the air.

'Are you implying that I'm somehow *implicated* in this grubby underworld saga?'

'I'm not implying it, dickhead, I'm fucking saying it.'

'How dare you!' he squealed, but suddenly cut his anger short. Perhaps his neck muscles were starting to give him a bit of trouble. Instead he set his mouth into a twisted approximation of sympathy.

'Simon, as your friend here says, you have had a disturbing day, so I am prepared to make allowances. Your judgement may not be what it should at the moment.'

'Gee, thanks.'

'Simon, Simon. I am Brian Blennerhassett.' He said it as if it were an elevated state of being rather than a pretentious name. 'One may say many things about Brian Blennerhassett, but I think you'll find one thing I have never been accused of is associating myself with vulgarians.'

'You *prick*,' I said, suddenly the champion of vulgarians everywhere.

'Simon, please,' snapped Odette. 'How could you think Brian had anything to do with that? Just look at him. He is harmless.'

The hurt look was back, this time aimed at Odette. He picked up his drink and took a series of aggressive little nips from it, like a dog lapping at water. We watched him, slightly appalled.

After what he considered a respectable pause, Brian Blennerhassett plonked his drink back on the table, ran a hand through his lank hair and looked at us both in turn.

'So,' he tweetered, the trademark supercilious grin again stuck to his face. 'You too have had an interesting day.' This, I assume, was what he considered a stylish comeback. The urge to slap him was overwhelming.

'Bongo told me all about it . . . actually, speaking of him, you haven't come across the chap on your travels, have you? We were due to meet in the Hairy Lemon after work, but the bounder stood me up.'

'Did you ring him?'

'Of course. Mobile turned off and no answer from his home.'

'Oh no. Oh shit.'

Brian Blennerhassett glugged on his drink again, oblivious to the filthy virus of concern he had sent racing into my bloodstream. My skin felt hot and itchy. I stared at Odette.

'We should go to his apartment,' she said.

Without another word to Brian Blennerhassett we stood up and left.

'Are you finishing these drinks?' he called after us.

Outside, the pavement was suddenly crowded with people keen to be anywhere other than the centre of town. They moved urgently, yet with a strange politeness, carefully trying to step around the delicate trigger of panic. We started marching towards Merrion Square, opting to catch a taxi on the way rather than risk the maddening wait at the bottom of Dame Street. We'd hardly got ten yards before I was suddenly gripped tightly by the arm and a scream of 'Howya, head!' made my inner ear vibrate.

Michael Flattery was one of those people you don't actually know, but you meet them a lot. He and his wife – a woman so blond, so plastic and so vacant she was probably created through injection moulding – were obscenely loaded, and lived for the Good Night Out. Anywhere that was expensive or hard to get in, the Flatterys had already been to, both of them demons for the culture: they'd go to celebrity chef restaurants, order steak, get plastered on some fabulously expensive wine and start singing Fleetwood Mac songs. Michael once (to his own mind famously) delivered a thunderously loud fart during a performance of *Riverdance*, and was also fond of mooning if anyone vaguely famous was in his presence. Oh yeah: the Flatterys were dead classy, and had a great sense of humour. Michael, after all, had made his fortune through a string of travel agencies, which he marketed with the achingly funny slogan *Flatterys will get you everywhere*.

'C'mere, head, here's one.'

He still hadn't released his grip on my arm. Gripping and talking were habitual to Michael, as if deep down he knew that, given the opportunity, anyone he addressed would run away. Despite the pencil thinness of his wife, Michael was starting to sag in all directions. Even his perpetually glassy eyes seemed to droop, making them hard to read. Sometimes I suspected that all the rugged bonhomie was an act to annoy me, which it often did. Either way, there was by now an established pattern to our conversation: because of some long-forgotten night when I told a couple of good jokes, Michael Flattery assumed that my thirst for new humour was unquenchable.

'So right this bloke, right? Goes to the vet and says me dog is sick right? And the vet says fuck him on the table there and I'll have a look. So he does that and the vet has a look at the dog and says to your man: your dog is dead.

'The bloke says: no fucking way. The dog was grand this morning. Can you not do more tests or something?

'So the vet says OK and opens a door and out comes a huge fucking Labrador that jumps on the table over your man's dog and gives it a load of woof woof, right? But the dog doesn't move. So the vet says: see, a dog would normally respond to that. Your dog is fucking dead.

'But the bloke isn't convinced, so the vet says: I can do another test. So he opens another door and a cat jumps out and up on top of the dog, says meow and all that. But the dog does nothing.

'So finally the bloke says: that's it. Me dog is dead. Jesus. So he says to the vet: how much do I owe you?

'A thousand pounds, says the vet.

'What? A thousand pounds, says the bloke, just to fucking tell me me dog is dead?

'Aw well, says the vet, my fee is only a hundred. The rest of it is for the lab report and the cat scan. D'yageddit?'

He released my arm to thump it. I smiled, mostly out of relief.

'Simon.'

Odette was standing beside a taxi, the back door already open. Without a word I walked away from the Flatterys and got in.

'Seeya so, head,' Michael called after me. I didn't reply.

'That was a clever joke,' Odette said to them. 'I must remember it.'

Even as the taxi pulled away, she was still smiling, and I realized that it was lingering on her lips for far too long. She was trying to appear calm, and by her standards making a bad job of it. She patted my leg, but kept her face to the window.

As he drove, the taxi driver yelled into a mobile phone.

'A bomb. A fucking bomb, I'm telling ya. O'Connell Street is wrecked. The cops have it sealed off . . . Well, I don't fucking know. Probably fucking unionists or something. Seeya later.'

He carefully clicked it off and peered in his rear-view mirror at us.

'Jesus,' he said.

'Yeah,' I agreed.

He switched on his radio. Already there were reports of the explosion, of chaos in the city centre. On a crackling mobile, Marcus Lynam gave an account of what he had witnessed. He kept repeating that he had parked his car in Marlborough Street, and if he hadn't, if he had turned left instead of right . . . It was almost apologetic. I remembered then that Marcus had been trying to contact Brian Blennerhassett, a fact which I had forgotten to relay to the Dick. This pleased me.

Two helicopters buzzed over us. A line of screaming ambulances swooshed past in the opposite direction. I took out my mobile, rang Bongo's flat. No answer. I threw it on the seat, as if this was the phone's fault. It was, of course, us who were to blame. We should have thought that they might go back to Bongo's; they had been there once already. We should have thought to warn him; he had phoned me up, I had spoken to him. He had said: I'm gonna stay home tonight, and I had agreed with this choice. My mind flitted between guilt and excuses I felt too disgusted to think out properly. I phoned again, still no answer.

Our car edged up Nassau Street. Merrion Square was already gridlocked, so the driver swung a left into Lincoln Place and tried nipping down the smaller roads parallel to Pearse Street. The area around the canal, however, had completely seized up. The driver held up his hands.

'This is the best I can do for you. Ye'd be better off walking from here.'

Odette threw the money at him and we ran.

This time she took the lead, my earlier athletic ability having now deserted me. My limbs felt leaden, like the force of gravity around me had suddenly increased five-fold. I couldn't keep up with her; each of my steps in nightmarish slow motion.

When I arrived she was outside the apartment, the door of it wide open, shards of broken wood scattered in fan shapes on the floor.

'He's not in there.'

I stood where I was, not wanting to see any more.

'It's empty but the door was kicked in and there is a lot of blood.'

I slumped down on the corridor tiles and lit a cigarette. I didn't look at Odette. I stared at the pastel-coloured wall opposite. I would like to say that at this moment I was racked with guilt and grief at the killing of my best friend, but I wasn't: the prospect of Bongo's death was still stored in the part of my brain labelled Highly Unlikely, along with alien invasions and my father getting a sex change. Instead I laughed.

'Lab report and cat scan. I get it now.'

At the time he'd told me, I'd barely registered it as a joke. Now it seemed to expand in importance and complexity, filling my numbed brain. A small trickle of blood cautiously eased from my left nostril. I made no attempt to wipe it away.

Eventually I stood up and entered the apartment. I walked around the upturned coffee table, the black globs splattered on the wooden floor, and down to the picture window. It was why he had bought this place: he loved the view. The roads below were stuffed with unmoving traffic. A grey twist of smoke rose from the city centre and formed a huge question mark. Sirens wailed in a crazed chorus.

I would stand there and bitch about Dublin: the thuggish struggle for fame and money, the bulging self-satisfaction; the overpriced restaurants for overpaid lugs; the prefabricated architecture, the prefabricated culture. What the place did to Me.

Bongo would say nothing; just look out the window and smile, because unlike me, he had an unambiguous relationship with his native city. He could see his home; what it had been and what it still could be. And because of him, sometimes I could see it too.

I smiled again, remembering the other Dublin he had brought me to.

Just before we recorded the album, we went on a mini-tour of the US: eight dates in a snowy New York, two in a rainy Boston. After the last New York gig, the band celebrated by gobbling down mouthfuls of dried, dull-looking buttons which Bongo had acquired and which, within an hour, had stewed our minds to a grinning mush; like mental patients recently electrocuted. Peyote. Cool.

Some of the others claimed they saw colours and halos around people; that they experienced what could have been profound insights. Not me. In all my years of drug taking, my experience has been strictly of two sorts:

a) I'm so wrecked I say nothing, but my mind clatters along like a rampaging rhino.

b) I giggle, and talk a lot of shit.

My experience that night in New York was of the latter category, along with the notion that I was insulated from the outside world by a syrupy bubble which protected me from cold and all harm, a notion which led me to abandon a two-hundred-dollar leather coat which I had bought just three days before. This, of course, was hilarious. Everything was: the members of Moon Palace had been reduced to little more than laughing, squeaking, snot-producing automata.

At some point we hooked up with an A&R man from a small New York label and agreed to go back to his apartment. I can't remember getting into the cab, but I have a vivid picture of crossing the Williamsburg Bridge back into Manhattan; we oohed and aahed at the massive stacked buildings like we'd never seen them before. Back in the apartment, he played us Art Blakey and the Jazz Messengers on his stereo. Artifoni, however, ignored the music, preferring to chat up the A&R man's girlfriend. By the end of the first track, 'Moanin'', Artifoni and his new friend had already repaired to the bedroom to do some moanin' of their own. Some minutes later the A&R man discovered them. He was less than pleased.

While the troubled couple screeched at each other, a semi-naked Artifoni bounded back to us, giggling maniacally and attempting to step into his leather trousers.

'Ooooh shite. I'm in trouble now.'

This, of course, was hilarious. We opted to vacate the building, laughing uproariously while the A&R tried to save his shattered relationship. Even as we leaned against a sharp wind down East Houston Street, we continued to snigger, stopping occasionally to howl like crazed dogs. But this was the Lower East Side at three in the morning. Groups of black men stood around flaming oil cans and stared at us. One or two shouted over, prompting us to significantly pick up the pace of our walk. We stopped laughing. A hairy hand of paranoia reached out to grip us, and not just because of the neighbourhood looming around. The whole city, it suddenly seemed, was angry. It glowed with fury.

Luckily we all had a powerful hallucinogenic drug in our blood-streams to help us cope with this crisis. Even though none of us could remember the A&R man's name (and Artifoni hadn't asked the girlfriend hers), we reasonably assumed that he might be annoyed with us: a situation which in all probability would lead to the members of Moon Palace being beaten, kneecapped or beheaded by the powerful hoodlum friends which the A&R man had doubtless already contacted. Rather than wait for our flight to Boston the next day, we decided to get out of town. We went back to our hotel, the Gramercy Park, had a quick drink to steady our nerves, got packed, checked out and then piled into a drab-looking Ford Transit van Bongo hired with his credit card.

To get from New York to Boston, a journey of just over two hundred miles, is fairly straightforward: from Grammercy Park we had to go back the way we had come, passing dangerously close to the Lower East Side and the A&R man's waiting hitmen. Just as the sun began to peek over the giant huddle of buildings, we crossed the Manhattan bridge onto the I-278, switched onto the I-95 and circled back around Manhattan to link up with the I-684. From there we travelled north, moved onto the I-84 and then eastwards on the I-90. Yes: perfectly straightforward for a group of men fleeing for their lives while under the still-considerable influence of mind-altering drugs. That we managed to even get out of New York was impressive; that we actually did get to the general area of Boston was amazing.

Instead of the I-90, we took the I-91 and ended up about fifty miles north of Boston, though at the time we had no idea of this: all we knew was that we were in New Hampshire and had no idea where New Hampshire was in relation to anywhere else. The peyote was wearing off now and we were coming down with a considerable crash. Bongo drove and, in an attempt to get us back on the right route, had made a number of impulsive navigational decisions. We ended up on a thin road snaking its way through snowy mountains; giant swirls of whipped cream. We had lost all hope that Boston might lie around the next turn. The few signs we saw were for places so small we couldn't find them on the map. We became silent and cranky, and sniped at Bongo for taking the wrong turns, for giving us the drugs in the first place, and at Artifoni for getting us in this mess. But we did it with little conviction: we knew our stupidity had been collective. It was a good idea at the time for all of us, and in truth we'd enjoyed our little adventure.

And then we arrived in Dublin.

Dublin, New Hampshire, is a town of about fifteen hundred people, most of whom live in rambling, colonial-style houses which peek out from behind trees, hinting at stately old American grandeur. The town is typically spread out, but centres on a wide, quiet street which sweeps up a hill, past plain wooden buildings with small windows and up to the sky-blue town hall, its spire reaching towards where Mount Monadnock squats, a gigantic block of blinding white and deep blue. This is old America, a place of money and decent Yankee values, where people walk slowly and speak gently, where Mark Twain used to come on holiday and where they still publish the *Old Farmer's Almanac*. We hadn't expected to see this. It was *The Waltons*: twee and bright, pristine under a blanket of snow.

It struck us silent: not just because it was pretty but because of its familiarity. The effect of too much television, I suppose. This felt like home; it was a place we had been nostalgic for without having ever visited. It was a vague copy of where we had come from, yet it felt more like the real thing.

Bongo crawled the van up the main street, turned around and drove back down. Without a word of discussion we pulled up outside the Dublin Inn and got out.

They gave us funny looks when we walked in, but they were polite. They warmed up though when they learned where we were from, when they noticed our awkwardness. We felt shabby and inappropriately dressed, and it reminded me of how I would dye my hair green, just to annoy my father, then suddenly realize how immature and pointless this was.

It was near enough to midday, but they served us breakfast: crispy bacon, scrambled eggs and real hash browns, not the sodden, frozen variety you get here. We went to our rooms and slept for a while, though not well; despite our exhaustion, we shared a gentle sense of expectation about this place; that we shouldn't waste our time here. Eventually we all got up, dressed in our warmest and most respectable clothes and trudged around the white town. We took pictures of each other outside the town hall, had hot chocolate in a café, even visited the library. Dublin was established in the mid-1700s by what the Americans call Scotch-Irish and what we call Protestants. In the nineteenth century it was something of a haven for writers and artists, most notably Mark Twain, who, while he was there, had a series of photographs taken of himself contemplating good and evil.

On the advice of the librarian, we drove out to the frozen stretch of Dublin Lake and sat in the boats. They were arranged by the lakeside in tidy rows, trapped in the icy stillness until spring came. We blew breath clouds and talked about home.

That night we went to an Italian restaurant, the only one in town, drank Chianti, ate shrimp and listened to a passable blues band. We chatted to the owner, who also owned a music store: about instruments, the two Dublins, the weather. Nothing of importance.

Later I lay in bed and carefully tasted the mesmerizing effect this place had upon me. I fell into a dead and gentle sleep. I dreamed of my mother.

The following morning I didn't want to leave. I could quit the band, live here, become a writer. During breakfast I said little to the others, wondering how I would phrase this announcement. I still wondered as we packed, shook hands with the owners of the Dublin Inn, got in the van and drove to Boston. I could go back, I thought. After the tour, after the album. After the band split up, I thought it again.

But I didn't want to risk it; risk finding out that in Dublin, New Hampshire, like everywhere else, people lie and steal and let their hearts fester. As with my mother, the imagined memory was far more potent. It was, and is, a soft, innocent Dublin, where writers sit on porches and contemplate morality. I've never been back there.

thirteen

We took a taxi back into the city. She whispered questions.

'Have you any money?'

I dug a hand in my pocket and produced about five pounds, all in change.

'No, I mean do you have any money in the bank?'

'Less than I have in my pocket.'

'A credit card?'

'Hasn't worked for months.'

I stuffed my total assets back into my jeans, then asked:

'What for?'

'Plane tickets. I think you need to get out of the country. I will bring you back to France. You will be safe there. Don't worry, I will take care of the tickets.'

It was still quite early, about half eight, but we knew we couldn't stay where we were, standing in Bongo's apartment while his blood went stiff and crusty on the expensive rugs. I nodded agreement, though in truth I wasn't worried about who would buy the plane tickets; I barely registered her words. I was caught up in a red blur of death. Mary Barton, the Russians, me, Bongo: we were all part of the same food chain, them supplying, Bongo and I the eager consumers; our lives and deaths nothing more than random strings of occurrence. It was the law of the universe: shit travels downhill, and once I'd dodged out of the way, Bongo had been buried by it. This is how, implicitly and explicitly, I have lived my life; the way everyone I know has lived their life. Morality is a myth to stop kids misbehaving on Christmas Eve.

Yet I don't want it to be; I wish it wasn't.

Tough shit, Simon.

Now that the fictions between myself and Odette had dissolved, she abandoned her studied ignorance of Dublin and suggested the bar of the Fitzwilliam Hotel on Stephen's Green: a venue, she knowledgeably informed me, where we were unlikely to bump into any gangsters. There, she would book us a room and our flight to Paris in the morning. She told me this in a low, almost shamed tone, as if embarrassed by her failure. By way of a consolation prize, we could have a drink first.

I waved my assent, let myself be led in there, sat down, have drinks ordered on my behalf. The bar was surprisingly full, given what had happened. Then again, city life is relentless: our taxi driver on the way back into town informed us that one side of O'Connell Street had already been opened up, a decision he seemed to approve of. Town was a bit more quiet than usual. Lot of cops on the street. On the other hand, a lot of people were going into the city to have a look at the damage. Looters and memento-hunters were getting arrested. Fourteen people dead. Over fifty injured. The smoke cleared away. The sirens turned off. Back to business.

The Fitzwilliam always reminded me of some of the trendier New York hotel bars: all low light, warm colours and vaguely art-deco yet comfortable furniture. They gave you nice crispy bits to eat and it was never too noisy. Mixed crowd, a scattering of young suits, a bit of overspill from the Shelbourne, well-heeled tourists, kind of place where you feel slightly uncomfortable if you drink pints. But I did anyway. I gulped Guinness and stared at the floor. Odette watched me but didn't interrupt my silence.

I finished the pint, placed the glass on the table, and without looking at her said:

'Can I have another please?'

She placed her hand on mine. Pinched me, hard. I jolted with shock.

'Sorry,' she said, not unkindly, 'but you have to concentrate.'

Two magenta crescents shone up at me from the back of my hand.

'Ouch,' I said, rubbing it.

'Sorry.'

I looked away again. But she knew I was listening.

'Simon, you have been through a . . . *terrible* day. But please don't think about this now. Don't dwell on Bongo, because the most important thing is that we get you on the plane tomorrow.'

Now aware of my surroundings, I could see that waddling across on her big shoes was Tara Beirne, a woman I had known for over ten years but knew precious little about.

'I do not want to be a killjoy,' continued Odette, 'but drinking will not help, Simon. We need to be alert for tonight.'

Tara Beirne had one of those non-specific jobs you can get in record companies and European-funded media centres: Co-ordinating Executive in charge of New Projects, that sort of thing, though I have a vague recollection that for a few minutes she was a model/girl band member and Going to be Huge; the usual.

'Simon. Hi!'

Odette shot her a filthy look, but this was not the norm: the thing about Tara Beirne was that everyone liked her, or at least couldn't find any reason to dislike her. This was for two reasons:

a) She was the living embodiment of the word 'perky'. Tall, rosy-cheeked, pretty and with cropped blond hair, she had a decided preference for clothes that used as little material as possible. There was a distinct element of bounce in all her movements; even the slightest hand gesture would bring the rest of her with it. In conversation, most men addressed Tara's breasts rather than Tara; something Tara, most men liked to believe, did not notice.

b) Tara was unrelentingly positive. She never said anything bad about anyone or anything: her universe was divided into 'great' or 'fantastic'. 'Good' was about as bad as it got for Tara Beirne. Tara enjoyed being positive, and I have no doubt believed in its deeply therapeutic and spiritual benefits. I suspect she regarded herself as a sort of doctor of the soul, with a mission to heal any bitter hearts she encountered by jamming in her huge hypodermic needle of love.

'Simon, how are you?' she crooned, crouching just low enough at the table to rest her breasts upon it. Another of the miraculous healing gifts bestowed upon Tara was the ability to know how someone was feeling; especially if they hadn't told her. Armed with this, she could produce dazzling variations on her opening line. In my case, this divided into two phrases:

a) 'So what's happening with the band?' This was the one she used before the break-up of Moon Palace, a query she would augment with various *ohs*, *ahs*, *greats* and eventually an orgasmic *fantastic*.

b) 'Simon, how are you?' with the stress on *you*, because Tara was interested in me as a person, and because there was no more band, and therefore nothing important, to ask me about.

The tone of her voice and our relative physical positions also seemed to change after the band. While Moon Palace was still an entity, all the conversations seemed to be with me standing, her looking up while gasping at some tedious story about a gig in Cork. Post-band, I always seemed to be sitting down, her leaning over me like a compassionate nurse with a terminal patient, her talking in a slow tone that indicated to me (and anyone else listening) that I was indeed one of the wounded. Before it was an honour and a thrill to chat with the bass player from Ireland's most promising band; now she was doing me a favour.

'Fine,' I said; what I always said. Her breasts bounced, pleased with the news.

'That's great, great. This bomb, though. It's wild.'

She seemed almost pleased about it. I made a noise.

'So what you up to?' she asked.

'Well, today I was kidnapped by gangsters, my daughter got thrown off a balcony, that bomb was actually my fault, I'm full of cocaine, the cops and most of the crimbos in the city are after me. We're trying to flee to Paris but I'll probably be dead by midnight. And do you know what? I don't care.'

Is what I should have said.

'Ah, you know. TV.'

'Great,' she intoned, like a doctor encouraging a cripple to walk. 'Music?'

'Er, no. Documentary.'

'Wow. Great. Interesting.'

She nodded her head to emphasize the interestingness of documentaries.

'How's Bongo?'

It was what she always asked, but right then it was as surprising as if her head had split open and revealed a green barnacled witch inside. I clamped a hand to my mouth, nodded at her, but could say nothing. Tears filmed my eyes and I could feel Odette reach across the table and touch my shoulder.

Tara Beirne's breasts trembled with sympathy. 'Wow,' she said, sensing an emergency code red for her heart-doctoring skills. Almost hungrily, she put her hand on my other shoulder, giddy at the prospect of draining my emotional pus.

'Oh, what's wrong, Simon?'

'Look,' snapped Odette, 'please leave him alone.'

'OK, but—'

'Look: fuck off!'

With the accent it sounded like *fakiff*, leaving Tara unsure if she had been insulted or not. To cover the doubt, she smiled brightly. I stood up, causing Tara to wheel off-balance and roll backwards onto the floor. Her breasts bounced with alarm. I headed for the door.

But it was annoyance I felt, not grief. Odette was wrong: during my silence I hadn't been thinking about Bongo; it was myself I had been feeling sorry for. I didn't want to think about him, and was furious that I nearly did in front of, of all people, Tara Beirne. Bongo would have found this funny.

Odette caught me just as I was leaving the hotel. She grabbed my arm, I shoved her away. She grabbed me again, and this time delivered another pinch. I watched with horror as a second set of crimson half-moons rose on my skin. I screamed.

'Will you fucking stop doing that!'

The murmur in the hotel lobby fell away like a shot bird. Each head rotated and a moustached manager took a few cautious steps towards us. I looked at them all, then at Odette, and suddenly didn't want to scream any more. I was woozy from the exertion. Odette gestured an apology. The manager stepped back but kept watching.

She led me to a sofa, wiped my eyes, kissed me on the cheeks like a mother. I sniffed back snot and blood.

'Sorry,' I muttered. 'Lost it there.'

Dilly Golding, the social diarist, pranced into the lobby of the Fitzwilliam Hotel. Sheathed in a tight black dress, she nakedly stared at my upset, at the cruel extent of my deterioration since she'd seen me earlier that day on Stephen's Green. I looked up at her. She scuttled into the bar.

'It's OK, baby, OK,' soothed Odette.

An arm threaded around my waist, she led me outside and into the light of a dimming sun which had managed to dodge around the purple clouds. It was going to rain. We walked slowly along the green and towards Grafton Street, swaying like lovers who've spent a Saturday afternoon in the pub. Dublin can be heaven.

Odette looked at her watch.

'Perhaps we should go for something to eat.'

I nodded.

'You choose.'

'Planet Hollywood!'

I had sudden doubts about her taste until I realized that it wasn't her who had offered this suggestion. The words had come from two huge and shabby men standing several metres behind us, one of them wearing what looked like a turban but was in fact a huge and crudely wrapped bandage. The Russians had obviously made their dining choice for the evening. Until they spotted us.

Understandably, I had a certain sense of déjà vu about this situation, and thus required little in the way of guidance from Odette as to what to do. I started running before she did.

Thankfully for me, our Russian pursuers had also been spending too much time at the fridge: within what seemed a matter of seconds I could hear them wheezing behind us, and for a moment I fancied that the exercise might simply prove too much and they would give up. But a glance behind told me this was unlikely: their reddening faces were set into bug-eyed, manic scowls, the big-baby smiles and waves torn away like cheap curtains. They wanted to kill us; repeatedly, if that were possible.

Running down Grafton Street was more an issue of dodging than speed: buskers, tourists, a tall man dressed in a blue sheet reading aloud from *Finnegans Wake*, herds of Spanish students, half-cut office workers, baggy-jeaned kids off to buy some E; they came at us like a set of moving traffic bollards, some of them stopping to look back as we swooshed by.

Hare, Hare, Hare!

A bouncing clump of grinning, orange Hare Krishnas stood in front of Brown Thomas and beat a soundtrack to our strides.

Hare, Hare, Hare!

I turned us left onto Suffolk Street. We were all slowing down now, each breath requiring a singular effort. We made for the Stag's Head, tried slipping down the alleyway to Dame Street, but they saw us and followed. We crossed Dame Street and tried doubling back around the Central Bank, but that didn't fool them either. At this stage the speed we were travelling at hardly constituted running at all. It was a jog, a tactical battle where one team would try to outfox the other with a sudden burst of speed. When they slowed down, we did too, anxious to preserve what little energy we had left. My chest felt cleaved with pain, like a scalpel had been left inside it by a careless surgeon. My legs were wobbly and uncertain, wheeling me as much side to side as forward, my arms swinging as I tried to claw the abrasive air out of my way.

We progressed like this halfway up Dame Street, Odette occasionally grabbing me by the collar and panting encouraging noises, but once we were level with City Hall, we received our first and only piece of luck: the traffic lights changed just as we scooted across Parliament Street, forcing the Beer Boys to dodge around irritable traffic suddenly coming at them from three directions, along with a cavalcade of women dressed in Edwardian clothes and riding old-fashioned messenger-boy bicycles. As if I had planned it all along, I led Odette into the Front Lounge, where I stumbled up the steps into the back section, skidded around the vulgar-but-ironic pink fountain and slammed headlong into a group of gay men. They retaliated with shoves and yelled abuse. I staggered off. They indignantly wiped the spilt drink from their leather waistcoats.

The Front Lounge, I had realized, has another entrance on Exchequer Street, where, in a positive welter of irony, it calls itself the Back Lounge. With our head start on the Russians, we could run through the pub, turn left and double-back down Dame Street and into Temple Bar, where, seeing they had only been in town a short time, they were unlikely to find us.

The Beer Boys, however, were well named. They already knew about the Back Lounge. They were leaning against a wall opposite, a gun drawn, smiling again.

''Allo,' said one, a phone pressed to his remaining ear. 'You wait.'

We slumped to the ground. It was a relief to stop running.

Within half an hour we were in the basement of a crumbling Georgian building off Mountjoy Square. A Volvo estate had collected us, driven by a tall skinny man with three studs in his nose and nothing to say. The earless Russian had sat up front, the other behind us in the boot, his gun barrel inches from the back of my neck. They didn't bother with blindfolds.

The basement had an uncovered concrete floor, and the grey walls were also naked save for a number of squares and rectangles formed by damp which had edged out around long-gone pictures. There was no furniture except for two office chairs, the swivelling kind which sit on a central column attached to a star-shaped set of legs. We were made to sit in these. Mine was in the centre of the room, as if I was about to take part in some amateur version of *Mastermind*. Odette's was by a wall, as if she was to be a member of the studio audience.

After several minutes of debate between the Russians, I was lashed to my chair, one sleeve inexplicably pulled up, my arms tugged down straight by ropes wrapped around the central column. Odette, however, was left alone. We exchanged puzzled looks.

The Russians returned to a standing position by the door and remained there, shifting uncomfortably on their feet like teenagers just arrived at a party. No-one spoke. I could hear occasional footsteps on the pavement outside, muffled shouts, cars burring past. Through a grimy, narrow window I could see the street from ground level, the occasional pass of headlights turning the basement monochrome.

Eventually, the sound of a door opening upstairs reanimated the Russians. They stood to attention, like children playing soldiers. There was a rumble of footsteps on the stairs, and into the room walked a crumpled, elderly man, his hands plunged into nondescript corduroy trousers. He wore a cardigan, and under this a Manchester United jersey.

He was, however, unlikely to be an off-duty player, because he was also immensely fat. The jersey seemed strained to breaking point under the huge mass of flesh it had been called upon to contain, virtually all of which had collected in the man's stomach: it rose out from his chest at a dramatic angle, as if he had stuffed a sack of sugar up his shirt and hoped no-one would notice.

The Russians and the fat man exchanged a nod as he waddled in. He glanced at me like I was a piece of work he had come to inspect, then turned to face Odette. She gazed evenly up at him. Her limbs were carefully arranged to imply defiance, but her chin trembled.

He shook his head, as if deeply disappointed with what he saw. Hands still in his pockets, the fat man bent down and whispered into Odette's ear. She glared at him but failed to reply. Again he whispered something, and this time she whispered back, angrily gesturing with her hands but careful not to touch him. The Russians looked out the door, trying their best not to listen.

The fat man turned to look at me again, as if to confirm something he had seen earlier. He tutted in disgust, and for the third time whispered to Odette. She whispered back, hissing the words, pushing them to the almost audible. He recoiled from her, like a nun who has just heard an obscene joke.

They stared at each other.

Eventually he extended a flat hand.

'No,' said Odette.

The fat man took a step backwards. Using all of his considerable weight, he swung one of his meaty fists precisely into Odette's chin, snapping her head sideways, wrenching from her the *Doh!* sound I had heard that morning. Blood squirted from her nose and mouth like water from a burst pipe. She fell forward and rested there, her hair shrouding her collapsed face. Thick globs of red pattered into her lap.

I watched this, amazed at the force of his punch, at how this tubby little man could hide such animal power within himself; at how this power could instantly rob a speaking, breathing person of the myriad qualities which for a lifetime had defined their existence: transform them into a slumped lump of meat, clothes and hair suddenly redundant and ridiculous.

Yet I watched it more in sadness than horror. It was what I expected. Odette would be another victim of my actions, and so, at last, would I. After Bongo's flat, I knew it was only a matter of time. It was the natural order of things. I caused all this.

With Mary Barton, there was never any pressure. She knew about Angela, knew about the baby, but never once asked about them, never once forced me to think about the moral slackness of what we were doing; quite the contrary. She would treat me as if

I was a single man, and only she was cheating: she assumed the guilt for the two of us. No pressure.

She gave me detailed accounts of her life: her daughter, her brother, her parents; the repellent Jimmy and his crimbo mates: all of it set in concrete the impossibility of escape for her. No pressure; such a lack of pressure that I didn't feel guilty about Angela. I felt guilty about Mary Barton. She, after all, had everything I wanted in a woman. No threat of commitment and unlimited access to heroin.

That started in the band, around the time of the American tour. At first we smoked it to please Artifoni, who for some months had been withering our ears with testimonials for smack. And he was right: it was wonderful. It seemed to solidify our future path, provide the power of will over thought, the capability to banish from the brain anything that didn't please. It turned a slum into a garden.

So I kept smoking it. Not a lot: maybe a couple of times a week. Sometimes I didn't touch it for a month, just to reassure myself, then I'd go back to it again. I never used a needle, never felt addicted, never got pains or sickness. But during the periods of abstinence I would miss it, there would be a gap; like the tan mark around a lost watch.

All thought of abstinence halted when Angela became pregnant. I was a pig for heroin, and only after some months with Mary Barton did it begin to dawn on me what I was doing, where I was headed to. I should have ended it with Mary as soon as I realized, but couldn't face the pain; mine and hers. I sensed her dependence on me, as I depended on her drugs. I couldn't face her being hurt and thinking badly of me. I couldn't be the villain here.

On our last night together, she delightedly told me that Jimmy – now out of prison after the assault case – was shitting himself because the fake-Georgian house in Castleknock was full of smack, the cops having stumbled upon the usual hiding place. She had revelled in his discomfort, and so on the following morning, as a final tragic and heroic gesture, I bravely left the police an anonymous tip, then rang Mary and told her it was over between us; I couldn't take the guilt. But I wanted her to know that I did love her (I could say it now; I was leaving), and because of that, Jimmy wouldn't be bothering her any more.

Jimmy got fifteen years. I stopped smoking heroin. It wasn't easy, though there were no dramatic physical side-effects: something like a bad flu for a few days, and then a sadness which lingered like an annoying scab. But it passed, or at least faded in intensity. The desire popped up occasionally, and when it did, there were always drink and other drugs to stuff it down again. Funny: I never told Angela. It was booze and laziness she threw me out for. The least of my vices.

Mary rang me some weeks later. Just for coffee. No pressure. She was shining: staring at me like I was a wonder, squirming with grateful giggles at even my weakest of jokes, mentioning Jimmy with conspiratorial grins. By leaving her, I had changed her life. Her gratitude was so overwhelming, I tottered between guilt and pride. I was Jesus with a cured leper.

Now she was speaking of her future, something she had never done before, never with any conviction. Now it was a possibility, a puzzle to be unlocked. There was a new scheme every time we met: she would simply leave Jimmy, tell him straight, she would move to Cork and get a job, she would clear his bank accounts and abscond to Australia, all of them thought out aloud for my comment or approval, all of them dissected by herself for possible danger.

I opted to pay no attention to this, to say nothing, like a dinner guest involved in a particularly complex parlour game who doesn't want to appear stupid. A game was all it was, because that's all I recognized it to be. No different from when we were together.

No different: it was mild fantasizing, which aimed occasionally to tease or shock me, like when she said her latest scheme was to take over Jimmy's old patch, sell smack for a year, then leave the country.

'What do you reckon?' she asked, a flirty girl.

'Oh yeah, great. Did I never tell you? When I did my Leaving Cert, my first choice was the drugs baron course. I didn't get enough points, though.'

She squealed an embarrassing laugh, wriggled closer to me across the table.

'No, really I could,' she said, as if encouraging me to try a new sexual position. 'I could hire some blokes from Romania or whatever. Emigrants. Put it about that they're Russian Mafia. That would scare the shite out of the Drummer. You could give me a few names from your emigrants programme.'

'Oh, great plan. It's a winner.'

I laughed, forcing it, pointed at my crumbling Filofax.

'They're all in there. In the hitman section.'

I went to the toilet, to escape the pathos of her plans, to get me standing so I could leave when I got back to the table. When I returned she handed me the Filofax, winked.

That was the last I ever saw of her.

You may find it hard to believe that I took so long to remember this meeting, to admit the connection between this and all the events of 16 June. Perhaps I didn't want to, and not because I needed to absolve myself: I simply couldn't believe it of her, couldn't imagine the kind of wolfish desperation that drove her to trudge around dank bedsits, meeting anxious-looking Poles, Czechs and Romanians; studying their eyes and the shake in their hands to divine if they were capable of the cold viciousness she required: a quality she eventually found in two large, grinning Russians. Now, even with all the facts, I still can't.

The fat man looked at the unconscious Odette for some seconds, like an artist studying what he has created. He rummaged in one of his deep pockets, produced a set of car keys, nodded to the former employees of Mary Barton and ambled from the room. They remained standing and silent as we listened to him breathily trudging up the stairs and out the front door.

They relaxed then: restaurant owners who had managed to charm the notoriously grumpy food critic. They studied me indulgently, then whispered and laughed, like there was a surprise present for me they had forgotten to wrap. One of them leaned behind the door, and with a magician's flourish produced a number of items encased in crisp plastic wrapping: a small metallic bowl, some alcohol swabs, a little bottle of water (non-sparkling), a fat, fifty-millilitre syringe with a needle attached and a bag of demerara-coloured heroin.

I looked at my rolled-up sleeve and nodded. I may have even smiled. There are worse ways to die. I thought of Alan and me, his first time smoking a joint. He giggled, then grew maudlin. *What would Mammy say if she saw us now?* He always called her Mammy, like she was a real person he had met rather than a blank space in his memory.

At first, the Russians were fastidious. The bandaged one did the cooking, taking care to wipe his hands and all the instruments with the swabs before placing some of the heroin and water in the bowl. He then set about heating this with a plastic lighter.

His companion, however, seemed less than satisfied with these preparations and kept interjecting instructions. The bandaged Russian did not welcome this advice and eventually yelled at his friend, petulantly flinging the bowl to the floor. He gestured to his companion to take over, but this offer was declined, apparently because the two-eared Russian was somewhat squeamish about needles.

The preparations began again, but this time with far less attention paid to swabbing the various implements. Once a quantity of the heroin had been liquefied, the bandaged Russian said something to his friend, who then tiptoed over to me, like I was half asleep and he didn't want to disturb my rest. He swung his jowly, phlegmatic face to within inches of mine and whispered:

'Cigarette?'

Thinking he was offering me one, I declined. But he continued saying the word with all the plastic sweetness of a receptionist, until I realized that he wanted one from me. I nodded towards the left pocket of my jacket. With great delicacy he took out the packet, extracted one cigarette, slid the packet back where he had found it and gave the fag to his companion. As if I was a valued member of the team, a vital part of this shared endeavour, the bandaged one nodded his thanks to me, then broke off the filter. This he placed on the needle of the syringe, then drew up the mixture.

He approached me, muttering in his own language as a doctor might to a small child, reassuring him that this isn't going to hurt. The other Russian turned his back, unable to watch.

But although the bandaged Russian did have something of a bedside manner, he had little in the way of medical training: he brutally plunged the needle into my arm, missing the vein. Not realizing his mistake, he tried injecting, but this burned me and I squirmed in my chair. A blister swelled on my skin. He apologized for his mistake.

After two more attempts, the tell-tale squirt of blood finally appeared, prompting a relieved *ahh* from the big, one-eared Russian. He tenderly pushed the mixture into my bloodstream. I watched it go and almost immediately felt my skin flushing hot, had to swallow down a slight wave of nausea. I felt sleepy, but fought against this: I wanted to be conscious of what was happening to me. My name is Simon Dillon. I know I am going to die soon.

Somewhere above us, a doorbell rasped. The Russians exchanged annoyed glances, had a brief argument. The bandaged one sighed loudly and stomped out of the room. We listened to his heavy footfalls on the stairs, a door groaning open, and then a tetchy conversation which see-sawed between whispers and shouts. The remaining Russian smiled at me, as if suddenly embarrassed by his partner's bad manners. He turned his back again, unable to face the sight of me with a large syringe dangling from my tethered arm.

'Sergei Ivanovich! Sergei Ivanovich!'

Relieved by the distraction, Sergei Ivanovich smiled, waved a hand at me as if to indicate that I should stay where I was, realized the stupidity of this, put his hand down and hurried out the door. He clunked up the stairs and the argument resumed, this time with more gusto. I couldn't make out what anyone was saying, though at one point I thought I heard the word *pizza*, repeated over and over.

I looked around the dank, blank room, looked at Odette's broken form, but couldn't bear to for long. I looked down at my chair. From between my knees protruded a metal handle, to be used for lowering or raising its height. I knew, because I've worked in a few offices in my time, that if I pushed down on it while standing up, the chair would raise itself until it simply fell off the central column. My captors, I mused, probably didn't know this, office technology not being a major part of their work.

This thought occurred to me in a distanced, distracted manner, as if it had no real bearing on my immediate predicament. It was simply the dull mechanics of my brain, fooling itself that it would have something useful to do beyond the immediate future. Indeed, I had left the thought alone, moved on to conjuring up images of everyone I'd known before it finally occurred to me how useful this observation was. And even then I was too lazy to act on it instantly.

I know this seems illogical: I had, after all, nothing to lose; any escape attempt would make no difference. But to my soapy brain, all options were simply varying methods of death: if I was caught, I reasoned, this would only make my inevitable demise more painful.

I coaxed myself into trying it with the promise that it was highly unlikely to work. Yet once I had managed to balance myself on one leg and hit the lever with the other, it was appallingly easy. The chair shot up, spun backwards off the central column and clattered on the floor, my ropes quickly unravelling to release me. I was standing, free, a window beside me, the syringe still wobbling in my arm like a blood-sucking insect. I brushed it with my fingers. Despite the rush I had experienced, the syringe was mostly full, and for a moment I toyed with the notion of giving it a quick squeeze; just a bit more of a hit. But I pulled it out, slapped a hand to where the blood seeped from my vein.

That was when the terror hit.

Fear we all know in varying degrees. But it is fear precisely because at the time we can recognize what it is, have a chance of controlling it. Terror is swamping, a long fall into an optionless hole where all the humanizing connections in the brain are unplugged, one by one. Love, loyalty, dignity are extinguished, revealing the burning animal beneath.

Perhaps this is self-justification; I can't really say. I can only tell you how it felt. On the quick descent to my primal self I knew they would be back any second. I knew Odette was unconscious and I would be unable to carry her. I scrambled out the window and into the darkness.

fourteen

It hurts to betray someone. More them than you, perhaps, but it hurts nonetheless.

Then again, this pain, such as it is, is easily ignored. I concentrated on the physical problems: slithering up onto the wet pavement – it had rained during our incarceration – creeping on all fours across the road and making my spastic dash towards Mountjoy Square. It was only a few dozen yards but it emptied me, sent stabs of pain across my chest and into my left arm. I clung to the railings of the park like a man on a rough sea crossing, slowly working my way along until I found a broken gate. I staggered inside, located a large congregation of bushes and threw myself behind it.

The wet grass was so cool, it was almost painful against my burning skin. I licked it, desperate for moisture, and for the second time that day threw up, though on this occasion with less success: a black liquid that once was Guinness flowed out of my open mouth. I crawled away from the pool of my inner detritus, flopped down and tried to lie still while the cramps subsided in my stomach.

I lay there for some time.

Perhaps I fell asleep; I'm not sure. Certainly the heroin was doing its insidious work, lulling me to stare up at a starless, lumpy-black sky. I thought of my father, and considered what Broder had told me about the Lash Keogh case: I had been right. There was something wrong with him: Mathew Dillon was corrupt, a crook, a bad guy, one of them.

One of us. The terms could only have meaning if I was sixteen again, armed with the binary arrogance of my teens. He was part of that group of well-suited, grinning-for-the-cameras men who run this city, who keep a cold eye out for one another. Or perhaps his was just one of many groups, or no group at all: he was simply unlucky or weak or stupid. It was something he had done, possibly done many times, but without any wider significance. It wasn't a trademark of his generation; I didn't buy that. I knew plenty of well-on-their-way publishers and publicans and public relations consultants who all knew one another, who would declare: we will be different. But the collective pronoun was already there: the *We*, the sense of exclusivity. A change of style, not content, while the rest of us, the Great Forgotten, continue as we've always done: unable and unwilling to make many or any real choices; accepting as presents the spiritual and material crumbs from the higher table.

And do I really care about any of this? Probably not.

I'd do it too, if I got the chance.

I thought of my daughter, sailing off the side of a building. *Daddy!* she would exclaim, apparently amazed at my very existence, thrilled that she too should have one. All this, and a daddy too.

I thought of kicking through the snow in Dublin, New Hampshire, of a filthy bedsit I once had on the Lower Kimmage

Road with an old-fashioned electricity meter that I fiddled with a huge magnet.

I thought of a time years ago with Bongo and a few other people. We took acid and went to Herbert Park and talked pretentiously about God. I found a pound of sausages, squeezed them and declared *a pound of sausages!*, knowing then their sausagy essence.

I thought of this guy I know. What's his name? Early twenties, skinny, Elvis Costello glasses. Nice fella. Described to me with a babyish innocence how two Australian girls jointly fellated him outside a bar in Ibiza.

I thought of Angela, sucking on a chubby joint, her hair in dreadlocks, the way she had it in Amsterdam. Her face still thin: that flirtatious dimple when she smiled. *Yes, I would like to have children some day. Really. Stop laughing.*

These thoughts were not unpleasant; there was a quiet clarity to them that managed to soothe the noisy jangle of my mind, dripped coolness into my aching limbs. But I knew they couldn't last: nibbling at their cusp was the certain knowledge that none of it mattered; at least not now: now the huge sky above me was shrunk to a single point and I was alone, for one moment master of my own fate.

It reminded me of the first time Mary and I arranged to meet in a hotel. I got pretty stoned beforehand, and I was deeply frightened as I walked into the foyer of the Shelbourne, to confront what I was capable of doing without drink or chance to blame. Yet as I hobbled in there, as I forced my legs to move one after the other, I felt exhilarated, I caught a glimpse of my own power. It was wrong, and that was the whatness, the *quiddity* of it. It was pure, and just for that moment, I understood myself and everything I had come from. Or imagined I did.

But as I say, these thoughts were irrelevant: mental junk food before the inevitable tumble back to the immediate. *Your name is*

Simon Dillon. You have taken heroin. You have to do something now.

Eventually I stood up, took a series of deep breaths, coughed, felt a bit better. The dizziness had evaporated. Don't get me wrong: I wasn't about to attempt some puerile grope at redemption. It was a choice, nothing more; a diamond carelessly thrown in my lap. I knew, from a previous visit I had completely forgotten the circumstances of, that a muck-brown public toilet squatted in the north-west corner of Mountjoy Square. I made my way to it. I drank metallic tap water, splashed my face, and with the aid of a lighter snorted three lines of cocaine. I headed for the gate and padded back to find Odette.

Nothing would please me more than to relate a heroic tale of how I outfoxed the evil Russians, but in truth I had no idea what I was going to do. It even took me some minutes to find the right house, something I finally achieved by sliding along the pavement on my belly and peeking through the basement windows.

She was conscious, slowly moving her head back and forth as if it were being pushed by invisible hands. I could see she desperately wished to rub her face, push back her hair and feel the clotted blood around her nose. But her arms had been tied. Apart from Odette, the room was empty.

It struck me as strange that the conversation upstairs could have gone on as long as this. Unless they had already finished it, discovered my escape and gone out to search for me. No: one of them would stay behind to guard Odette. Unconscious and now tied-up Odette. With an electric start I realized that remaining on the street might be more dangerous than going into the house. I looked up at the front door. It was wide open.

Thus it was panic, not heroism, that drove me back into the basement, and even then my first thought wasn't for Odette but for her bag, left discarded by a wall. The gun might still be in there. It was: glinting, heavy and impossible for me to use. I didn't take it out. It probably had a safety catch I wouldn't be able to find, and if the Russians saw me with a gun they would be even more likely to shoot.

''Imon.'

She knew I was there, but seemed unable to keep looking at me, as if my image kept flicking around to different parts of the room. Her nose was black with crusted blood and the left side of her chin was starting to swell, ridged with a long purple shadow. She tried to smile, but it obviously hurt her.

I tried untying her ropes but my hands were too sweaty. Instead I used a lighter to burn through them. She rubbed her face, tenderly felt her jaw and emitted a low moan.

'Can you walk?' I asked, knowing she couldn't.

She nodded yes, knowing it too. I grabbed her bag and threaded one of her arms across my shaking shoulders, slowly bringing her upright. With her free hand Odette held her head, as if afraid it might fall off. There was no way I would be able to get her out the window. We would have to brave the stairs and the prospect of a face-to-face encounter with the returning Russians. I considered taking out the gun, then changed my mind, then changed it back again. We had taken about half a dozen painful steps into the corridor behind the room, but I kept stopping to think, kept glancing back at the window like a hassled commuter setting off for work and sure he's forgotten something.

''Imon, c'mon.'

She breathed the words rather than said them, like a whisper from a ghost. We mounted the steps, one by one, and soon could see the open doorway, the rectangle of purple sky which at any moment could be filled in by the black shapes of men who would kill us. With every step I started, imagining they were there, but they never appeared. In utter disbelief I led Odette out of the front door, across the road and back into the woody refuge of Mountjoy Square. She collapsed onto the grass with a moan.

I left her there for a while, and watched her chest swell with each new valued breath. Eventually I dug around in her bag, found some tissues, wet them in the toilet and placed them over her face. She sighed with pleasure and gestured her thanks.

I sat, and waited for her to move. Even as I looked at the wreckage of her face I wanted Odette to get up, get better and tell me what to do. Perhaps that was why I went back for her; I was more scared of being on my own than of the Russians.

After a time, she did sit up, though not well: she swayed to the side, nearly flopped back over. I helped her to the toilet where she washed, illuminated by my flickering lighter. I could hear her crying, but more out of anger than anguish. I hugged her for a while, and finally she pushed me back and stood without my help. It was time to go.

She still wasn't steady on her feet, but we managed to creep around the parked cars of Mountjoy Square and down into the plastic shabbiness of Parnell Street. The eastern side of O'Connell Street was still sealed off after the bomb, so we turned left into Marlborough Street and, once Odette managed to lean against a lamppost and not give the impression of being drunk, we hailed a taxi.

I told the driver to take us to Rathmines, for no reason other than it was a few miles away and a part of town I hadn't been to for years; I was unlikely to meet anyone I knew. Thankfully, the driver didn't want to talk, bar the usual recitations of horror at the bomb and what's the place coming to. Odette put her head in my lap and I watched the nightlit streets slide past. Even now, people were walking, singing, kissing. I had an impression of what it was like to feel safe, to be unaware of the dry twigs that underpin ordinary life.

When we got there I was reluctant to get out of the car, but couldn't think of an excuse to stay. Odette was still unable to make any decisions, so I opted to head for the only sensible refuge available to us: McDonald's. She went to the toilet, while I queued behind a group of drunken African women. They sniggered quietly and pushed each other, like laughing out loud was something they were not normally permitted to do. A skinny man in a motorcycle helmet walked up to the counter, pretended to look at the gaudy menu, then slowly scanned all the other customers. I turned my back to him. I ordered two Big Mac meals, sat beside a large plastic locomotive, nibbled at my food, listened to a muzak version of 'London Calling' and kept an eye on the door.

Odette came back, and despite a distinctly lop-sided aspect to her face, was much improved. She smiled, after a fashion, and patted her bag.

'I have smelling salts. Useful.'

She glugged back all her Coke, poured out the ice onto an elaborate patchwork of paper napkins, rolled it up and put it gingerly to her jaw.

'Are you not going to eat?' I said, having not eaten much myself.

She picked up a chip, as if to please me.

'Can't eat that,' she said, pointing at the burger. 'Can't open my mouth.'

She smiled, even though it hurt.

'Thank you for saving me. What happened?'

I decided to tell the truth. But she was untroubled by this.

'You came back.'

'But I left you. I ran away.'

'I am here. That is what's important. And I have let you down.'

Two Asian men walked in and sat by the window. Ignoring the signs forbidding it, they lit up cigarettes. One of them blew smoke rings, then glared at me. I looked away, picked up my burger and took a mouthful.

'No, you haven't,' I said, trying to sound concerned.

'I have. I have been so . . . *stupid*. I should have figured this out before.'

I stopped chewing.

'And now you have?'

'Yes, it was obvious,' she said, thus implicating me in her stupidity. 'Russian Mafia: it was a ridiculous story. Who could believe that?'

A spotty assistant manager was now talking to the two smoking men. He put an arm on one hip in an attempt to appear forceful. The men grinned back, revealing years of poor dental work.

'So there's no Russian Mafia?'

'No, just Mary Barton. The stupid bitch.'

She sighed the words, like a broken-hearted parent. The Asian men had put out their cigarettes and were now on their feet, attempting to shake hands with the assistant manager as he coaxed them towards the door.

'Sorry, Odette; you've lost me.'

She carefully eased the disintegrating ice pack from her face and tumbled it back into the Coke carton.

'What Gavin McCabe told us was true. Mary hired the Russians and they took over Ferndale from the Drummer. The Drummer sent men after them, but the Russians scared those men off. The Drummer cannot beat the Russians, so what does he do?'

I was never any good at quizzes. I shrugged helplessly. The muzak player was now performing 'Three Times A Lady'.

'He offers the Russians a job, of course. He pays them a lot of money to kill Mary Barton. So they kill her.'

'OK, but what's that—'

'Wait.' She was frowning and staring at the table, as if she might forget what she was about to say if she didn't get it out quickly.

'The Drummer sees this as an opportunity. He tells no-one that

232

the Russians are now working for him. He puts out this story that the Russian Mafia are moving into Dublin, and he gets his Russians to start killing people from all the gangs, even his own gang, so it looks like he is also a victim in this.

'That is why you were questioned this morning, why they wanted to know how well you knew Mary. They thought: maybe he knows what the Drummer is up to. Maybe Mary Barton told him on the phone just before she was killed.'

She smiled at me. Bitterly: like a betrayed wife.

'Oh, but you are a good liar, Simon. You must have had lots of practice. They believed you, so they let us go. Even the Drummer doesn't want to kill a judge's son if he doesn't have to.

'Of course when they later learned of your affair, that changed their mind.'

I had now finished my burger and was starting on Odette's, mildly astonished at how I could do this and discuss the prospect of my death.

'But she could have told lots of people,' I ventured. 'Her brother.'

'Her brother would be too scared to speak out, and even if he did, who would believe him? Mary did not know anyone else like you: you are the son of a judge, you are a journalist, or so they think. If you say the Drummer is behind this, then people will listen.

'That is why they tried to kill you with heroin, to discredit you in case you had told someone. Then the papers would say: he was crazy on drugs. He was in a rock and roll band. It is a tragedy, but no big surprise.'

She sat back and exhaled deeply, spent by her explanation. Her fingers drummed irritably on the yellow table.

'Hang on,' I said. 'I have to get more Coke.'

Queuing was a relief from the squealing pitch of Odette's

explanation: she had spewed it out at me, as if the information burned her insides, like the knowledge of a cruel betrayal. So it was about me; some of it anyway. For a day I was a dangerous threat to the Drummer's secret kingdom, a threat he sought to diffuse by leaving me dead and full of drugs in Mountjoy Square. He was in a band. It's no big surprise. My life and death again defined by what I couldn't manage to be.

When I returned to the table Odette was patting make-up onto her bruised chin. She grimaced, as if the very notion of make-up disgusted her.

'OK, two questions,' I said. 'How does killing all these people benefit the Drummer?'

She flung her make-up kit back into her bag.

'Because gangsters are stupid.'

She said this a bit too loudly. The spotty assistant manager, cleaning a nearby table, paused to put a hand on his hip.

'In each gang, there is only one person, maybe two, with any brains. If you have too many clever people, they keep trying to rip each other off, and the gang cannot work. So if you have seven gangs in Dublin, that means seven clever people. You get rid of those brains,' she swished her fingers across her throat, 'and the gang dies.'

'OK. So?'

'So if you want to take over the territory of another gang, eliminate the boss. If you want to take over all of Dublin, kill all the bosses. But this is difficult because they are well protected. Except . . .'

Finally, I twigged something. I stuttered it out like an excited bingo player with a full house.

'Except they are all meeting tonight in the Sidebar. What McCabe said.'

234

'Yes, Simon. They all arrive. They have a few drinks, they talk about their problem. After an hour or so the Drummer goes to the toilet and *quelle surprise*! The Russians show up. Everyone is dead except for Monsieur Drummer and he is King.'

'Fuck,' I said, wishing I could produce a more intelligent response. 'Fuck.'

She watched me, a slightly deranged smile playing about her face. I ate the last of her burger and wished she'd stop looking at me. To counter this, I asked:

'Why the Sidebar anyway? I know just about everybody there and I've never met any gangsters.'

She sighed, as if bored now.

'Because it is neutral ground; somewhere they would never normally go. They can get a private room. And the Drummer owns forty per cent of it.'

'What? Forty per cent of the Sidebar?'

She nodded.

'Fuck off!'

'No. It's true.'

It had never occurred to me before who might actually own the club. I knew the manager well: a Belfast man named Phillip Ryan who suffered from a lisp and a good deal of secret ridicule due to the poor arrangement of what little hair he had left. I had assumed the Sidebar belonged to him.

'But . . . won't the others know this?'

'No,' she pronounced.

'But like . . . he's going to have the fucking OK Corral in his own club. The cops are bound to find that he owns part of it.'

She smiled again, as if the prospect of all this death gave her a sexual pleasure. She widened her eyes.

'Perhaps they will, Simon. But they know the Drummer is

clever, and it would be stupid to have a gunfight in your own club. If they find out – if the Drummer lets them find out – it makes him look innocent.'

She threw up her hands in helpless admiration.

'Fuck,' I said. I was starting to annoy myself. 'Shouldn't we . . . warn somebody about this?'

'No,' said Odette: with such a granite finality I opted not to pursue this any further.

'So are we still going to Paris?'

She gave her wounded smile again.

'You have another question,' she said, knowing what it was.

'OK. How did you figure all this out?'

'I think you know that, Simon. I think you know who that fat man was.'

'The Drummer.'

'Yes.'

'You know him?'

'Not for much longer. *Ce mec, c'est une ordure. Je vais lui trancher son gros bide et sucer ses tripes sanglantes.*'

'What?'

She ignored me.

I decided not to pursue this either; it hadn't seemed like she was saying it to me. Odette dipped her hands under the table and rummaged beneath her tee-shirt. There was a metallic click, then the screech of adhesive tape being torn from skin. She gave no indication of pain.

'Here,' she said, handing me a minidisc. 'You keep it. The fat man is not so clever. He told me most of this when we had our little chat.'

She tried to smile, but again it mutated into a grotesque twist of her mouth. Suddenly, she seemed overwhelmed by bitterness, every muscle in her face emitting the tart odour of ill-suppressed pain. I didn't dare ask where this came from, but knew that her role as my protector was now secondary to something else; something crackling with hate.

'We're not going to Paris now, are we?'

'No,' she said. She looked at her watch. It was 11:20. 'We're going somewhere else.'

As I say, I'm useless at quizzes. But I could make a good guess.

fifteen

Less than an hour later Odette had me marching down the twisted road off Earlsfort Terrace that leads to the Sidebar, an arm firmly curled around one of mine. I had my hands in my pockets, but they kept shaking anyway.

Her plan had a crazed simplicity: we would go in, Odette would contact some of the other gang leaders and explain to them what the Drummer was up to. If further evidence was required, she would bring these people over to me – I was to remain in another part of the club, out of sight – where the minidisc would be played for them on her Walkman.

Once this truth was revealed, it would set me free: they would be too busy killing each other to bother with Simon Dillon.

Simon Dillon hadn't been consulted on whether he agreed with this scheme or not. As soon as Odette had become bent upon it, my opinions, or lack of them, were irrelevant: this was her new, bloody production of *Macbeth*, which would take the stage with or without me. And anyway, all I had to do was sit in a dark corner and not be seen; I could do that. I could.

Yet the closer we moved to the club, the more the primordial creature within me squirmed to win control of my rubbery limbs; howled in complaint at the unnatural stupidity of walking in here, of trying to force back the millions of years of slippery evolution which commanded above all else: stay alive. Run. All doubt had been squeezed away: if I entered this place, I would be killed.

And I was right.

It being the sort of establishment that trades on a thick air of inaccessibility, the Sidebar didn't have a sign or even much of an entrance: simply a brown metal door with a pair of hulking, dickey-bowed bouncers, lumpy shadows in the thin single light. Of course, this being the Sidebar, they called themselves *hosts* and generally said more than the grunt'n'nod most members of their profession dispensed. It was *good evening, how are you tonight?* Unless they didn't recognize the face: then it was *are you a member?* knowing you weren't, because no-one actually joined the Sidebar; there was no card or badge or form to fill out. Membership was earned by the simple means of them knowing who you were already: an impossible conundrum if you were not from the right caste; not even a little bit famous, rich, important or, like me, still trading on it. That said, the first couple of hundred ordinary punters who turned up would be allowed the honour of paying through the nose in return for admittance; their function being to fill up the bar while everyone else paraded through to the VIP Room: reminding them, and us, of how lucky we all were.

As we rounded the corner Odette motioned me to a halt. She fluffed her hair to obscure her bruised jaw and walked on alone.

'Iz Grafton Street?'

'No, love, you need to go back up the ways.'

The two of them launched into an elaborately helpful account of how Odette could negotiate a path back up the ways. She grunted appreciatively in stage-franglais.

Back up the ways around the corner she shook her head.

'There are two other men by the far wall, watching everyone go in.'

She cocked an arm on her hip and looked at the ground, distractedly stroking her injured jaw while she thought. I looked at her and began to doubt that she could ever have been truly beaten into helplessness; it was no more than an occupational hazard. Another shitty day at the office.

'We need to get them away from there,' she said.

I looked at my watch, suddenly inspired.

'There is a back door.'

It was locked, of course, right at the bottom of a filthy and usually unnoticed alleyway. But that's what I expected. From my brief and bitter flirtation with DJing, I knew that it was nearly midnight, and that the main DJ would be turning up within the next ten minutes or so to start his set. Chances were I'd know him.

Odette nodded, almost impressed. We picked our way to a clearing in the rubble of bins, boxes and bottles from the Sidebar. There was a stench of stale alcohol, like last night's regrets.

Five minutes later Dave Regan loped into view, balanced between two metallic cases like some high-tech worker on a paddy field. Not having given this part of my master plan a great deal of thought, I simply called out his name from the darkness.

The cases clattered to the ground as Dave wheeled around madly, trying to identify which part of the wall had suddenly grown lips and spoken.

'Dave, Dave, it's me. Simon Dillon. Sorry, man, sorry about that.'

'Jesus, you scared the shite out of me,' he said, rather redundantly. 'What's going on? Why are you hiding down here? Are you trying to avoid someone or something?'

Dave Regan was never shy about jumping to a conclusion; sometimes even the right one. As far as Dave was concerned, the world was a sweetshop of opportunities, which was why he was far more than just a DJ; in fact gigging at the Sidebar was probably his least profitable venture, maintained only to keep up the all-important Profile. Dave ran clubs, owned several record labels, promoted gigs, directed music videos and by unpopular wisdom owned a few pubs down the country. More recently he had been promoting himself with a few Voice of Young People appearances on television: he'd bleat about how his generation would be different, without being specific as to how. It was marketing, made to sound like a sort of idealism. Dave was a perfectly formed Celtic Puppy.

'Dave, I need a favour.'

'Yeah?'

It's not that Dave was a particularly unpleasant person; it was just that asking him for something free was like asking a junkie to mind your heroin while you went to the shops. Dave, I knew, had a key to the door, but wouldn't let us in if he thought there was any risk to him. More importantly, he wouldn't let us in if he thought he wasn't going to get anything out of it.

'Could we go in the back door?'

He shook his head. He looked like an old garda raiding an after-hours pub.

'I dunno about that. I dunno. I'm not supposed to. They trust me with the key. Why, who are you avoiding?'

'Ah, just some people out the front.'

'Who, like?'

'Look, I can't say. I'd just really appreciate it if you brought us in.'

By my usually high standards, this was deeply ham-fisted lying. Dave and I could both hear the tremulous, desperate notes in my voice, making me even less eager to tell him the truth, which he wouldn't believe anyway. Nonetheless, Dave was achingly keen to find out what it was.

'Look, Dave, I'd really appreciate this. I'll owe ya. Big time.'

'Really?'

Dave already knew I'd owe him for doing this; what he wanted to know was how much, what kind of currency I was prepared to flash. This was how he operated, keeping a mental list of social debits and credits to be spent when he needed them. What he required was an amount, some measure of just how much debt I wanted to get into. I could think of nothing.

Thankfully, he did.

'Who's your wan?' he asked, nodding at Odette.

'Dave, you've got to promise me that you won't tell anyone this, OK?'

Dave nodded enthusiastically. The likelihood was that Dave wouldn't tell anyone; unless it was to his advantage to do so.

'Well, it's just that Michael Attwood is in town. You know Michael?'

Dave didn't know Michael, but I knew that already. Michael Attwood was, however, a huge UK promoter who Dave would very much like to get to know. I didn't know him either, bar a brief handshake at Dingwall's a few years before, a photograph of which subsequently appeared in *Hot Press*. At the time it had been enough to convince half of Dublin that Moon Palace were an insincere smile away from being millionaires.

'Oh,' said Dave, noncommittal but leaking a greedy interest. 'You're still in contact with him then? You have a deal or something?'

'Well, not really.' I decided not to stretch his credulity too far. 'It's just that she's his wife.'

Dave looked at her again.

'So?'

'Well, she told him she was going back to the hotel for a rest.'

Dave looked blank. For an otherwise bright guy, he seemed to be a bit slow on this one.

'But she was really with me and we don't want him to know.'

'Oh my God!' ejaculated Dave. 'Sorry. Bit thick there. Ah, Jesus, no problem.'

He threw an arm around me, suddenly a friend of forbidden love everywhere.

'Don't worry. Not a word from me,' he whispered. He nodded at Odette as he unlocked the door, almost too excited to speak. He waved her in.

'So is he upstairs now?'

'I wouldn't say so, but he should be here soon. I'll introduce you.'

That was enough. Dave ushered us in, the transaction complete: he would guard my grubby secret, and in return I would introduce him to the UK promoter never to arrive. As we tramped up the stairs and the thump of music grew larger in my ears, I should have warned Dave that tonight the Sidebar was to be used as a conference room for some of the biggest gangsters in Dublin, and that those gangsters would at some point probably start shooting at one another. But he wouldn't have believed me; if it had been the other way around, I wouldn't have believed him. I didn't know people like that came here. There was a lot Dave Regan and I didn't know.

We emerged behind the bar and Dave quickly waved us out. It's strange, entering a place you usually inhabit under the influence of drink and whatever else you can afford that night. My memories of the Sidebar are all of darkness, noise, shouted conversations and the odour of whiskey deep in the back of my nose. Now, though, it was a rather shabby series of half-empty interconnecting rooms with stained carpets. The faded velvet seats sagged forlornly. The place had a tragic, dispirited air; a waiting room for the hopeless.

We were located at one end of the sweeping mahogany bar, luckily for us quite a distance from the entrance to the VIP Room, where we assumed the meeting would take place. Behind were toilets, the DJ's booth and the Purple Room: a part of the club which had grown so tatty, the owners had been forced to choose between darkness and redecoration. They had opted for the former.

At the entrance to the VIP Room a bulky, shaven-headed man I didn't recognize was standing with the bouncers, while all the familiar faces were being turned away: a few journalists, a radio DJ, a television executive, a publisher with three of his ex-girlfriends, assorted musicians and ex-musicians, models, actors, Brian Blennerhassett (of course), a staggeringly drunk writer, an artist who made things out of wire, marketing and advertising types and lots of people with nondescript jobs who liked to hang out with all or any of the above. I knew stories about most of them, many of them bad; probably a lot of them untrue. They knew stories about me as well. We were all armed and ready to draw, creating a tense calm; a social cold war. I felt a mix of nostalgia and disgust.

As they went up in turn to receive their humiliation, all of them remonstrated; some even grew angry. But the shaven-headed man stared them away: now they would have to stay outside the VIP Room, with people who had paid to get in. Oh, the horror.

A small group of dishevelled men in straw boaters and stripy jackets anchored at the far end of the bar tried to start a singsong. The dispossessed VIPs looked at them with lazy detestation.

We ordered bottles of Beck's, and I explained the geography of the Sidebar, social and physical, to Odette. She nodded and sipped her beer through the non-bruised side of her mouth.

'OK,' she said. 'I will go for a look. You stay here. Stay out of sight.'

'How are you going to get in there?'

'I will get in. Do not worry.'

She wandered off, beer in hand, a girl on a night out. For my final time that day, I headed for the toilet.

It wasn't that I particularly craved more drugs, but I had an urge to indulge in the familiar, and the jax in the Sidebar was one I knew well. Naturally, the management there didn't encourage drug taking, though if you were going to design a toilet to facilitate such a pastime, this was it: roomy, bright and equipped with a black marble sink unit ideal for chopping up white powder. It also had a chair which, when sat upon, brought you to nose level with the marble.

The coke burned my nostrils. I had taken so much during the day I now found it difficult to snort, yet still the Charley managed to burn through to the back of my throat, filling my mouth with that familiar, sparky taste, stroking my head and shoulders with a warm flush of well-being, a sense that no problem was beyond solution. Sherbet for grown-ups: the beautiful, bitter flavour of the humming nighttown Dublin I have embraced so many thousands of times. Familiar and hostile. Tender and cruel. All I treasure and all I loathe. I love cocaine.

What was left on the marble I rubbed into my gums, numbing my lips in the process. I sniffed a few times, checked my nose, had a piss and went back to the bar.

From where I stood I could see many familiar faces, but not anyone who looked like they might be there to attend a criminals' convention. Odette seemed to have disappeared. I sipped my beer, and realized that I would have to make it last until she returned: I had no money left. I shut my eyes and tried to conjure up pleasant images; imagined other countries. Australia. Maybe I'd go there and visit my brother. He'd invited me, in that vague way of his. *Australia is great. Maybe you should, you know, if you're stuck for somewhere to go. You know.*

'Young Simon Dillon! Are you sleeping?'

I fearfully opened one eye. The men in the stripy jackets had migrated down the bar and were now collected around me. In the middle of them, Brendan Boylan's fleshy magenta face loomed up to mine.

'Did we wake you?' he barked.

'No, no. I was just . . . wishing I was someplace else.'

'Ahh,' he said, as if he actually understood. He held up an unsteady finger. '*Ineluctable modality of the visible:* . . . er, can't remember the rest of that line.'

'Pardon?'

'What you see, Simon, is what you get. That's life, I'm afraid.'

The faces of the men arrayed around Brendan Boylan chuckled approvingly, though they were hardly men: not one of them older than twenty, and all with the unrealistically confident air of university students. Brendan Boylan was, of course, a friend of my father. He lectured in English Literature at Trinity College: just one of the reasons why he liked to observe the Bloomsday festivities. Another was that he took some pride in the fact that a character in *Ulysses* had the same surname as him, while he also greatly enjoyed having an excuse to drink all day and end up in nightclubs which he normally wouldn't visit.

'So how are you? And how's the old man? Must go out and see him.'

In fairness, Boylan was one of the few people who could say this and not be a complete hypocrite: after my father went weird, he had been out to Dalkey a couple of times.

'OK. The same,' I said, finishing off my beer. I wondered would he offer to buy me another.

'And don't you have a daughter? Think I saw her last year. Pretty little thing. *Runs, she runs to meet me, a girl with gold hair on the wind.*'

I smiled, trying hard to project the idea that I knew what he was talking about. Over by the VIP Room, I caught a glimpse of a fat man being ushered through the crowds.

'So did you hear about this bomb? All those people. My God, I thought those days were long gone. Do they know who did it? I can remember Nelson's Pillar being blown up, that'll tell you how old I am. What are you drinking there, Simon?'

I quickly turned my attention back to Boylan.

'Er, actually I'll have a whiskey please. Cheers.'

'Good man, Simon! I'll have one too.'

He plucked out a fifty-pound note, slid it to one of the students and pointed him towards the bar. Taking one last glimpse at the VIP Room, I moved in closer to the huddle of stripy jackets.

'So you were doing your Joyce stuff today?'

'We were indeed, Simon, though most of the places mentioned in the book aren't there any more. Still, it's good fun. You should come along next year. I'm surprised you haven't, what with your father's interest.'

'Yeah, yeah. Actually, I've never even read it.'

'Really? I'm astonished. Why not?'

'Well . . . all that stuff is for tourists really.'

'Yes, yes, yes. *Bloomsday* might be. But the book, Simon. You really haven't read it?'

'Yeah. No. Couldn't understand it, to be honest.'

Brendan Boylan groaned with playful exasperation as the drinks arrived. We clinked glasses and threw back our whiskeys, sucking in air as the liquid scorched our throats.

'Simon,' he continued. 'Everyone says that. Yes, you do have to give it a bit of work, but the text is really about a simple and universal theme that applied to life when it was written, and still applies today. Especially today with all this fucking money and greed and aimless existential emptiness.'

He nodded at his surroundings, as if the aimless existential emptiness of the Sidebar was self-evident.

An arm suddenly appeared between us. The hand at the end of it curled into a thumbs-up sign in front of my face.

'Howya, head,' merrily screamed Michael Flattery. He retracted the arm and backed off in the direction of the Purple Room. 'Lab report and cat scan, what?'

I nodded and smiled thinly. Brendan Boylan watched him go, as if he was some rare and terrifying beast. Without any further comment, he turned back to me.

'*Ulysses* asks one very simple question: what is it that binds us together? *What is the word known to all men?*'

He paused, presumably to give me a chance to guess what this word might be. But I'm no good at quizzes.

'I dunno.'

Brendan Boylan opened his mouth to tell me, but instead of the answer, thick globs of blood tumbled out. It smeared his chin and splatted onto his jacket, like a messy eater after a plate of spaghetti bolognese. He dropped his glass, the sound of its crash obscured by the thumping music, and fell forward upon me. Suddenly pinned to the bar, I saw the clean faces of his students, laughing at what they assumed was a joke. I saw the skinny blade sprouting from the back of his neck, and beyond that, the one-eared Russian: his face curled in irritation, like a man who has just missed a bus. He shook his head, still apparently astonished that he could have failed to hit me at that range. He took two steps forward and grabbed the shoulder of my jacket.

I didn't react. I couldn't drag my gaze away from Brendan

Boylan's still-quivering face: resting on my shoulder, his mouth open, frozen in the act of revealing the word known to all men. I felt his clotted blood dropping in warm lumps onto my hand, saw that it had left a large angry smear on my jacket. My stomach convulsed.

'Brendan?' said one of the students.

'Come,' instructed the Russian.

I screamed.

In a spew of disgust, I catapulted Boylan's stiffening body away from me. It crashed into the Russian, spinning the two of them backwards against the far wall. The students roared and dropped their drinks. I ran.

In the wrong direction. The VIP area, I quickly realized, was probably even more dangerous than where I was. I slid to a halt and double-backed, but by then the Russian was almost on his feet, swiping wildly at my legs as I scooted past him. I headed for the Purple Room, a trail of Boylan's blood splattering behind me.

Even in the relative darkness there, each set of white eyes widened as I tumbled upon Dilly Golding, the social diarist. Quickly righting herself, she took in the tragedy of her tight black dress, now stained with vodka, gore and diet Seven Up.

'Everything's ruined!' she squealed. The first thing she'd said all day.

She cocked a furious eye at me, to ensure that I realized the full extent of my crime. But instead of more reprimands, Dilly Golding delivered a gasp. She hunched her shoulders and shrank from me: I was a crimson-smeared madman, his torn jacket fluttering at the shoulder. People I had been meeting here for years also started and stood back, as if I was the carrier of some lethal contagion. They were defenceless, unable to pretend that they hadn't seen me or the damage I had done. I ignored them, urgently scanning the room for another door I might have forgotten about.

'Dillon. Bollix.'

Thankfully, not everyone in the Purple Room was so observant. Ray Coffey stood with an arm pointed in my direction, like we were duelling swordsmen finally to meet.

'Dillon,' he said again, and waved me towards him.

Ray Coffey was not well named: he had eschewed the delights of caffeine some years before in favour of alcohol, which he consumed with the regularity most people reserved for coffee. He was a radio DJ with something of a following, and even though still in his twenties, was tormented by the notion that success had already dodged his friendly advances. I knew this because I had drunk with him many times. Not because we were friends: simply because we both came here far too often, and would sit together while we waited for someone more interesting to turn up. I would drink until I became bored. Ray Coffey, however, was sixteen stone, and capable of consuming alcohol until well past the point of sensibility or reason. Invariably, he would try to hit someone; anyone: violence gave a completeness to his night's entertainment.

'Dil-lon!' He swung an arm holding a half-full pint of urine-coloured lager. It splashed on the carpet.

I scuttled over to Ray Coffey and positioned myself behind him. I pointed at the door.

'There's a bloke—'

'Wha'?'

'There's a bloke coming and—'

'Wha'? Dillon!'

It was too late to explain: the bloke had arrived and was already attempting to elbow Ray Coffey out of his path.

'Whatyoufucking?' slurred Coffey, shoving the Russian back. He dropped his pint and puffed out his chest like a mating bird. The Russian, distracted by this challenge, shoved again. Coffey grabbed him by the throat. The Russian reciprocated. Thus locked together, the two combatants staggered around the Purple Room like mechanized men. The others watched in startled awe.

Michael Flattery cheered them on.

'Go on, ya bollix ya!'

I ran back towards the bar, but even before I reached it I knew the battle behind me had been disappointingly brief. There was a crunch of broken glass, a few screams and the sound of Ray Coffey already bitter in defeat.

'Fuckingbastard. *Bastaard.*'

I didn't look around, deciding now to dash for the door behind the bar. The Trinity students were crouched like monkeys around Brendan Boylan's prone body, their hands clamped to their shaking heads in disbelief. I made to swerve around them, but something viscous on the floor swept my running legs from under me. Suddenly I was airborne: like a novice swimmer, I belly-flopped into the centre of the grieving group. The students crashed back in all directions, while again I came face to face with the dead, open-mouthed lecturer.

There were more yells and trundling limbs, and then my head was being raised up, my hair gripped by a thick, sweaty hand. Over the throb of the music he breathlessly yelled:

'Love you!' *Lave Yoou.*

I clamped my eyes shut and waited for the gunshots. Three of them came, with such a graceful rhythm they could have been mistaken for part of the music. The grip on my head was released, and a body thumped down on top of me. It smelled of garlic.

To this day, I don't know who killed the Russian. Odette said it wasn't her. Perhaps it was a gang member who recognized him. At the time I gave it no thought because I didn't realize what had happened; I believed I was dead: crushed in a sandwich of fresh corpses, their bodily juices leaking across my limbs.

Only when I realized I couldn't hear the music did it occur to me that I was still alive; that the mirrors which covered the walls of the Sidebar were crashing all around me, disintegrating under the burning *ratatat* of gunfire. And curiously, it struck me that this was probably happening far earlier than the Drummer had planned: his Russian employee had blown the surprise by coming out of hiding to kill me. Everywhere I go, I fuck everything up.

I opened my eyes, but it was too smoky to see, too thunderous to hear: blocks of shadow struggled against each other, like a giant maggot had become trapped in the club and was frantically thrashing in all directions. Dozens of legs flew past, bodies fell to the floor nearby, but from where I was pinned I couldn't tell if they were dead or frozen with fear. The shots came singly and in great terrifying spurts, each of which triggered another round of coughing and screaming. With a loud pop, what light there was disappeared, increasing the elemental blindness. Now none of my senses could deliver any information. A choking yoghurt of blackness enveloped everything I knew: so dense, it was inescapable; so infinite, it made me doubt if light and shape had ever existed, if I hadn't just imagined them. A fresh delivery of souls to hell, squeezed from the grey sunken cunt of the world.

It was the fear of suffocation which eventually forced me to move. I pushed my way out from between the dead men, but found I could still breathe no better. I tried to feel my way towards the bar, retching as I did so, then realized that something above me was visible: the skinny sets of red LCD meters, still obediently jumping in thrall to the music. Dave Regan had obviously vacated the DJ booth. I crawled towards it.

One thing about being a DJ: it's quite easy to cheat. You can spend two hours fussing around a pair of turntables, scratching the discs, your cans pressed to your head, lining everything up with mathematical precision, while all the time the music you appear to be playing is coming from a minidisc underneath the desk. Of course it's considered bad form; the DJ equivalent to miming on stage. But I'd heard of it happening. Dave Regan was probably one of the people who told me about it. But there it was, *Mix 17* written on the display.

I was surprised by this. Dave was money-mad, but he did seem to be genuinely into music and the club scene. Perhaps his many business interests just got a bit too much for him. I felt for the stop button, pressed it and ejected the disc.

Curiously, this seemed to increase the level of screaming, as if the music was the last sensory link with what was normal about the Sidebar. There was more running, more shots cracking out in the darkness. I got up on my knees and felt for the mixing board. Music from the DJ booth is pumped to the dance floor below, the bar and the VIP Room, but at different audio levels. I put everything at full blast, felt in my pocket, and inserted Odette's minidisc. The display came up: *22 tracks. 12:23.*

Twelve minutes. Shit.

Frantically, I began clicking through the tracks to find what I wanted: rustling, a car engine, me laughing, Gavin McCabe's thick, milky accent: *What's this got to do with me?* – aural snapshots of the day we'd had. The sounds melted into the cacophony which stuffed the Sidebar, until a sandy Dublin tone boomed out like the voice of God.

Fucking disappointed in you.

More screams, but after a few moments the noise fell away, eventually down to a level which resembled normal. Now I could make out distinct noises: breathing, crying, urgent whispers. There would be near-silence, then movement, the occasional shot, yells in response. But for most of the time everyone there listened to what the Drummer had to say. There was a curious sense of community about it: welcome to hell; this is why you are here.

Your father would be ashamed. What are you playing at? This guy is a fucking wanker. Get some fucking sense into your head. I'm asking you now. Them Russians is working for me now. It's my game. It's going to be fucking huge, and you should be in it.

The track lasted no longer than thirty seconds, but it was enough: immediately a furious stampede of bullets rampaged around the building, seeming to come from all directions at once. More mirrors shattered, their contents jangling to the floor. I pressed the play button again, but this time God's voice had no effect, his children too concerned with trying to send one another to his side.

I crouched as low as I could and crawled out of the booth. In front of me I heard something yelled in Russian, and noticed then that the gunfire seemed to be concentrated at the far end of the bar, by the entrance to the VIP Room. It had also transformed in texture from an indiscriminate blanket of noise into something far more ordered: shouts, then shooting, then shouts; a conversation punctuated by violence, an almost boring routine of death and insults.

'O'Connor, ya fat cunt.'

'Fuck you.'

'*Nyet, nyet!*'

'He's there, there!'

Furniture crashed over as the combatants breathily stumbled in the darkness. The battle seemed to be moving even further away now, towards the far end of the Sidebar.

'There he is.'

'Fuck off!'

'Ya tubby prick.'

'You're fucking dead. I'm gonna kill your whole family. Slit their fucking throats.'

'There he is, there, there. C'm'ere, Tom.'

'Don't fucking come near me.'

'Drum this, you fucking obese cunt.'

A thunderous drumroll of automatic gunfire forced me to jam my hands over my ears. I turned around and moved in the other direction, away from the storm of bullets drenching the cornered Martin O'Connor. Goodbye, drummer boy. I may even have smiled. An overturned table blocked my path. I tried to go around it, but it was too big, forcing me to stand and attempt to scramble my way over. And it was then that I felt the clean buzz of pain slice through me, starting in my chest and shooting down my arm. I saw a sudden burst of light, and knew it was behind my eyes, not before them. I fell backwards and felt my body crunch into broken glass. I thought: so this is being shot. It's not so bad. And I realized I didn't mind dying. I just wanted to avoid pain on the way there.

Somehow it grew even darker. The noise seemed to abate. I saw lights, could have been torches, and then Brian Blennerhassett leaning over me, shaking his head while he went through my pockets. I tried to say something to him: not a word, just noise, but I was unable. Then I felt I was being lifted up, but I knew I wasn't. I was stuck to the cold floor, dying, while the smell of blood and alcohol pricked at my nostrils.

sixteen

So that's what happened to me on 16 June.

Since I've been in hospital, I've had a few visitors, all of whom have been able to contribute their fragment to the story of what happened after I was swooped away in a flashing ambulance.

My first visitor was probably the greatest surprise. Judge Mathew Dillon hobbled into my room two days after I arrived, a bewildered and slightly embarrassed look perched on his gnarled face. He sat beside my bed, but at an angle, so I couldn't get a clear look at him. He made a weak attempt at being jaunty, like I was in hospital for a minor sporting injury sustained in a foolish yet manly tackle on a prop forward three times my size. He told me that the Drummer and both the Russians were dead, shot in the Sidebar. He said it in an uninterested, throwaway manner, as if it had hardly anything to do with me, as if it shouldn't. Guards are saying it was a gangland battle, he told me. All over now. They are even rebuilding the spire. Everything back to normal.

I smiled, having some idea now of what normal was. He looked away.

But I wasn't being vindictive. I knew he never would describe to me the strange correlations of power which curled through Dublin: he wasn't about to list all the dirty little favours he may have proffered over the years, or outline how he had robbed the Lash Keogh of his children to oblige the biggest drug dealer in the city. He was too old, broken and distracted to start explaining, to search out a reason why. If he ever had one.

In truth, I didn't care. He was here, and that was enough; he'd left his house for the first time in two years to visit me and, strangely, I was glad to see him: his weakness and mine now made us equals. Not that I was ever going to tell him this. I was too old and too distracted as well. He kept talking, and I let him. *I rang your brother in Australia. He sends his regards. Coming home at Christmas. Has a new girlfriend. Serious, I think.*

Eventually he brought up his cane as if making ready to leave. He put his hand on my bed, not close enough to touch me, but enough to indicate a lessening of distance between us. He looked around him, and to my window said:

'You're safe now. Nothing to worry about.'

He hobbled to the door without looking at me, paused there and asked:

'Angela and the baby. Should they visit you?'

I told him no.

He placed a bony hand on the door, and as he heaved it open, I saw another man waiting there. The man nodded at my father, said: I'll catch you up. Leaning one arm against the open door, the man took a step into my room and halted there. He looked down, as if what he was about to say was written on his shoes.

'How are ya?' muttered Leo Broder.

I shrugged; looked at the television above my bed.

'You seem better anyway. You were in a bad state getting into the ambulance.'

I turned to look at him. Broder's face was milky pale, his cheek pock-marked with scratches. He held his left leg at an uncomfortable angle: a clue that his limp was worsening.

'You were there?' I finally said.

'At the end, yeah. We got a report of the shooting. I brought you into the ambulance. Fucking bedlam in town that night, with the bomb and everything. Total panic. There was a shooting star. We had people ringing in thinking Dublin was under attack from rockets.'

He attempted a smile. I didn't reciprocate, not knowing how to react to a man who had betrayed me.

'Anyway, it's over now. The Drummer's gone, you heard that. The others have already carved up his territory. Different faces, same bollocks.'

I nodded again.

Broder extracted a packet of Marlboro, opened it, then realized he was in a hospital. He shrugged and suddenly looked foolish. With exaggerated care, he placed the cigarettes back in his pocket. He looked at the floor again.

'Well, when you're back on your feet, maybe we should . . . you know.'

'Yes,' I said softly. 'We should.'

Surprised by my quick agreement, he continued to stand uselessly in the doorway; robbed of the chance to deliver his rehearsed speech, relieved he didn't have to.

'Right, so. Great,' he said.

I didn't know if I had forgiven Broder for giving me up to the Russians; I still don't. But right then it seemed somehow wasteful, even strangely cruel, to recriminate. Everyone is faithless, and he had, after all, put me in the ambulance. He had brought my father here. Perhaps I will meet him. Perhaps not.

I didn't even notice him limping backwards out the door. I had gone back to what my father had said: *should Angela and the baby visit?* He always called her the baby. Half the time he couldn't remember her name. The simple weight of my refusal had surprised us both, yet I knew that even the thought of Emily was almost more than I could bear. The sight of her would have been unendurable: knowing how pleased she would be to see me, knowing that in a few short years the mental image of her father will be eroded to just a word. *Daddy.* She will imagine what I was like, and pretend this is a memory; just as I have done for my mother.

You see, I am dying.

I didn't get shot. I had a heart attack.

Two of them, actually, in quick succession. Turns out I have a disease of the heart: for years it has been slowly rotting in my chest, deadening me from the inside out. Eventually I would have noticed it: shortness of breath, pains in my arms. I, however, bypassed all that by having a rather stressful day and snorting an enormous amount of cocaine: so much of it, they had to flush out my system or it would have killed me that night. Or so the nurses say. They've tried to jolly me along by playfully admonishing my rock 'n' roll lifestyle (their words), but I've found it hard to be chirpy. I have to breathe oxygen for half the day, I ache for cigarettes and I've little to do but feel the dull tick of the time bomb in my chest. I need a transplant within six months, a year at the most. They say they'll get a donor, but when I ask them how they know this, they change the subject.

So I lie in bed, and before I started writing this I would watch people venting their problems on daytime television: a universe of blame and accusation. If there is a moral force, perhaps what happened to me is an example of its work: my guilty life ebbs away in return for that of other, far less blameworthy individuals. My daughter. Bongo.

He didn't die. Quite the reverse: he didn't turn up to meet Brian Blennerhassett that night because he has fallen in love. A woman at his work with whom he had been flirting for some time went for a drink with him that evening. Many drinks, actually, then dinner, then her place, where they remained for the following forty-eight hours without contacting anyone. The Russians did break into his apartment, but it was their blood on the carpet, courtesy of their encounter with Odette.

Bongo himself didn't tell me any of this, because he hasn't been in to see me, and I don't blame him. If he hadn't got lucky that night, he would be dead now, and it would be my fault. He was my best friend, my only friend, and I never thought to warn him. I never told him about Mary Barton. I should have.

I learned all this from my third visitor, whose arrival was nearly as surprising as the others'. Brian Blennerhassett came in holding a bundle of music magazines which he nervously deposited on my bedside cabinet. He was sweating slightly and didn't sit down, just stood there adjusting his dark glasses and giving me a thin, uneasy smile. Finally, he put his arms behind his back and began, like a lawyer in a TV show about to give his dramatic closing address.

'You are no doubt wondering why I'm here.'

I was wondering if I was having a hallucination. Yet, as with my father, I found my anger had evaporated or, more correctly, been dwarfed into insignificance. In another set of circumstances, I would have been preparing to throw Brian Blennerhassett out the window for stealing cocaine out of my pocket. Despite the fact that it wasn't my cocaine and I almost killed myself taking it. But that would have been then.

He held up a finger.

'The Charley. Do you remember me taking it from you?'

I nodded.

'Yes,' he said, sounding slightly disappointed.

'When I met you earlier on, you were very obviously under the weather.' He paused, to underline his generosity in not further mentioning my trying to choke the life out of him. 'And at that point I did surmise that you had consumed a considerable quantity of powder.

'Later on in the Sidebar, when all the shooting started, I was crawling along the floor and happened upon you by chance. You were obviously injured but alive, so I reasoned that it would not further your cause any if the hospital authorities discovered any class A drugs about your person. That's why I took it out of your pocket.'

'Really? You're a fucking saint.'

I was breathless when I said this, so it lacked much of the venom I had intended. Brian Blennerhassett smiled.

'Only later did I learn that it was Bongo's coke. So I returned it to him. I also paid him for the impressive amount you managed to direct up your nose. I said the money came from you.'

I picked up my oxygen mask and took three large breaths. It was the closest thing to a cigarette I had. It also allowed me a few seconds to think about what he'd said. If this was true, he'd done me a favour, and for once I could not see an ulterior motive. I was flummoxed. He knew it, and was obviously enjoying himself. He sat down.

'I know you may find that confusing, Simon. Take comfort in this: I didn't do it for you.'

'What are you up to?'

'I did it for Bongo.'

'Bullshit.'

He swiped a hand in front of my face, as if trying to bat away my cynicism. He brought the hand back up and took off his dark glasses.

Brian Blennerhassett has only one eye. There is a glass replacement in the dead socket, but it's a travesty, a cheap ball bulging out of his head which mockingly draws attention to what's not there. The remaining eye is rheumy and almost colourless. He looked at me with it. He was shaking slightly.

'I was born this way. Disabled. My sight isn't that great. The sunglasses are prescription. I had a difficult time of it in school. A horrible time.

'For someone like me, things do not come easily. Any degree of success. Friends. Women. I could be working now as a switchboard operator or some such job, but I chose not to. I defied the world and reinvented myself. What you see is what I chose to make up.

'Oh, I know you and many people think I'm a sham. But I see no greater honesty in the way you have presented yourself to the world.'

I looked away, took a blast on my oxygen.

'There are many people like me, like Bongo, like you, who for varying reasons do not make friends easily. Bongo is my friend, and I value that a great deal. And you, if you were not bent on self-destruction, should value it too.

'And because Bongo is my friend I know the pain he has felt over the years on your behalf, because of the band, your many and varied failures. For his own perverse reasons he loves you unconditionally and I did not want him upset because you were finally thrown into prison for possession, even though I might have quite enjoyed seeing that myself. And I certainly didn't want him to think that his *friend* stole cocaine off him.

'He is hurt enough right now due to your myriad other sins.'

We talked for a little while more, but in an uncomfortable way, as a father might converse with his pouting baby son after giving him a slap: behind Brian Blennerhassett's practised vowels was a tone that betrayed his pity for me. He left, and I cried.

She finally arrived after I'd been a week in hospital, wearing a wide-brimmed hat and a sheer summer dress that fell around her body like it was in love with her. She looked like she'd just come from a wedding. Odette kissed my forehead, my eyes, my lips, my hands. Despite my illness, I sprouted a very healthy erection. Not good for my heart, I suppose, but it made me feel better.

The bruising around her jaw had almost gone. She sat on the bed, holding my hands and regarding me shyly.

'Sorry I took so long to come here. I had to get out of town for a few days.'

It took her a few minutes to begin, but when she did, there was a clear sense of rehearsal: not to hide the truth but the opposite, to be simple and honest, to tell me what happened without messy justifications. And this, I could see, was difficult for her.

The morning we first met, she had told Bongo that her father was from Westmeath. Robert Doherty, however, didn't stay there for very long. He was wild; a dark-eyed devil, who by the age of sixteen had already broken his parents' hearts. He had done two stretches in reform school, and would have done a third but for a soft-hearted garda who let him off the bus to go to the toilet.

Robert headed for Dublin, and for a while slept rough, surviving through petty theft and God knows what else, until he met an older, more accomplished delinquent by the name of Martin O'Connor. O'Connor was then many pints and pies away from becoming the Drummer, preferring more active pastimes such as bank robbery and the occasional spot of arson. He too had done time, but even then was developing the techniques to ensure that he never had to go back: recruiting tough yet slightly stupid men to take the risks for him. Robert Doherty, however, didn't quite fit this category, possessing a predatory cunning equal to his capacity for violence: qualities which soon recommended him for the job as the Drummer's second in command. Together they patiently built up a patchwork of fiefdoms around the city, and were by popular wisdom the first to organize the large-scale importation of heroin into Dublin.

They did well for themselves, Robert and Martin, and remained friends: Martin was best man at Robert's wedding, when Robert married Martin's sister, Margaret. She was already pregnant with Odette.

Margaret, however, proved less fond of Robert than her brother was. The marriage lasted less than three months, and in an attempt to protect her unborn child from its father's criminal influences, Margaret fled to Lyons, where she had worked some years before, cleaning up hotel rooms after rich Arab tourists. They remained there, though Margaret did not have to return to her former profession; Robert agreed to support his emigrant family, in return for visitation rights. Margaret reluctantly agreed, but on one strict condition: that Odette never be brought to Dublin.

She never was, but that was hardly necessary: Robert Doherty brought Dublin with him. He came over at least once a month, and dazzled his daughter with stories of his life in Ireland: a tale of lovable, working-class villains, not doing that much harm, just trying to get by in a poor country, while more sinister forces constantly threatened their way of life. Daddy taught Odette that family and good friends were the only people she could trust; anyone else was a threat. He paid for her karate lessons, and when she was sixteen sent her to Switzerland to learn the use of firearms.

Odette was bright: after school, to please her mother, she enrolled to study law in Paris. But it was a token effort on both their parts; the stories and pictures of Dublin had so infected Odette she now hated her coiffed and polished peers. After just a few weeks, she quit university and joined the army, where she remained for the next six years, overseas mostly, serving in Africa and the Middle East. She was on leave in Jerusalem when she heard her father had been killed. Her mother begged her not to, but Odette was too far gone with guilt and grief to listen; she should have done it years before. She flew to Dublin.

The Drummer met her at the airport, there to comfort his weeping niece. But he didn't realize how much her father's daughter she was. All Odette Doherty wanted to know was who had killed Robert, where they were and what weapons were available. The Drummer gave her everything she asked for: her father had been killed in a row over money with two UVF guys engaged in a modest amount of dealing around Lisburn. Within forty-eight hours they were dead. Robert Doherty lived on.

It was a return to the family business: not discussed and hardly thought about. There was no role for Odette in Dublin – she was a woman, after all, and equality legislation has yet to make itself felt in the Irish underworld – but the Drummer did have a position in mind for his niece: a professional killer. As I'd witnessed myself, a beautiful Frenchwoman, unknown in Dublin, can get in just about anywhere.

Which she did, though not that much; Uncle Drummer was careful not to overuse Odette's talents. In the meantime, she developed her own business. She remained in France, but never worked there. Ireland, other European countries and occasionally the US or Canada were her markets. She would fly in, do the job and fly out again, unknown to her victim or the local police.

For added security when she was in Dublin, the Drummer offered Odette the option of staying with Jimmy Barton and his wife, Mary. Jimmy, of course, was hardly ever there, so Odette and

Mary, despite Odette's profession (they never spoke of it), became friends. Mary visited Odette in Paris and sometimes Odette would return the favour by meeting with Mary in Cork or Galway.

Over time, Mary began to confide in Odette, and eventually told her about an affair she was having with a drunken reporter; an affair which eventually ended, though Mary never forgot about it.

The night before she was killed, Mary Barton rang Odette in Paris and told her she was scared. She couldn't find the two Russians she had hired and feared that someone had bought them off. She said she was heading for a safe house, but was worried that she wasn't able to contact me on my mobile. She was afraid that someone might discover the connection between us, putting my life in danger. She asked Odette to come over. Even if it's too late for me, she said, please look after Simon.

Look after Simon.

'I had seen your picture. Mary told me about the pubs you liked. You were easy to find. When she called me that time it was the first I had heard about these Russians, so I too had to find out what she had been doing.

'I didn't tell you this before because it would have scared you. You wouldn't have trusted me.'

I nodded, thinking of how little I had trusted her anyway.

'The Drummer is your uncle?'

'Yes. *Was* my uncle.'

'You killed your own uncle?'

It came out sounding like a judgement. Given that she had done it to spare my life, this did seem a little ungrateful. Yet Odette seemed unfazed by my tone of voice.

'Well, no. The others got him first.'

She said this softly, as if it was disappointing news.

'But I would have. My uncle tried to kill me. Simon, I loved my father. Whatever he did, I loved him. He looked after me and my mother. He looked after his friends. In his way, he was honest.

'But I have been uneasy about the life I have led. Killing. Apart from my day with you, I had given it up. That day was for Mary. Jimmy Barton was a pig, and some time ago I realized my uncle was a pig as well. Not like my father. Not at all.'

Her mouth screwed up as she said this; like a grieving wife who still cannot accept the death of her husband. She looked down at her hands. Her entwined fingers wrestled with one another, and for an instant the sheen of her self-possession slipped away: she was a teenage girl, forced by the adoration of her father into a tense moral logic which could only be maintained through sheer will. To be herself required denying her own intelligence, shutting off the prospect that her father was just as much a monster as the Drummer and, by extension, so too was she. She had imprisoned herself in a labyrinth of doors she did not dare open, leaving her nowhere to go, no person to become: without the myth of her father to emulate, she was nothing, could be nothing. The myth was too costly. For a time, it filled her up. Now, it had emptied everything out. The children waving behind the barbed wire would eventually die.

Our alliance had been an accident of time, nothing more: if it had been a year or two earlier, she could have been the one sent to kill me. I was stunned by the depth of my pity for her.

'Not at all,' she repeated. 'Not like Mary. She was beautiful. I know you did not love her. You were honest. But she loved you. I think she started all this for you. She told me once that if she had money, she would bring you away somewhere you liked. Was it also called Dublin?'

'Yes . . . yes. In New Hampshire.'

'Yes. Mary was not stupid. I think she knew she was being foolish, but she did it anyway. For just the chance of love.'

Only a French person could say that and not sound silly.

She stroked my face.

'And I could see why she loved you.'

She left shortly afterwards, and I knew I would never see her again. Said she was flying back to see her mother: since Robert Doherty's death, they haven't got on that well. Odette blames her mother for keeping her from Dublin; Odette's mother blames herself for letting her go.

She kissed me, and gave me her hat.

'A memento: like Homer Simpson.' *Seempson.*

Once alone, I realized I still had an erection, so I turned on my side and masturbated onto the stiff sheets, tears streaming from my eyes. It wasn't my unfulfilled lust for Odette or my memories of Mary Barton; it had hardly anything to do with sex at all. It was Life: this was the closest to a life-affirming action I could come up with, and afterwards I lay there, the tears still matting my face, my thoughts fixed on the baby daughter I had refused to see. I didn't want to die. I still don't.

Odette's mention of the other Dublin has brought to mind something I told you before: there is a series of supposedly famous photographs taken of Mark Twain while he was staying there. There were seven of them, entitled *Progress of a Moral Purpose*, and it was a spoof, really. The pictures just showed Twain sitting alone in a rocking chair, wearing his trademark white suit and explosion of hair. He smoked a cigar and sat in various poses, but on each of the photos he made notes of what he was supposed to be thinking. This is what he wrote:

a) Shall I learn to be good? I will sit here and think it over.

b) There seem to be so many diffi . . .

c) . . . and yet I should really try . . .

d) . . . and just put my whole heart into it.

e) But then I couldn't break the Sab . . .

f) . . . and there's so many other privileges that . . . perhaps . . .

g) Oh, never mind. I reckon I'm good enough just as I am.

At the time I first saw this, I thought it amusing enough, in a turn-of-the-century-man-of-letters way. Now I don't really know what he meant. Perhaps he was simply taking the piss out of a more puritanical era. Or perhaps he was saying that an effort to be better is impossible: even to sit on a veranda and consider the question is more luxury than most people have.

But this was all weeks ago, and I've done little since. Scratched my itchy limbs, watched TV, typed this account, tried to sleep when my body would let me.

Yet there has been some change: I'm starting to wish I'd called Angela and told her to bring in Emily. There's still no sign of a heart donor, but they say I'll be well enough to get out of here in a few days. At least I'll have that. And maybe then I'll go and visit my daughter. Maybe I will, Yes.

Acknowledgements

Many thanks to: Rob for sweaty vests and the e-mail address. Declan for how to be in a band. Philip for fill her up. Mary J. for the slit wrists. Brian for the nicknames and the singing story. Colette for the French. James Joyce for the use of the hall. Jimmy G. for how to be a DJ. Jonny G. for not telling me how much he asked for. Deborah for all the Liga. Aelred for being wolfish. Teddy for the use of his name. Bridget for not being surprised at any of this. And Sencha, Keelin and Ellie, just because I said I'd mention them.